PRAISE FOR LINDA TURNER:

"Ms. Turner mixes delicious humor with heartfelt emotion."
—*Romantic Times*

"Ms. Turner develops a luscious romance
with great sensitivity, capturing all the wonder
of the first moments of love."
—*Romantic Times*

PRAISE FOR INGRID WEAVER:

"Ms. Weaver combines topnotch suspense
with hot-blooded romance to provide the
very best for your reading enjoyment."
—*Romantic Times*

"Ms. Weaver's tight blend of sizzling romance
and exciting suspense provides super
entertainment for romance fans."
—*Romantic Times*

PRAISE FOR JULIE MILLER:

"With skilled characterizations and plenty of excitement,
Julie Miller gives readers pure enjoyment."
—*Romantic Times*

"Julie Miller's crisp writing style highlights her well-developed
characters, complex intrigue and strong plot."
—*Romantic Times*

Dear Reader,

The editors at Harlequin and Silhouette are thrilled to be able to bring you a brand-new featured author program for 2005! Signature Select aims to single out outstanding stories, contemporary themes and oft-requested classics by some of your favorite series authors and present them to you in a variety of formats bound by truly striking covers.

We want to provide several different types of reading experiences in the new Signature Select program. The Spotlight books offer a single "big read" by a talented series author, the Collections present three novellas on a selected theme in one volume, the Sagas contain sprawling, sometimes multi-generational family tales (often related to a favorite family first introduced in series) and the Miniseries feature requested previously published books, with two or, occasionally, three complete stories in one volume. The Signature Select program offers one book in each of these categories per month, and fans of limited continuity series will also find these continuing stories under the Signature Select umbrella.

In addition, these volumes bring you bonus features...different in every single book! You may learn more about the author in an extended interview, more about the setting or inspiration for the book, more about subjects related to the theme and, often, a bonus short read will be included. Authors and editors have been outdoing themselves in originating creative material for our bonus features—we're sure you'll be surprised and pleased with the results!

The Signature Select program strives to bring you a variety of reading experiences by authors you've come to love, as well as by rising stars you'll be glad you've discovered. Watch for new stories from Janelle Denison, Donna Kauffman, Leslie Kelly, Marie Ferrarella, Suzanne Forster, Stephanie Bond, Christine Rimmer and scores more of the brightest talents in romance fiction!

The excitement continues!

Warm wishes for happy reading,

Marsha Zinberg

Marsha Zinberg
Executive Editor
The Signature Select Program

COLLECTION

Linda Turner

Ingrid Weaver

&

Julie Miller

CorNeReD

Published by Silhouette Books

America's Publisher of Contemporary Romance

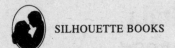 **SILHOUETTE BOOKS**

ISBN 0-373-28528-0

CORNERED

Copyright © 2005 by Harlequin Books S.A.

The publisher acknowledges the copyright holders
of the individual works as follows:

FOOLING AROUND
Copyright © 2005 by Linda Turner.

THE MAN IN THE SHADOWS
Copyright © 2005 by Ingrid Caris.

A MIDSUMMER NIGHT'S MURDER
Copyright © 2005 by Julie Miller.

This edition published by arrangement with Harlequin Books S.A.

® and TM are trademarks of Harlequin Books S.A., used under license.
Trademarks indicated with ® are registered in the United States Patent
and Trademark Office, the Canadian Trade Marks Office and in other
countries.

Visit Silhouette Books at www.eHarlequin.com

Printed in U.S.A.

CONTENTS

Dear Reader,

I've written a lot of stories over the years, but I can't remember the last one I enjoyed so much. There was something about the hero and heroine and parrot in "Fooling Around" that I just loved. And I have my late, great, wonderful grandmothers to thank for that. When I was growing up, Ludie Mae, my maternal grandmother, used to tell me stories about her aunt and her pet parrot. Whenever someone in the family had a baby, the parrot would fly to a perch on the roof of the house and yell, "New baby in town!" Don't you love that? I can just see the parrot sitting on the roof of a Victorian house in small town, Texas, spreading the good news.

In honor of Grandmother, who felt as if she was thirty-two at the age of ninety-two, I had to add the parrot.

Then, there was my paternal grandmother, Evelyn. She had spunk. She joined the circus with my grandfather and traveled all over the country, singing opening acts and hanging by her teeth. She eventually lost her teeth, but not her gumption. She was the type of woman who would have owned her own detective agency.

So this story is for both of my grandmothers, who are, no doubt, dancing in heaven and having a wonderful time. I hope you enjoy reading their story as much as I enjoyed writing it.

Best wishes,

Linda Turner

FOOLING AROUND
Linda Turner

Prologue

It was a dark and stormy night, and normally, Josephine London would have been curled up in bed with a good murder mystery. Instead, she sat at her small kitchen table and stared at the letter she'd just found in her afternoon mail.

Dear Miss London,
I am writing to inform you of the death of your great-aunt, Boonie Jones. She died quietly in her sleep two weeks ago and was cremated, as she requested. As you may or may not know, your late father was her favorite nephew, and it was always her intention to leave you all of her worldly possessions. As the executor of her estate, it is my duty to inform you that you have inherited her home in San Antonio, as well as her ownership in

a private detective agency. I have included a full
accounting of her possessions, as well as several
documents that you need to sign and return to me.
You will also find in the paperwork a personal letter from Boonie that she requested I give you upon
her death.

If you have any questions or wish to talk to me
about your great-aunt, please feel free to call me.
She was a wonderful person.

Sincerely,

Gene Stevens

Stunned, Josephine read the letter again, then again.
She had a Great-Aunt Boonie? Why was she only just
now finding out about her? Granted, her father had died
when she was just a baby, and her mother had remarried
a year and half later. After that, there'd been little chance
for her to get to know any London relatives. Her stepfa-
ther was in the air force, and they'd lived all over the
world while she was growing up. Not surprisingly, her
mother had lost touch with her father's family years ago.

And all this time she'd had a great-aunt who had, according to lawyer Gene Stevens, adored her father. And
now it was too late to get to know her…except through
her letter. With fingers that weren't quite steady, she
broke the seal on the envelope and pulled out a letter
written in a delicate feminine scrawl. Transfixed, she
began to read.

Josephine, even though I haven't seen you since
you were a baby, I have always loved you. You are
your father's daughter, and he was a darling boy.

A day hasn't gone by since he died that I haven't missed him. I'm sure you must feel the same.

As Gene has no doubt informed you, I have made you my sole heir. It was the last thing I could do for your father and you, and I do it joyfully. You should know, though, that I didn't do this blindly without knowing anything about you, sweetie. I had you checked out.

I hope that doesn't horrify you—you must indulge your old aunt. I tracked you down to Seattle on the Internet, but was unable to travel, so I called one of my contacts in Seattle to do the legwork for me. Needless to say, I was quite shocked by the report I received. You have no beau, no male companion, no fun in your life! You go to the bookstore, to work and church, and appear to spend the rest of your time in your apartment reading romances. Josie, why are you letting life pass you by? There's a whole world out there just waiting for you to explore. And you're holed up in your apartment reading about what you're missing!

Please don't take this as criticism, but rather the worries of an old woman who only wants the best for you. You're smart and pretty and, from all reports, an excellent school librarian and a wonderful person. Your father would be proud of your character and academic accomplishments—and worried that you're sitting on the sidelines watching life pass you by. I, too, am concerned. I want you to have love and adventure in your life… which is why I'm leaving everything I own to you. The business and house aren't worth a fortune, but I laughed through life and can promise you that by the time you get this letter, I died with no regrets. I wish the same for you and can think of no greater legacy I can leave you than the means to really start living life. Enjoy, sweetheart. Be happy. Love life.

Your loving aunt,

Boonie Jones

Reeling, Josephine didn't know if she wanted to laugh or cry. Boonie Jones was absolutely right about her. She lived a nice, quiet, boring life—and only found love in the pages of books. She kept telling herself that one day she was going to do something about that, but she never had. And now Boonie had left her everything she owned, including a private detective agency. She was a librarian, for heaven's sake! Now what was she supposed to do?

Chapter 1

Josie had always considered herself a practical woman, but the day after she received news of her inheritance, she quit her job and notified her landlord that she would be moving out at the end of the week. On Saturday, she squeezed the last of her personal things into her Volkswagen bug and headed for Texas.

She'd lost her mind, she decided. There was no other explanation. All her life, she'd played it safe. She didn't speed, didn't drink, never took any drug stronger than an aspirin. And she never, ever took a chance and went out on a limb. So what the heck was she doing?!

Having an adventure, just as Boonie had suggested, she decided, and was shocked to hear herself giggle. She couldn't remember the last time she'd giggled. Maybe she was going through a midlife crisis. That had to be it. Granted, she was only twenty-eight, but what other explanation could there be? She'd just walked away from her *life,* and she couldn't stop smiling. And she hadn't even notified her aunt's attorney that she was driving to Texas to claim her inheritance!

She should have called him, but part of her had been afraid she'd change her mind at the last moment and run back to Seattle.

So she'd mailed the papers he'd asked her to sign, then continued on her way. It was, to say the least, a long drive, but she'd never driven across country before and she thoroughly enjoyed it. By the time she reached San Antonio, she couldn't wait to explore her new home.

First, however, she had to meet Wiley Valentine. After reading more of the paperwork Gene Stevens had sent her, she'd learned that her aunt and Wiley Valentine had been co-owners of the detective agency. And now he was her partner. She almost laughed aloud at the thought. This was so wild. She felt as if she had somehow stepped into the pages of a book.

Wiley Valentine. She hadn't spoken to him yet, but she loved his name. Was he as wiley as his name? In her mind, she could already see him. He'd be tall and scruffy, in need of a haircut and shave, and have a twinkle in his eyes. Obviously, he was too stubborn to retire—he was still working after her eighty-six-year-old aunt had died—but Josephine didn't doubt that he was still as sharp as a tack. Otherwise, he would never have been friends with Boonie. She couldn't wait to talk to him.

Checking her map and the address of the AAA Detective Agency, she soon pulled up in front of an old single-story brick building that looked as though it had been there since the siege of the Alamo. The agency name was painted in a half circle on the plate-glass window, and when Josephine pushed open the front door, a bell tinkled merrily in greeting. Delighted, she took a quick look around and had to grin. There were files piled carelessly on two old-fashioned rolltop desks, a faded map on the wall and a brass hat rack in the corner loaded down with all types of hats and scarves and even wigs. Even though she'd never met Boonie, she could just see her aunt and her partner laughing together as they disguised themselves before going to work.

Then, suddenly a man in the back room growled, "You can't keep making such a mess with your coffee. I'm tired of cleaning up after you."

"Kiss my grits."

"Don't get smart with me, Ethel. I'm not in the mood. I didn't get much sleep last night."

"Take a nap, sweet pea. I'll watch the place."

"Yeah, right. Just shut your yap and leave me alone."

"In your dreams, sweetheart. I was born to sing. La-la-la-la…"

Laughter bubbling up inside her, Josephine slapped a quick hand over her mouth and stifled a giggle. Ethel sounded like a parrot, but she was awfully sassy. Maybe there was a television on in the back.

Stepping further into the office, she called out, "Hello? Is anyone here?"

"C'mon back," the man retorted. "We're back here."

We're? Josephine wondered. Was he talking about the bird or was there someone else with him? Not quite sure what to expect, she crossed the front office and stepped through the open door into what turned out to be a small kitchen. Normally, the parrot standing on the table, dunking a vanilla wafer in a cup of coffee, would have been more than enough to stop her in her tracks. Then she got a good look at the man seated across the table from the bird.

This couldn't be Wiley Valentine, she thought, confused. Somewhere in his mid thirties, he was far too young to be her aunt's partner. "I'm sorry," she said huskily. "But could you tell me where I could find Wiley Valentine?"

Sitting back in his chair, Wiley observed her with a grin. Well, wasn't she cute? A little prim and proper in her starched white blouse and linen slacks, but that didn't bother him. A woman was like a present, a surprise just waiting to be unwrapped, and he'd yet to meet one he didn't find fascinating. He bet this one held more surprises than most. If she'd let her hair down out of the ponytail she'd scraped it into and loosen up enough to smile, she'd be downright pretty. Of course, she wouldn't unbend easily—he only had to look at the stubborn set of her chin to know that, but he'd had fantasies about a woman like her. He'd just never had a chance to indulge himself. Maybe—

"Excuse me?" she said with a frown, interrupting his daydreaming. "Do you work here? I'm looking for Wiley Valentine."

"Watch out, sister," the parrot piped up. "He's a hottie."

His gaze had drifted from her chin to her mouth, but at Ethel's tart remark, he laughed and tossed the parrot another cookie, which she promptly caught and dunked in her coffee. "I'm Wiley," he said, flashing his dimples at her. "What can I do for you?"

Stunned, Josephine just looked at him. This was

Wiley? Her aunt's partner? The man she'd assumed had to be eighty, if he was a day? This man with the lean, rugged good looks and wicked eyes full of laughter was her partner? He couldn't be!

"I thought you'd be older," she said, stunned.

His mouth kicked up into a crooked grin. "I'm old enough to do anything that's legal and a lot of things that aren't, sweetheart. What'd you have in mind?"

Still reeling, she hardly heard him. "I'm Josephine London," she said. "Boonie's niece."

The words were hardly out of her mouth when he burst out laughing. "Well, I'll be damned!" Rising abruptly to his feet, he reached for his wallet, pulled out a fifty-dollar bill, and held it out to her. "Here. I owe you."

Surprised, she blinked. "I beg your pardon?"

"I had a bet with your aunt," he said, grinning. "I bet her you'd sell the house and your share in the agency without ever putting your big toe in Texas. Looks like I was wrong." Cutting the distance between them in half with one long stride, he reached for her hand and closed her fingers around the money. "Take it. You won fair and square."

"But I didn't make the bet!"

"Doesn't matter. I promised Boonie I'd pay you if I lost the bet."

With his fingers still curled around hers, Josephine felt a warmth settle in her stomach she couldn't understand. Swallowing, she said faintly, "You don't have to do this."

"Oh, yes I do," he said, chuckling as he gave her hand a squeeze and released her. "You didn't know your aunt. She was the most easygoing, generous woman I ever met, but when you gave her your word, she expected you to stand by it. If I didn't pay you, she'd be rattling chains and haunting every step I took. I don't know about you, but I'd just as soon avoid that."

He was serious. Fighting a smile, she lifted a delicately arched brow at him. "You really believe in ghosts?"

"I believe in Boonie," he retorted. "Trust me, that woman could do anything she set her mind to. Why do you think I jumped at the chance to be her partner? If she decided she wanted to take me to task from the other side of the pearly gates, she'd find a way."

She sounded wonderful. "I wish I'd had the chance to know her," Josephine said wistfully.

"She was a trip," he told her. "Her one regret was that she wouldn't be here to see your reaction to everything she left you." He nodded to where the parrot sat on her perch at the table. "There's your first new possession. Her name's Ethel Merman. I should warn you she's got a smart mouth. She won't let you get away with anything."

"You got that right, buster," Ethel piped up. "Don't forget your manners. Stand up straight. Give us a kiss."

Torn between horror and amusement, Josephine looked at him in disbelief. "You're kidding…right?"

"Oh, no," he chuckled. "She's all yours."

"Oh, but I couldn't! She doesn't even know me."

Far from sympathetic, he only grinned. "She's part of a package deal. It's all or nothing. If you refuse any part of the bequest within the first year of possession— Ethel, the house, or the agency—everything goes to a pig farm south of town."

Josephine couldn't believe he was serious. Surely

her aunt wouldn't have made such provisions in the will. But there had been a codicil to Boonie's will that had stated that if she refused her inheritance, a second codicil would then kick in. She hadn't paid any attention to it because she hadn't planned to refuse her inheritance. Of course, she hadn't known at the time that Boonie's worldly possessions included a parrot with an attitude.

Studying the redheaded parrot with a worried frown, she told Wiley, "I know nothing about parrots."

"Don't worry," he chuckled, "she'll tell you everything you need to know. And if you're not careful, she'll be running your life for you within the week."

"Sit and have a cup of coffee," Ethel said in a singsong voice. "Take a load off."

Josephine laughed, she couldn't help herself. "Thank you. I don't mind if I do."

Wiley grabbed a clean coffee cup from a shelf on the wall, filled it with the steaming brew, and joined her at the table, taking a seat opposite her. "You know, just because the will says you have to keep everything a year doesn't mean that you have to stick around here," he said casually. "You can go back to your life in Seattle and I'll take care of things here. Then, at the end of the year, I'll buy everything from you at fair market value. Hell, I'll even take Ethel. She's like family, anyway."

Studying him, Josephine had to admit that when she'd first heard of her inheritance, she had considered making him that very offer. But Boonie's letter had touched her in a way she'd never expected. When she examined her life, she was forced to admit that her aunt was right—she *was* sitting on the sidelines, letting life pass her by. How could she refuse Ethel—or sell the agency—when Boonie had not only left her everything, but opened up a whole new world for her?

"I appreciate the offer," she said huskily, "but I can't. That would be a slap in the face to Boonie. So it looks like we're partners, partner," she added with a grin, holding out her hand. "I can't wait to get started."

Whatever reaction she'd been expecting, it wasn't the sudden scowl on Wiley's face. "This is a joke, right? You're just yanking my chain?"

"Why would I do that? Boonie left her share of the business to me. She obviously thought I could handle it."

"But you're a librarian! You don't know anything about being a private investigator."

"So I'll learn," she said with a shrug. "Like you said—I'm a librarian. I'll read up on the subject."

Chapter 2

Wiley liked to think he was one of those easygoing souls who could roll with whatever life threw at him, but he was not amused. When Boonie had told him she was leaving her share of the agency to her niece, he hadn't been concerned about a librarian who lived a thousand miles away causing him any problems. That's why he'd made the bet with Boonie—there was nothing he liked more than a sure thing.

Yeah, right, he thought grimly. Here she was in the flesh and now he had to deal with her. "Some of the jobs we get are dangerous," he warned. "You could get hurt."

"Did Boonie ever get hurt?"

"No, but she could take care of herself."

"So can I," she replied indignantly. "And I don't believe she would have left me ownership in the agency if she truly believed working here would put me in danger." When he continued to frown, a half smile curled one corner of her mouth. "You just don't want to work with me, do you? Is it something I said?"

"She's a babe!" Ethel warned suddenly. "Run for your life!"

"That's enough, Red," Wiley growled.

Struggling to hold back a smile when Ethel sniffed, Josephine said teasingly, "Oh, I get it. It's because you think I'm too young. You like working with older women."

"I never said that."

"That's okay. You didn't have to. I can read between the lines—I'm a librarian, remember? So I'm too young. Are you saying I'm too immature to do the job?"

"Of course not!"

He only had to look at her to know she didn't lack for maturity. And maybe that was the problem. He knew from the background check that Boonie had done on her that she was twenty-eight, but there was something about her prim and proper demeanor, her quiet confidence, that he didn't know how to deal with. She was different from the women he knew.

"I like her," Ethel said brightly. "Let's keep her."

In the silence that followed the parrot's announcement, Wiley's eyes met Josephine's, and they both started to laugh. "I warned you she'd be running your life if you weren't careful. She said the same thing about me when Boonie and I became partners. And I have to admit, she's a damn good judge of character. There's been a number of clients she warned me and Boonie not to take, and she was right every time."

"So you don't have any objections to us working together?"

He had objections, but he kept them to himself. "You have as much right to be here as I do," he said simply, and reached for a ring of keys on a peg by his desk. "Boonie's house is just around the corner. C'mon. I'll walk you over."

She started to follow him to the door, only to hesitate. "What about Ethel?"

"Oh, she'll come, too. Watch." Holding the door open, he turned and grinned at the parrot. "C'mon, Miss Merman. Let's go home."

"Quitting time!" she sang gaily, and flew through the door.

"Oh, my God!" Josephine cried in alarm. "Will she come back?"

"She'll be at Boonie's before we will," he retorted, chuckling. "When Boonie first got her, she'd take her back and forth to work in her cage, but then Ethel accidentally got out one day. Boonie was worried sick. I thought she'd lost her for good, but Ethel was waiting for her at home, sitting on the porch swing, singing 'Margaritaville.' I never laughed so hard in my life."

Josephine grinned. "How did she develop such a huge vocabulary? Boonie must have spent a lot of time working with her."

"Boonie loved that parrot like she was her own kid," he replied with a chuckle. "They'd listen to the stereo together and sing all their favorite songs. They even played Scrabble together."

"Who won?"

"After Ethel's vocabulary improved, it was usually a draw."

Amused, Josephine could just see Ethel and her aunt

playing Scrabble. "The more I hear about Boonie, the more I hate I never knew her."

"She was special," Wiley agreed. "I never knew another living soul like her."

Leading her across one of the arched foot bridges that spanned the San Antonio River, he nodded at the small yellow house that sat on a corner lot a block from the river. An old faded red Volvo coupe sat in the driveway. "That's her place," he told her. "It's all yours now, including the car."

Whatever Josephine had been expecting, it wasn't the little Victorian house surrounded by a jungle of tropical plants. As Wiley had promised, Ethel was perched on the back of a wicker porch swing, singing "Cheeseburger in Paradise."

Walking up the front walk, Josephine laughed. "Obviously, she likes Jimmy Buffett. I guess Boonie did, too."

"She had all his CDs," Wiley replied with a grin. "The first time I heard her and Ethel harmonize, I laughed until I cried."

He unlocked the front door for her, but he didn't give her a guided tour. Instead, he handed the keys back to her and stepped back. "I won't go in. You must be tired, and you need to explore the place on your own. I'll warn you up front that it's pretty dusty. I cleaned out the refrigerator after Boonie died, but I'm sure you'll want to give the place a good cleaning before you unpack your things. Why don't you take the rest of the week to settle in?"

"Oh, no, I couldn't leave you in the lurch that long," Josie replied quickly. "I'll come in in the morning. I can unpack in the evenings, after work."

"But I've got a surveillance job in the morning," he argued with a quick scowl. "You need to wait until I can be there to show you the ropes."

"Don't be silly," she assured him. "It's not like I'm going to run out and investigate a messy divorce on my own. I'm just going to read some of the files on your back cases and learn how you and Boonie operated the business. I'll be fine."

She could see the doubt in his eyes and half expected him to object again, but something in her expression must have convinced him she wasn't going to change her mind. With a sigh of defeat, he gave in. "I won't be coming in in the morning at all, but my cell phone number is in Boonie's address book. If you run into any problems at all, call me immediately. I can make it back to the office in fifteen minutes."

"I'll be fine," she repeated, smiling. "I promise I won't burn the place down."

He looked far from satisfied, but there was little more he could do. "Call if you need anything," he said, then left her alone with Ethel.

In the silence that followed his leavetaking, she should have felt like she was snooping in someone else's house, but she'd never felt more at home. There were faded photographs of what Josephine could only assume were family members everywhere, including dozens of her father she'd never seen before. Wandering around the small house, she could almost feel her aunt's love for her family. The pictures were obviously for her own enjoyment—many of them weren't even framed, but were tacked up in the kitchen and her small office where she could see them as she worked.

On the nightstand next to Boonie's bed, Josephine found her favorite. It was a picture of her father with two women taken on the day he graduated from high school. Young and smiling, looking barely old enough to shave, he smiled into Josephine's eyes and made her heart ache. Why had she never realized before that she had his smile?

Smiling through sudden, unexpected tears, she shifted her gaze to her father's companions and knew without a doubt that the woman on his right who was beaming proudly was his mother. The other woman had to be Boonie. With a twinkle in her eye and her floral hat set at a cocky angle, she looked like the kind of woman who would own a parrot and be a private investigator.

"What's for supper?" Ethel demanded, interrupting her thoughts. "Polly wants a cracker."

"Your name's not Polly," Josephine said, chuckling as she went in search of some food for her in the kitchen. "And I don't have a clue what I'm supposed to feed you—"

"Steak and potatoes. It'll put hair on your chest."

"Really?" she laughed. "Well, that may be fine for you, but that's not my goal in life. I'll bet you eat some kind of bird seed."

"Yuck! Let's have a beer!"

"I don't think so," she said dryly. "How about some birdseed instead? Here it is, right here by your perch. Now if I can just find something for me to eat, we'll both be set. Wiley cleaned out the refrigerator—maybe there's something in the pantry…"

But a search of the pantry turned up nothing but several cans of sardines and a box of cereal. "Well," she said with a grimace, "I'm not really big on sardines. Maybe I'll order a pizza—"

"With extra cheese!"

"We'll see," she said with a grin, and went in search of the phone book.

Heading back to the office the next morning with Ethel flying ahead of her, leading the way, Josephine couldn't remember the last time she'd been so excited. With Wiley gone for the morning, she had the place to herself. She couldn't wait to explore the case files. She'd found Boonie's diary on her nightstand last night and spent hours reading her aunt's private thoughts. At first, she'd felt like a voyeur, but then she'd gotten caught up in the story of who Boonie Jones really was, and she'd read until two in the morning.

How she envied Boonie the life she'd led! She'd been a free spirit with the most amazing sense of adventure. She'd married a man she'd only known for a week and loved him for fifty years. Together, they'd traveled the world, working for the government as diplomatic spies. When they'd decided to settle down, they'd tossed the name of dozens of cities in a hat and pulled out San Antonio.

Amazed, fascinated, green with envy, Josephine was forced to face the emptiness of her own existence. Unlike Boonie, she'd played it safe her entire life, never taking a chance on anything. She'd worked hard, done what was expected of her, and even though she'd been lonely, she'd convinced herself that it wouldn't be forever. One day, she promised herself, she would meet a good man, fall in love, and live happily every after. All she had to do was be a good girl and follow the rules.

It should have been easy. But she was twenty-eight years old and had never been in love. There wasn't even a man in her life! And as she'd read Boonie's diary, she'd realized that all these years when she'd thought she was on the road to living the American dream, she was just treading water. Her life was one big bore.

Thanks to Boonie, that was about to change, she thought, and felt her heart skip a beat in excitement as she unlocked the front door of the office. Ethel swooped in the second she opened the door, leaving Josephine to follow more slowly. This was really part hers, she thought as she set about getting the office ready for the day. Quickly flipping on the computer and turning on lights, she found her eyes going again and again to the old-fashioned wooden file cabinets that lined one wall of the office. She couldn't even imagine the stories they could tell. She couldn't wait to get at them.

"Tea time," Ethel sang from her perch. "Let's have a cookie."

"We just got here," Josephine reminded her, only to grin when the parrot gave her a look that she was coming to know all too well. It was her "feed me" look, though how she managed to convey her thoughts without blinking an eye, Josephine didn't have a clue. She just knew she had to feed her quickly or she'd never hear the end of it. Last night, when Josephine hadn't fed her the second she claimed she was hungry, Ethel had claimed she was a victim of parrot abuse. Josephine couldn't remember the last time she'd laughed so hard.

"All right, all right, I'll feed you," she promised.

"Hurry, please. I'm fading away."

Delighted with her response, Josephine sent up a silent prayer of thanks to Boonie. Without even knowing her, she'd made sure her life would never be boring again.

Hurrying into the kitchen, she found the tea and a stash of vanilla wafers, which were Ethel's favorite, along with the tray Wiley had used for her tea yesterday. A few short minutes later, she returned to the front office with enough tea and cookies for her and Ethel, made sure the parrot was happy, then settled at Boonie's desk to read.

She'd barely opened a file, however, when the bell over the front door rang merrily and a tall, middle-aged Hispanic woman walked in. In the process of sipping her tea, Ethel glanced up sharply and seemed to stiffen. Josephine expected her to say something sassy, but instead, she growled, "Watch it."

"Sshhh," Josephine said under her breath, then turned to the woman with a smile. "Good morning. Can I help you?"

It was a simple question, but apparently the wrong one. To Josephine's horror, the woman's eyes filled with tears. "I'm sorry," she choked when Josephine rushed forward in alarm. "I swore I wasn't going to do this, but I'm just so afraid my husband is having an affair."

Understanding, Josephine murmured, "That explains why you're here. Please, sit down. Let me make you some tea while you tell me all about it. Oh, I'm Josephine London. And you're…"

"Olivia Sanchez," she sniffed.

"And your husband's name?"

"Roberto Sanchez."

Handing her a cup of tea, Josephine sank into her chair and reached for paper and pen. "How long have you been married?"

"Nineteen years," Olivia said with a painful sigh. "I loved him from the moment I first met him. I always thought he felt the same. But lately, I'm not so sure."

"He's changed?"

She nodded grimly. "He's never home anymore, and when he is, he's different. I can't tell you how, but a wife knows when her husband is looking elsewhere. He's seeing someone else—I'm sure of it."

Her heart pounding with excitement—this was her first case!—Josephine asked her all the pertinent questions she could think of: home address, where her husband worked and spent his free time, friends who might cover for him, the make and license number of his car and so on. "We'll do everything we can for you, Mrs. Sanchez. Is there a private number where I can reach you?"

She gave her her cell phone number, but cautioned, "Please don't leave a message if I don't answer. My husband knows the code to access my messages."

"No messages," Josephine jotted down at the top of her notes. "Trust me, your husband will know nothing about this visit. Does he handle the finances? How did you plan to pay? If your husband pays your credit card bills, I would advise you not to charge our services."

"Oh, no, I have cash," the older woman assured her. "It's my pin money. What is your fee?"

Josephine didn't have a clue what to charge her. Then she spied a sign on the wall that posted not only the hourly fee, but the retainer required to secure their services. Nodding toward the sign, Josephine said, "I hope we will be able to get answers for you quickly, but I can't make any promises."

"I want the truth," Olivia Sanchez said flatly, pulling a fat envelope of cash from her purse and handing it to her. "If you need more, just let me know." Standing, suddenly anxious to be gone, she looked over her shoulder, out the storefront window to the view of the busy street. "I must go," she said huskily. "Thank you for your help."

She was gone before Josephine could do anything but promise to call her as soon as she knew anything. She sympathized with the woman, but the minute the door closed behind her, she couldn't contain her glee. Turning to Ethel with a huge grin, she cried, "Did you hear that, Red? I've got my own client!"

Far from impressed, the parrot cackled, "Look out! We're in trouble now."

Chapter 3

"Who's in trouble?"

Whirling to find Wiley stepping through the front door, Josephine grinned. "Nobody. Look!" With a flourish, she waved the envelope of money Olivia Sanchez had given her. "It's five thousand dollars!"

Wiley's dark brows snapped together in a frown. "Oh, God, Ethel's right. What'd you do? Rob a bank? Where'd that come from?"

"Our new client. She wants us to check out her husband. She thinks he's playing around on her."

"And she just waltzed in here with five thousand dollars in her purse? Who the hell is she? One of Donald Trump's exes?"

"No, of course not. Her name's Olivia Sanchez. Her husband's—"

"Roberto Sanchez," he finished for her, horrified. "Tell me this is a joke."

His reaction stopped her in her tracks. "You know him?"

"Not personally, thank God," he retorted. "Dammit, Josie—"

"Josephine," she corrected him automatically. "I don't—"

"Like nicknames," he finished for her, his frown deepening into a scowl. "You're not going to have to worry about that if Roberto Sanchez finds out you're helping his wife check him out. He's the head of the Mexican mafia, *Josie*. People who cross him end up wearing cement shoes in the river."

Shocked, Josephine paled. "He couldn't get away with something like that. He'd be in jail."

"Oh, God, an innocent!" he moaned. "Please tell me you don't believe liberty and justice for all really exists."

Heat colored her cheeks. "You don't have to get sarcastic. I realize that the system has flaws."

"You're damn straight it does," he said grimly. "And the bad guys with the bucks know how to use those flaws to their advantage. Roberto Sanchez has more money than God, sweetheart. *Drug* money. And he knows every cop and judge and law-enforcement officer in the state who's on the take. Trust me, you don't want to have anything to do with him. You've got to call Mrs. Sanchez and tell her you made a mistake. You can't help her."

"But she's already paid us!"

"Give her the money back with interest if you have to."

"Can we do that? What if she's offended? She could go to her husband—"

"When she hired us to check him out?" he argued. "I don't think so."

"She's not going to tell him the truth, silly," she retorted. "She'll claim she wanted us to check out a new housekeeper or a business she wanted Roberto to invest in and we insulted her by refusing to take her money. Won't he be furious that we offended his wife?"

Frowning, Wiley wanted to tell her she was worrying about nothing. But was she? He'd never met Sanchez personally, but it was a well-known fact around town that the man was macho and arrogant and had a quick temper. If his wife came crying to him that her money wasn't good enough for the AAA Detective Agency, there was a very real possibility that he would try to find a way to make them pay for upsetting his wife. And when Sanchez made people pay, someone usually got hurt.

Swearing softly, he growled, "You made your point."

"So I can take the case?"

"No. *I'll* take it. You don't have a license, and there's no time for you to get it right now. I've got to get evidence on Roberto Sanchez as quickly as possible so we can send his wife on her way."

"But what about your other cases?"

He shrugged. "I'll have to put them off. Anyway, nothing else is so urgent that it can't wait a week or so."

"You can investigate him in a week?" she asked, surprised.

"If he's fooling around on his wife, it won't take me long to get the evidence."

"How?"

"You don't need to worry about the details, Josie. I

know what I'm doing. You just stay here and answer the phone and I'll take care of Sanchez."

Disturbed, she hardly noticed his use of the nickname she'd never really cared for. Instead, her eyes narrowed at his dismissing tone. "I have a right to know what you're going to do. I'm your partner, not a glorified receptionist."

"I never said—"

"You're very charming," she cut in smoothly, "but I'm not some bimbo you can schmooze and run right over. Just because I have no experience in investigating doesn't mean I can't understand the business. Believe it or not, there are people who consider me to be quite intelligent."

Her tone was light and amused, but her chin was set at a stubborn angle and when her brown eyes met his blue ones, she made no effort to disguise the fact that she was more than a little irritated with him. Far from impressed, he glared right back at her.

Then, suddenly, his eyes started to dance and his mouth twitched into a crooked grin. "I'm not going to tell you how much you look like Boonie right now. She didn't let me get away with anything, either."

Josephine felt her heart miss a beat and sternly warned herself not to be taken in by a flash of male dimples and the wry glint in his laughing blue eyes. She might as well have told herself not to breathe.

"Stop it!"

"What?" he asked, wide-eyed.

"Don't play innocent with me," she told him sternly, struggling not to be charmed. "I'm serious!"

"I know," he replied, grinning widely. "I am, too."

"Oh, really? I hadn't noticed."

"There you go again, sounding just like Boonie," he said with a chuckle. "She would have liked you."

Just that easily, he melted the last of her temper. "I would have liked her, too," she admitted softly. "I started reading her diary last night. She was fascinating…and a woman who knew how to stand up for herself," she added pointedly. "I'm sure she'd be terribly disappointed in me if I didn't do the same. So…are we partners or not?"

"Of course we're partners. I never said that we weren't."

Far from amused by his sidestepping, she gave him a stern look. "You know what I mean, Wiley. Am I going to have to fight you every step of the way just to be included in the day-to-day running of the agency? If so, tell me now so I'll know what to expect."

For a moment, she thought he was once again going to evade the question. He hesitated, but he didn't, to his credit, blow her off. "This is an adjustment for me, too, Josie," he said quietly. "Boonie and I were partners for a lot of years, and I trusted her completely. She was a damn good investigator. I don't know you. You're not licensed—"

"All I ask is you give me the chance to learn," she interrupted. "I'm not here on a whim. I quit my job in Seattle—I'm not going back. Thanks to Boonie, this is my life now. I plan to make this work, so I *will* get my license, and I hope one day I'll be the kind of investigator that she would have been proud of."

His eyes searching hers, Wiley couldn't doubt her sincerity. She might look all prim and proper, like the librarian she'd been only a matter of days ago, but she had the same kind of gumption that had made Boonie so special. He didn't doubt that she *would* get her license, just as she'd promised. In the meantime, however, she'd already proven she could get into a hell of a lot of trouble if she was left to her own devices. For no other reason than that, he had to take her with him.

Boonie, what have you gotten me into? he thought with a silent groan.

I didn't want you to be bored, sweetie. You two will be good for each other.

He could hear the words in his head as clearly as if Boonie stood before him, grinning at him without the least bit of sympathy. She'd always had a wicked sense of humor. Holding out his hand to Josie, he grinned crookedly. "Looks like we're partners, partner."

Her eyes lit up like a Christmas tree. "You mean it? You're not going to give me a hard time?"

"Well, I wouldn't go that far," he retorted, grinning, "but not where the business is concerned. In the meantime, you might as well get your feet wet and go with me to check out Sanchez. I've got some things to do, but I'll be back around three. You'll need to go home and change into something appropriate for a date."

Thrilled, Josephine could have hugged him. "I'll be ready," she promised. "I don't have a clue what I'm going to wear, but I'll be ready."

She grabbed her purse and started to hurry out, only to stop in her tracks when Ethel whistled sharply. "I'm sorry," she told the parrot with a laugh when she turned to find her almost frowning at her. "I completely forgot about you. C'mon, let's go."

Ethel didn't say a word. Instead, she sailed through the door the second Josephine opened it for her. Watching her head for the Riverwalk and fly through the towering cypress tress that lined the river, Wiley grinned. "You offended her. She doesn't like being ignored."

"I'll have to remember that," she said dryly. "I'm not used to having a pet that can talk back."

"Oh, you ain't seen nothing yet," he laughed. "Just wait."

Josephine didn't see how Ethel could be even more vocal than she already had been, but as she hurried toward Boonie's house, her only concern was her first case. Wiley had said to wear something appropriate for a date, which sounded simple enough … except that she'd never dated much. It wasn't that she didn't want to—she just didn't seem to meet anyone she was interested in going out with.

There was, however, something about Wiley—

Oh, no! she thought, stiffening. She wasn't going there. She wasn't interested in Wiley as anything other than a partner. Granted, her heart seemed to skip a beat every time he smiled that crooked smile of his, but that was perfectly natural. He was a good-looking man. What woman wouldn't catch her breath when he flashed his dimples at her?

Confident that her reaction to him was nothing out of the ordinary, she reached Boonie's house to find Ethel sitting in a tree in the front yard. "Hurry!" the parrot called out in a singsong voice. "'We're late, we're late… for a very important date!'"

"Cute," Josephine chuckled as she unlocked the front door and held it open. "But it's not a real date. I'm just supposed to dress as if it is."

"You've got a hot date," Ethel retorted stubbornly. Immediately flying into the bedroom, she perched on the footboard of the antique iron bed that had been Boonie's and considered Josephine with knowing eyes as she pulled open her closet door to consider her clothes. "Loosen up! Don't be so uptight. Wear red!"

"Too flashy—I don't want to stand out in a crowd," she said, then had to laugh. "I can't believe I'm having a conversation with a parrot! I must be losing my mind."

"Join the club!"

Amused, Josephine chuckled. "Stop that! I have to concentrate on getting ready. Now what am I going to wear? And don't say red!"

Ethel took her at her word and held her tongue as she began to preen her feathers. When Josephine turned to survey her closet, she grimaced at the sight of her wardrobe— black and gray, grim business suits she'd worn to work. But she wasn't a librarian any more and she was doing just what Boonie had wanted her to do—living a life of adventure. Now she just had to figure out how to dress the part.

Her gaze landed on a sundress that she'd bought on a whim last year. It was the kind of dress she'd always wished she'd had the nerve to wear—short and sassy, with spaghetti straps that showed off bare shoulders. After she'd bought it, however, she'd felt too self-conscious to wear it. She couldn't bear to take it back, so it had hung in her closet for months. It was perfect for a date.

So try it on.

Even though she'd never spoken to Boonie, Josephine could almost hear her whispering in her ear. Did she have the nerve to wear it? she wondered with a pounding heart. She'd never shown so much skin, but it did have a matching jacket that made the entire out-fit more demure.

Grimacing at the direction of her thoughts—she sounded like a prude!—she reached for the sundress. It wouldn't hurt to try it on.

A few moments later, Josephine stood before the mirror attached to her closet door and felt excited and nervous and giddy all at once. She had no reason to apologize for wearing the jacket. It was as short and sassy as the dress itself and almost flirty.

Or at least it would look that way on someone who had more curves, she admitted ruefully. On her, it looked…modest. And there was nothing wrong with that. Once she stepped into her sandals, neatly con-trolled her hair in a ponytail, and applied some makeup, she looked fine. Granted, she wasn't the kind of woman who would ever knock a man out of his shoes, but she was all right with that. She'd much rather be interest-ing than drop-dead gorgeous.

Satisfied that she was ready, she never knew how she got through the next few hours. She tried to relax with Boonie's journal, but she kept watching the clock and listening for Wiley's knock. She found herself pictur-ing everything that could go wrong and started to ques-tion the wisdom of going at all. What if she did something that tipped off Sanchez that he was being fol-lowed? She could put Wiley in danger…

When there was a sudden knock at the front door, her heart jumped in her throat. On her perch, Ethel stirred, but Josephine didn't notice…until she pulled open the door and the parrot whistled sharply in appreciation. "Hey, baby. Wanna fool around?"

Mortified, Josephine blushed to the roots of her hair. "I'm so sorry!"

Wiley only grinned. "Don't apologize. Where do you think she learned that? Boonie was always making cracks like that." Suddenly noticing her dress, he said, "Hey, look at you!"

Holding her arms out from her side, she smiled self-consciously. "You said to dress for a date. Is this all right?"

For a moment, Wiley couldn't find words. All right? That depended. There was nothing the least bit suggestive about the way she was dressed. The pink-and-white short-sleeved jacket she wore was open at the throat, showing little skin, and her matching dress only hinted at the soft, gentle curves beneath. Still, she somehow managed to catch his attention, and that stunned him. He was usually drawn to women who liked to walk on the wild side, not sedate librarians who spent most of their time with their noses in books.

So why was he tempted to touch her to see if her peaches-and-cream complexion was as soft as it looked? Then there was her mouth. Why was he only just now noticing how kissable it was?

Confused—and more than a little irritated with the direction of his thoughts—he jerked his attention back to the matter at hand. "You look fine," he said stiffly. "C'mon, let's get out of here. We've got work to do."

Chapter 4

Josephine stopped short at the sedate sedan parked at the curb in front of Boonie's house. "This is yours?" she asked Wiley in surprise. "I thought you'd drive something flashy like a Z3 or something."

"Actually, this is a rental," he admitted with twinkling eyes. "I've got a bike, but it's hard to do surveillance on a motorcycle. And I didn't think you'd be thrilled at the idea of snuggling up to my back. Of course, if you'd rather…"

"Oh, no!" she said quickly, cursing the color that heated her cheeks. "This is fine."

"It's also safer," he said, sobering as he opened the passenger door for her, then came around to slide into the driver's seat. "Sanchez didn't get where he is by being dumb. A man in his position has a hell of a lot of enemies, and he knows it. He's going to be looking for a tail just as a matter of precaution. If he spies us following him, he'll have a difficult time tracing the car back to me or the agency."

"You really think he might realize we're following him? Would he confront us?"

"It's always a possibility," he said as he put the car in gear and pulled away from the curb. "If he does, we just act like we don't have a clue what he's talking about and pretend we're out on a date. Then we'll leave as soon as we can without looking like he scared us off."

"But he'll recognize us if we try to follow him again," she pointed out. "He's not going to do anything if he knows he's being tailed."

Far from worried, he only grinned. "We'll wear disguises next time. Trust me, when I get through with you, your own mother won't recognize you."

"My mother's pretty sharp," she told him, "and I imagine Roberto Sanchez is, too."

"You got that right. The man hasn't evaded arrest all these years by being stupid. There's not a hell of a lot of people he trusts."

Checking his mirrors, he suddenly pulled over on a busy downtown street and nodded to the small office building located in the next block. "That's his office," he said as he put the car in Park and cut the engine. "According to the information his wife gave you, he always parks in the parking lot next door, right?"

She nodded. "He drives a silver Mercedes convertible."

They could both clearly see the Mercedes parked in the lot down the block. It was right in the front row and the only Mercedes on the lot.

Sitting back in her seat, Josephine sighed in relief.

"Good, he's still here. Olivia said he told her he would be late tonight because he has a business dinner immediately after work. She thinks he's meeting a woman."

"Time will tell," he said as he, too, settled back in his seat. "Powerful men like Sanchez aren't known for their fidelity."

The words were hardly out of his mouth when the front door of Sanchez's office building opened and the man himself stepped outside. Recognizing him not only from the photo his wife had left with Josie, but also from seeing his picture on the news, Wiley quickly started the car. "Looks like it's showtime."

Twenty seconds later, Roberto Sanchez pulled out into the traffic and headed west. When Wiley waited another twenty seconds before he followed, Josephine frowned. "What are you waiting for? We're losing him!"

He only smiled. "There's an art to tailing someone, Josie girl, and the first rule of thumb is not to get in a hurry. You don't want to run up on someone's butt."

"But you don't want to lose them, either," she argued. "And that's exactly what you're doing. He's turning!"

"Hold on, hold on," he drawled easily, speeding up and changing lanes. "I've got everything under control."

Ten seconds later, he took the same turn Sanchez had and spied him half a mile ahead of them. Wiley shot her a triumphant grin. "See...what'd I tell you? Trust me. I know what I'm doing. I've been doing this for a long time." Returning his attention to his driving, he stiffened, swearing. "Damn! Where'd he go?"

"He turned right into the parking lot of the bar on the corner," she said dryly. "You were saying?"

Far from chagrined, he only chuckled. "I knew there was a reason I brought you along."

Fighting a smile, Josephine rolled her eyes. The man had an answer for everything. "You brought me along because you didn't trust me to stay in the office alone," she said dryly. "So now what?"

"We're going in that bar."

He drove past it without checking his speed, and Josie felt her heart sink as she got her first good look at the place. "It's a dive. How are we going to go in there? The second we step through the front door, everyone inside will know we don't belong there."

"No, they won't. Because we won't look like we do now. I've got some wigs and stuff in the trunk."

Josephine couldn't believe he was serious. "You really think that's all it's going to take?"

"That and a little makeup," he said confidently. "Of course, if you don't think you can pull it off…"

"Oh, no you don't!" she said quickly, making him laugh. "You're not getting rid of me at this late date. I can pull off anything you can. Let's go."

She didn't have to tell him twice. Grinning broadly, he headed toward the nearest fast-food restaurant, where they could each use the public restroom to change.

Ten minutes later, Josephine stood in the restaurant's restroom and studied herself critically in the mirror. There was no question, at least in her eyes, that she still looked like a librarian. And there was no way that a librarian would ever step foot in a sleazy bar. If she wanted to look like she belonged there, she was going to have to make some major changes. First, she had to get rid of the jacket.

* * *

Sitting in a booth across from the restrooms, Wiley checked his watch and scowled. He'd changed into a faded black T-shirt and rough work boots, applied a fake tattoo and a shaggy black mustache, then slicked back his hair, all in the time it took to order a hamburger and fries. And Josie was still in the restroom! How long had she been in there? Fifteen…twenty minutes? A complete makeover didn't take that long! What the devil was the woman doing?

Frustrated, he couldn't help wondering if they'd already lost Sanchez. Just because the man was probably meeting his lover at the bar didn't mean the two of them would stay there for any length of time. Right this minute, they could be walking out the door!

Rising from the booth, he strode over to the women's restroom and knocked sharply on the door. "C'mon, Josie! We've got to get out of here."

"I'm coming," she called. "Just a second."

"We don't have a second," he retorted, trying to keep his voice down so half the restaurant didn't hear him. "We're running out of time—"

She jerked open the door and whatever he was going to say next was lost forever. "I'm ready!" she said brightly. "What do you think?"

She could have knocked him over with a feather. Stunned, he just stood there with his jaw on the ground.

Grinning, she laughed in delight. "I take it I surprised you?"

Surprised? That didn't begin to describe what he was feeling. He couldn't take his eyes off her. "How did you manage this?" he said hoarsely. "I didn't even recognize you."

Her brown eyes danced with triumph. "I just applied a little more makeup and took my hair down. Do you think I'll stick out like a sore thumb?"

Oh, yes, he wanted to tell her. She would stick out, all right, but not because she looked like she didn't belong there. He didn't know how she'd done it, but by letting down her hair, teasing the top, and changing her makeup, she'd somehow completely altered her appearance. When she'd walked into the office for the first time—was it only yesterday?—she'd been neatly dressed in linen slacks, a simple white blouse and wire-rimmed glasses, and she'd had *librarian* stamped all over her. There was, however, no sign of that woman now.

She had, no doubt, tried to make herself look like a hard-edged woman who frequented bars, but she'd failed miserably. She'd taken off her jacket, and with her hair loose about her bare shoulders and her mouth soft with lipstick, she looked feminine, touchable, kissable. Why hadn't he noticed before now how pretty she was? he wondered, stunned.

The blush that she'd brushed on her cheeks emphasized her high cheekbones, and her eye makeup, though deliberately extreme, seemed to make her eyes bigger, darker. And then there was her dress. It wasn't skin-tight, but it still managed to hug the curves of her breasts and hips in a way that somehow made him drool. Had she looked like this yesterday? She must have, but somehow, he hadn't noticed. It must have been those librarian clothes, he told himself. They'd hidden her figure. What else was she hiding?

Grinning, she waved her hand in front of his face. "Wiley? Hello? Are you in there?"

He blinked and was shocked to feel heat steal into his face. What was she doing to him? "Of course I'm here," he growled. "You look nice."

Another woman might have been disappointed with such a weak compliment, but she'd seen the look on his face, and there was no question that she'd surprised him. She'd struck him dumb, she thought, swallowing a giggle. That was the only compliment she needed.

"Thanks," she said, flashing her dimples at him. "You look pretty good yourself."

Pleased with her own gross understatement, she prayed he couldn't hear the pounding of her heart. How could a man who was already breathtakingly sexy look even sexier just by pasting on a fake mustache and a tattoo?

"Thanks," he said roughly, making her wonder if he could read her thoughts. "Let's get going. Hopefully Sanchez hasn't left."

He didn't have to tell her twice. They hurried outside to the car and headed back to the bar, where they both sighed in relief when they saw Sanchez's car still parked in the parking lot. Josephine expected Wiley also to park in the bar's lot, but he found a place on the street, instead. "Just in case we have to make a fast getaway," he said when she lifted an inquiring brow.

Her heart lurched at that, and suddenly, fears she hadn't allowed herself to consider before reared their ugly head. What was she doing? she wondered. She didn't know anything about being a PI! What if Sanchez discovered they were following him and pulled out a gun? He was the head of the Mexican mafia—he probably didn't leave his house without a weapon. If he confronted them, she didn't even know what to do!

"Josie? You're awfully pale all of a sudden. What's going on?"

Glancing up from her thoughts to discover that Wiley had cut the engine and walked around to open her door for her, she just sat there. "Maybe this is a mistake. You're right—I shouldn't be here. I don't have any training for this kind of thing. Go on without me. I'll just stay here and wait for you."

"Oh, no, you don't," he growled, taking her hand and pulling her to her feet beside him. "Don't chicken out on me now."

"But I don't know what to do!"

He grinned. "Just follow my lead. We're just a couple out on a date. That's all you have to remember."

He made it sound so simple, but nothing felt simple as he took her hand as if he had a thousand times before and led her toward the entrance to the bar. She wanted to run...and she wanted never to let go of his hand. This was crazy! she thought wildly. What was he doing to her?

They reached the door to the bar then, and Wiley pulled it open so she could precede him inside. The second he joined her inside, he slipped his arm around her waist. Startled, she started to ask him what the heck he thought he was doing, but the words never left her mouth. Across the bar, Roberto Sanchez was dead center in her line of vision. He wasn't looking at her or Wiley, but he only had to turn his head mere inches to see them. Without saying a word, she relaxed and leaned into Wiley.

"Good girl," he murmured. "Let's grab a seat at the bar."

"Whatever you say," she said quietly. Praying her

legs wouldn't give out on her, she let him lead her over to one of the stools at the bar.

Roberto Sanchez never noticed. His eyes were trained on his companion. Young enough to be his daughter, she wore a tight, low-cut blouse and jeans that looked as though they'd been painted on.

The minute they reached the bar, Wiley ordered them each a beer without consulting her, then angled her barstool toward where he stood. Josephine wanted to get a better look at Roberto Sanchez's girlfriend, but Wiley never gave her a chance. Before she could guess his intentions, he leaned down to kiss her.

Chapter 5

Her heart slamming against her ribs, she couldn't have been more surprised if he'd got down on his knees and proposed. But she didn't pull back. *Follow my lead.* His words echoing in her ears, she lifted an arched brow and looked him right in the eye as his mouth came closer to hers. "What are you doing?"

At her quiet inquiry, he only grinned and leaned down to nuzzle her ear. "Sanchez just looked this way," he murmured in a soft, rough voice that sent a delicate shiver sliding down her neck. "We have to make sure he thinks we're not interested in anything but each other."

Josephine hardly heard him. Her blood heated, and every fiber of her being seemed to quiver in anticipation. If she tilted her head just the tiniest bit, his mouth would brush her ear. Could she be that daring? There'd

been so few men in her life—her experience was practically nil. Did he know what he was doing to her?
Would he notice if she leaned into him? Would he realize she was inviting him to…

What? a voice in her head drawled. Kiss you? Of
course he would! The man fairly oozes sex appeal and
experience. He knows exactly what he's doing—which
is more than can be said for you! Have you forgotten
Sanchez? Wiley hasn't. The only reason he's coming on
to you in this filthy bar is because he's working! He's
trying to get the goods on Sanchez so he can put this case
behind him. He's not interested in you. Remember that!

Focus, she told herself silently. She might as well
have told herself to turn green. When she tried to concentrate on Olivia Sanchez and the pain and hurt in her
eyes when she'd come to her for help, all she could
think about was Wiley and how close he was. Then he
looped a casual arm across the back of her barstool and
began to play with her hair. Just that easily, her thoughts
scattered.

"So what do you think?"

Whatever cologne he was wearing should have been
outlawed, she mused dreamily as the spicy, masculine
sent wrapped around her like an embrace. She couldn't
seem to keep her eyes open when he was this close.
What *would* it feel like to kiss him? Instinctively, she
knew he was one of those men who knew how to please
a woman. He hadn't even really touched her and her
bones were already melting.

"Josie? Sweetheart? Why do I have the feeling I've
lost you? What planet are you on?"

It was the husky amusement in his voice rather than

his words that snapped Josephine back to her surroundings. Part of her was horrified that she'd nearly fallen for what he'd already warned her was an act, but then her sense of humor kicked in. Glancing up at him, she made no attempt to hold back a wry smile. "You're good, Wiley—I've got to give you that. For a minute there, you really had me going."

His blue eyes dancing with wicked laughter, he leaned close and rubbed her nose with his. "You're not mad?"

"Two can play at this game," she purred, and deliberately reached up to trace his ear with a seductive finger. "How'm I doing?"

His eyes darkened even as his grin broadened in appreciation. Capturing her teasing finger, he drew it down to his knee, where he held it captive. "You surprise me, Miss London. I didn't know you had it in you."

"You ain't seen nothing yet, Mr. Valentine." And with no more warning than that, she began to slowly slide her hand up his thigh.

Under her palm, she felt his muscles jump, but he made no move to stop her. Instead, his eyes locked with hers and he growled softly, "Truce."

She didn't move another inch. "Truce," she echoed softly.

Never taking his eyes from hers, he reached into his shirt pocket and pulled out something that resembled a cigarette lighter. A split second later, Josephine heard a nearly silent click and realized it was a camera.

"Wow," she whispered, not daring to look at Roberto Sanchez. "That's cool."

"So are you," he said with a grin. "I owe you an apology."

Surprised, she lifted a brow. "For what?"

"For thinking you would be a liability tonight. You've done great."

At their table in the corner, Sanchez and his "date" rose to their feet and started toward the front door. Catching sight of them from the corner of his eye, Wiley swore silently. They were headed right for them and there was no time to disappear into the woodwork. Without a thought, he reached for Josie.

"What—"

Snatching her into his arms, he covered her mouth with his before she could say another word. All he could think of was he couldn't let Sanchez get a good look at either one of them, not if they were going to be tailing him for the next few days. Sure, they had taken pains to disguise themselves, but Sanchez had the eyes of a hawk. Little went on within his sight that he didn't see.

Thankfully, he wasn't interested in a couple kissing by the bar. He and his date strolled past without slowing down, and a few seconds later, the door to the bar swung shut behind them. In a distant part of his brain, Wiley acknowledged that he needed to go after them, but he couldn't. Not yet. Josie filled his arms as if she'd been made for him. When she melted into him, he completely forgot why he was kissing his partner senseless in a rundown bar he normally wouldn't dream of taking a woman to. When she kissed him back, he forgot his own name.

Later, he couldn't have said how long he kissed her for. He just knew he wasn't ready to let her go when a woman seated at the far end of the bar laughed sharply, jerking him back to his senses. What the hell was he doing? he wondered wildly, swallowing a curse. They were working, not kissing for real. Or least, that was the way it had started out. When had it changed? And how? She wasn't even his type!

Abruptly releasing her, he stepped back, only to groan when she swayed and frowned up at him in confusion. "Why did you do that?" she asked huskily.

"Sanchez was coming this way—I didn't want him to see your face," he said in a voice as rough as sandpaper. "I'm sorry if I caught you off guard. Are you all right?"

"No."

A crooked grin curled the corners of his mouth at her honesty. "I know how you feel, but we don't have time to discuss it now. Sanchez is getting away. C'mon."

They rushed outside, but it quickly became apparent that they wouldn't be going anywhere except home. Roberto Sanchez was gone, along with his car and the woman he'd come there to meet. And they didn't have a clue where they'd gone.

"Damn!" Wiley swore. "This is my fault. I lost my head—"

Josephine's heart lurched at his words. So she hadn't been the only one who'd been caught up in the heat of that kiss. Not sure if she wanted to smile or run for the hills, she said, "At least we have a picture of them together. And maybe the woman didn't take her car. We could wait to see if they come back…"

She thought it was a good idea, but he merely lifted a sexy masculine brow at her. "So what are you suggesting? That we sit in the car for the next couple of hours and wait for them to come back? What are we going to do while we wait?"

Put that way, she had to admit that he had a point. Heat stealing into her cheeks, she sighed. "Okay, bad idea. Then why don't we write down all the license plate numbers of the cars in the parking lot and check them out when we get back to the office? One of them could be hers."

"If she didn't take a cab here," he said.

"The place is a dive, Wiley. Do you really think she took a cab here?"

He grinned. "I'm just covering all contingencies."

"Which is why we should check out all the cars in the parking lot."

"Okay, okay," he chuckled. "We'll run the plates through the DMV. Who knows? We might get lucky."

"Olivia Sanchez also gave me a list of her husband's favorite hangouts. We could drive by them and see if his car's parked out front. It's a longshot, but since we've already lost him, there's not much else we can do tonight."

He could think of a hell of a lot they could do together other than chase down longshots, but those were the kind of thoughts that were only going to get him in trouble. She's your partner, he reminded himself sternly, nothing more. "We might as well give it a try," he agreed, and quickly wrote down the plate numbers of all the cars in the bar parking lot.

Ten minutes later, they headed for an exclusive club on the north side of town. Not surprisingly, there was no sign of Sanchez's Mercedes convertible in the parking lot.

"I didn't think he'd be here," Wiley said as he headed for the second place on the list Olivia Sanchez had given Josie. "He's not going to take his lover anywhere he might run into a family friend who might tell his wife."

"She didn't need a friend to tell her," Josephine said. "She knows. She just needs us to give her the details."

"And when we do, she's going to flay him alive. If Sanchez wasn't such a scum bucket, I might feel sorry for him."

"He deserves it. If he wants to fool around, he should get a divorce."

"Trust me—he's not a man who feels like he has to answer to anyone, even a wife," Wiley retorted. "His life's about to get very interesting."

"Once we get the goods on him," she reminded him. "Right now, things don't look too hopeful."

"Don't give up hope," he said easily. "We're really just getting started."

They spent the next two hours checking out the list, but there was no sign of Roberto Sanchez or his Mercedes anywhere. Disappointed, Josephine sighed in defeat as Wiley headed downtown. "This has turned out to be nothing but a major waste of time. I'm sorry, Wiley."

"For what?" he asked, surprised.

"For getting you involved in this to begin with. I should never have accepted Olivia Sanchez as a client."

"Hey, don't worry about it. You're new in town—there was no way for you to know who Roberto Sanchez was. And it's not like I don't make mistakes," he added. "Boonie used to tease me all the time about the people I accepted as clients. Most of them didn't have two nickels to rub together. By the time I found that out, it was too late—I already felt sorry for them."

For all of two seconds, Josephine believed every word. Then she burst out laughing. "You a softie? I don't think so."

Far from offended, he only grinned. "I had you going there for a minute."

"You don't have a soft bone in your body."

"Sure, I do. Ask anyone. They'll tell you I like puppies and babies and bunny rabbits."

"And crocodiles and barracudas and dragons."

"True," he chuckled. "What can I say? I'm just one surprise after another."

"I'll remember that," she said dryly. He pulled into Boonie's driveway then and she was surprised when he cut the engine. "You don't have to walk me to the door. It's late. I'm sure you'd like to get home."

"It's not that late," he replied, unbuckling his seatbelt. "Anyway, I just live around the corner. I just want to make sure you're safe."

Josephine wasn't one of those women who jumped at every shadow, but she did appreciate Wiley's presence as they started up the front walk. "It takes a while to get used to a new house," she admitted. "I'm not usually a fraidy cat, but last night, it seemed like I heard every creak and groan the house made."

"The neighborhood is usually pretty quiet," Wiley assured her. "I can't remember the last time there was a break-in around here. That doesn't mean it can't happen, of course, but don't forget…you've got Ethel. She's better than a watchdog. She can scream like a woman when she's scared."

Grinning, Josephine chuckled. "She's a character, that's for sure. I never know what she's going to say next."

Unlocking the front door, she stepped inside with Wiley two steps behind her. Sitting on her perch in front of the television, which Josephine had left on for her,

Ethel perked up, her dark eyes sparkling with interest as she observed the two of them. "Sweety's got a sweety," she suddenly sang gleefully.

Stopping in her tracks, Josephine groaned. "She might be better than a watchdog, but at least a dog doesn't make smart remarks."

"Aw, come on," Wiley chuckled. "Could a dog be this interesting?"

When Josephine just gave him a baleful look, he turned to the parrot with a grin. "People with no sense of humor just don't know what they're missing, do they, Ethel?"

"Life's a party," the bird retorted. "Get down!"

When they both laughed, Ethel stretched her wings, but Wiley didn't give her a chance to get rolling with the wisecracks. Turning serious, he said, "How's it going, Ethel? Has it been pretty quiet around here?"

"Not a creature is stirring, not even a mouse," she replied. "Darn. Where's dinner?"

"In your bowl," he retorted. "Bon appetit."

"Yum," Ethel cackled, and turned her attention to eating.

Wiley grinned at Josie. "Looks like you're safe for the night."

"From mice and men," she said with a chuckle. "Thanks."

She walked him to the door, and when his eyes met hers, memories stirred between them. In the time it took to blink, they were back in the bar, back in each other's arms.

Later, Josephine couldn't have said how long they stood there, close but not touching, remembering. Then, just when she thought she would die if she couldn't step into his arms, he said thickly, "I've got to go. Good night."

No! she wanted to cry. But it was too late. He was gone.

Chapter 6

Josephine knew she was in trouble when she dreamed about Wiley all night long. Finally falling asleep around four in the morning, she woke at eight when she found herself reaching for him. Groaning, she rolled to her back, not sure if she wanted to laugh or cry. This couldn't be happening! She couldn't be dreaming about Wiley because of one kiss! She'd been kissed before, for heaven's sake. Granted, that was four years ago, and Arnold Shoemaker was no Wiley Valentine. He'd worn his belt cinched tightly at his waist and never did anything without consulting his mother. The only reason she'd gone out with him was because she was friends with his cousin, who had begged her to give him a chance. *He* had kissed *her,* not the other way around, and she certainly hadn't dreamed about him or the kiss later.

Wiley, on the other hand, was an entirely different

matter. Why did he have to be sexy? Sexy men weren't interested in her—they never gave her a second look. Or at least they never had before.

Wiley was just making sure Sanchez didn't get a good look at either one of you, that irritating little voice in her head reminded her. Don't get all warm and fuzzy on the inside. That kiss was strictly business.

Unable to deny the truth, she sighed. She knew better than to daydream. Women like her didn't get that luxury. She was a good person, a hard worker, intelligent and caring, but she wasn't was the kind men found exciting. She'd accepted long ago that she never would be.

That was okay, she told herself. She could still work with Wiley, still enjoy his company. Thanks to Boonie, her life would never be boring again.

Grinning at the thought, she rolled out of bed and stepped over to her closet. It was Saturday, and the office was closed. Maybe she'd spend the morning reading more of Boonie's diaries, then explore the Riverwalk later in the afternoon. She'd find somewhere nice to have dinner—

The doorbell rang then, startling her. On her perch in the living room, Ethel chimed, "Domino's! Time to eat!"

Josie laughed. "It's eight o'clock in the morning, silly. Trust me—I didn't order pizza."

Hurriedly slipping on a robe, she strode to the front door, wondering who could possibly be ringing her doorbell so early on a Saturday morning. She didn't know a soul in town except…

"Wiley!" she said, trying to look stern. "What are you doing here? Do you know what time it is?"

"Of course I do," he retorted. Leering at her teasingly,

he grinned at the sight of her Winnie the Pooh pjs. "Did I happen to mention how much I love Pooh?"

Struggling not to smile, she ignored the heat climbing in her cheeks and said, "You can't just drop by whenever the mood strikes you. Especially not at the crack of dawn on a Saturday!"

Far from chastised, he only grinned. "It's not the crack of dawn—the sun's been up for hours and it's time for a little adventure. Are you game?"

The wicked sparkle in his eyes had her heart tripping over itself. Wary, remembering all too well just how intoxicating his brand of adventure was, she hesitated. "For what?"

"After I got home last night, I was doing a little detective work on the computer and discovered that Sanchez not only owns a motorcycle but he's heavily into the riding scene around town. And there's a memorial ride and picnic today to honor a friend of his who was killed in an accident last month. I thought we'd go."

She blinked. "This is a joke…right? You want me to ride a motorcycle?"

"You don't have to make it sound like I'm asking you to strip naked and ride down the street like Lady Godiva," he teased. "I'll drive. All you have to do is sit behind me and hang on."

When she just looked skeptical, he said, "C'mon, live a little. Sanchez will be there—he helped organize it. We can tail him all day and have fun, too. How many times can you combine work and play? It's the perfect setup."

"But what about his wife? If the guy who died was such a good friend of his, won't she come, too?"

"Are you kidding? Olivia Sanchez is a high-class

lady who devotes most of her time to charity work for children. Trust me, she wouldn't be caught dead on a motorcycle. And while the cat's away…"

"The rat will play," she finished for him. "You expect him to bring his date from last night, don't you?"

He shrugged. "Maybe. Maybe not. He could bring someone else. After all, we don't know that he's just seeing one woman. He's a powerful man who probably never hears the word *no*. He could be cheating on his wife with a whole slew of women."

He had a point. Why would Roberto Sanchez limit himself to one woman when he could probably have anyone he wanted? "If this ride is with some kind of motorcycle club, won't Sanchez and his friends know we don't belong there?"

"It's a memorial ride advertised on the Internet," he replied. "There'll be a lot of people there Sanchez won't know. And you don't have to worry about him recognizing us from last night," he added, reading her mind. "I came prepared. Black leather covers up a host of sins."

He held up a large plastic bag which she'd only just then noticed and pulled out a biker jacket. "I've got everything you need," he told her. "Go ahead and try it on."

Josephine knew she should have said thanks, but no thanks. She really did need to rethink being a PI—it was turning out to be a lot riskier than she'd first thought. But when she should have turned Wiley down, the words just wouldn't come. Instead, she found herself wondering what she would look like dressed as a biker.

"You're tempted, aren't you?"

Looking up from her thoughts, she found him grinning knowingly at her. Caught redhanded, she had to laugh. "You don't play fair. How did you guess?"

His blue eyes twinkling, he shrugged. "I don't know. You look like one of those women who played it safe your entire life. There's nothing wrong with that," he assured her, "but there's got to be a secret part of you that longs to be daring."

She hardly knew the man, yet he knew her better than she knew herself. Before Boonie died and left her her share in the detective agency, Josephine would have sworn that she was completely satisfied with her safe, unexciting world. Obviously, she couldn't have been more wrong.

"All right, so maybe I've wondered what it would feel like to ride down the street on the back of a motorcycle or be a lingerie model and walk down a runway in my underwear. That doesn't mean I'd actually do it."

"Damn," he swore teasingly. "I never even thought of a lingerie model. I must be slipping."

"Don't get any ideas, Einstein," she warned, fighting a smile. "Black leather's one thing. Lingerie's a whole other category."

Far from disappointed, he only grinned. "One can only hope." Pushing the bag of clothes into her arms, he nodded toward her bedroom. "Go on. Go try them on. Let's see how you like being a motorcycle mama."

The old Josephine, the librarian who'd never done anything more adventuresome than pay her bills online rather than through the mail, would have quickly come up with an excuse and let him go on the bike ride alone. The woman he insisted on calling Josie—the woman who was secretly beginning to like the name *Josie*—

couldn't go back to the safe, quiet life she'd lived in the past. She was going, but this time, she wouldn't get caught up in the game they were playing and forget that their "dates" were just pretend.

Hurrying into her room, she dumped the contents of the bag out on the antique iron bed she'd inherited from Boonie, then laughed. Black leather pants and jacket, black tank top, curly red wig and sunglasses. She would have to ask Wiley where he'd gotten the outfit at eight o'clock in the morning and who had provided it. Pulling off her pajamas, she reached for the black leather pants.

A few minutes later, she stood before the mirror and stared at herself in amazement. Even with no makeup, she looked nothing like a librarian. In fact, she looked as though she'd never walked into a library in her life! And she loved it!

But she still had some work to do.

Sitting down at the old-fashioned dressing table that was still decorated with Boonie's favorite old pictures, she quickly pinned up her hair, then pulled on the wig. A few minutes later, she reached for her makeup. Grinning at herself in the mirror, she couldn't remember the last time she'd had so much fun. And the day hadn't even begun!

"What's she doing in there, Ethel?" Wiley asked the parrot as he paced restlessly. "How long does it take to change clothes and plop a wig on her head?"

"A lifetime," Ethel responded promptly. "Pull up a chair!"

"You nut," he said with a chuckle. "And no, I'm not pulling up a chair. We've got to get going. If she's not out in two minutes, I'm going in after her."

"Twooo minutes!" the parrot cried like a basketball announcer announcing the approaching end of a game. "You've got two minutes!"

The words were hardly out of the bird's mouth when Wiley heard Josie's bedroom door open. Whirling, he'd meant to tease her about primping, but he took one look at her and felt as if he'd been struck in the heart with an arrow. Black leather on Josephine London should have been outlawed. She looked incredible...and nothing like the woman he'd gotten to know over the course of the last few days. He could see her on a bike, on *his* bike, feel her arms around his waist, her body leaning into his as they raced down the highway as though they didn't have a care in the world.

"I guess I don't have to ask you how I look," she said, fighting a smile. "I take it you approve?"

"Approve?" he stuttered, snapping out of his daze. "You've got to be kidding! Of course I approve. You look incredible!"

"I feel pretty incredible," she admitted. "I should have bought a wig years ago! Do you know how freeing this is? My own mother wouldn't recognize me in this getup!"

If her mother was as prim and proper as Josephine, she would have a fit if she saw her daughter in black leather, Wiley thought with a grin. But that was a thought he kept to himself.

"Boonie would be proud of you," he told her. "You look nothing like the woman who walked into that bar last night."

"Thank you," she said huskily. "And thank you for letting me be a part of all this. I'm having the time of my life."

Surprised, he said, "You don't have to thank me, Josie. You're a partner."

"But you didn't have to make it so much fun," she replied. "I'm having a blast!"

She wasn't the only one. Wiley couldn't remember the last time he'd enjoyed a case so much. And it was all because of Josie. He'd been up at the crack of dawn, so excited about going with her on the bike ride that he hadn't been able to sleep. He'd gotten a friend who owned a bike shop to open his shop before seven, then he'd bought Josie everything she would need for their ride—all without even knowing if he could talk her into going with him.

He'd lost his mind and all perspective—he readily admitted it. If he'd had any sense, he would have avoided her like the plague this morning. But he couldn't stay away from her, and that scared the hell out of him. He'd never had such a strong reaction to a woman in his life. Every time she smiled, laughed with delight when she did something for the first time, she totally captivated him. Right or wrong, there was no way he could walk away from her.

"You ain't seen nothing yet," he told her with a grin. "Come on. Let's go see what kind of trouble we can get into."

They didn't have to go far…only as far as Wiley's bike. The second Josie gingerly climbed on the motorcycle behind him and slipped her arms around his waist, they both could have sworn they heard—and felt—the other catch their breath. Hearts started to pound, but neither said a word about the awareness that throbbed between them.

"Okay?" Wiley asked hoarsely.

No! she almost cried. How could she be all right when he was so close she could feel the heat of his body through the black leather they both wore? How could she be all right when nothing had ever felt so right in her life? Dear Lord, she was in trouble!

"Josie?"

"I'm fine," she said huskily. "I'm just trying to figure out where the seatbelt is."

"Cute," he chuckled. "Don't worry. You won't need a seatbelt. I don't take chances on a bike."

He might not, but she certainly did, she thought, swallowing a giggle as he started down the street with her clinging tightly to his back. There was no other way to describe getting on the back of a motorcycle with a man who made her heart race. And she wouldn't have changed it for the world.

Chapter 7

His hormones working overtime, every nerve in his body attuned to Josie and the feel of her arms around his waist, Wiley had to force himself to concentrate as he headed for the motorcycle bar on the northwest side of town where the riders were gathering for the memorial ride. It wasn't easy. With every curve, every dip in the road, Josie crowded closer. And everywhere her body brushed his, he burned.

How the hell was he going to get through the day? he wondered as they arrived at the bar and pulled up behind dozens of motorcycles lined up in the street. He was already drooling over her and the ride hadn't even started yet.

Thankful for the chance to put some space between them, he hurriedly dismounted, then turned to help Josie. She, however, was already off the bike and searching the crowd. "He's here," she said softly. "Over by the entrance to the bar. And he's not alone."

Wiley turned casually, as if he was checking out the size of the crowd, and spied Sanchez with his date just as the woman pulled off her helmet. Long blond hair tumbled halfway down her back, but it was her face that drew the eye of every man there. She belonged in a beauty contest. Wiley had never been interested in women with the perfect features of an ice princess, but he had to admit that she was incredibly beautiful.

Beside him, Josie gasped silently. "I can't believe it," she told him in a low hiss. "You were right. He *is* with another woman! What a sleaze!"

Wiley had to laugh at her outrage. "Welcome to the real world."

"You're jaded."

"I know people," he said with a shrug. "Take your helmet off and climb up on the bike. I want to take a picture."

Surprised, she just looked at him. "What?"

His lips twitched. "Climb up on the bike, sweetheart. I want to take *a picture.*"

When he nodded ever so slightly toward where Sanchez stood with his "date," Josephine could have kicked herself. For a second, she'd actually thought he wanted a picture of her. Thank God, she hadn't said anything.

Remember why you're here.

Repeating that mantra in her head over and over again, she still hesitated. Casting a quick glance at Sanchez and the blond knockout with him, she said, "Aren't you afraid they'll notice?" she asked in a low-pitched voice that didn't carry past his ears. "Sanchez might be suspicious."

"Trust me," he said dryly, "you're worrying about nothing. Even if he sees us, he won't think anything of it. I'm just taking a picture of my date. What's wrong with that?"

He made it sound so simple, but as she pulled her helmet off and carefully made sure her red wig was still in place, her heart was thumping like crazy. Gingerly, she climbed onto Wiley's motorcycle as he pulled out a 35mm camera she hadn't even realized he'd brought. Making no effort to hide what he was doing, he positioned himself on the opposite side of the Harley so that when he took a picture of Josie, Sanchez was in the background.

"Smile," he told Josie. "Say money."

Surprised, she laughed. "What happened to smile?"

"I just got it," he retorted, snapping the picture. A split second later, he pointed the camera just a few degrees to the right and, lightning-quick, took two pictures of Sanchez and his paramour.

Josephine was dying to look over her shoulder but she didn't dare. "Relax," Wiley said with a smile. "No one saw a thing. They're all staring at the blonde."

She released her breath in a rush. "Thank God! Can we leave now?"

"Are you kidding? We're just getting started. We need to find out the girlfriend's name. We won't be able to do that if we cut and run now."

"I was afraid you were going to say that," she groaned. "Doesn't this make you nervous?"

"Not at all," he said with a grin. "Think about it. What's the worst that can happen?"

"Sanchez could discover that we don't belong here."

"So what if he does? He's not going to kill us—there are too many witnesses. And why would he hurt us, anyway? He doesn't know who we are or what we do for a living. He can't even trace the plates on my bike—I changed them."

"Oh, God, why did you have to tell me that? Now I really am worried. What are you going to do if a cop stops us?"

"Tell him what we're doing and take the ticket," he said simply. "I'd rather do that than give Sanchez an opportunity to discover who I am and where I live. I like to take chances, sweetheart, but not that kind."

Put that way, she had to admit he had a point. "So what do we do? Circulate? You have to know that gives me the willies."

He laughed. "Don't worry, Sanchez isn't going to let anyone get too close. In fact, he won't stick around long. There's too many people around he doesn't know. As soon as the ride's over with, watch him—he'll be out of here."

"But he organized this to honor his friend," she argued. "Surely he won't leave early."

"Time will tell," he said ruefully. "C'mon. It looks like we're about to get rolling."

Her heart pounding, she carefully pulled her helmet back on.

Wiley had hardly settled in front of her on the bike when Sanchez, as the lead rider, took off, his girlfriend perched like some kind of trophy on the back of his motorcycle.

What followed was like something out of a surreal dream. Wiley fell into line halfway back in the pack, and within seconds, they were surrounded on all sides by what surely had to be other members of the Mexican mafia. Josephine felt her heart stop just at the thought.

Later, she couldn't have said where Sanchez led them. She wasn't familiar with San Antonio yet, not that that would have mattered. She was too busy watching Sanchez over Wiley's shoulder to pay attention to the direction they took. They visited all of the deceased man's old haunts, winding through the city until Josie didn't have a clue where she was. Then, just when she was convinced they were going to ride down every street in town, Sanchez turned into the grounds of what looked like an old park.

"This is the old polo fields," Wiley told her quietly. She didn't see any sign of anyone playing polo, but there were picnic tables under the trees where Sanchez had arranged for barbecue to be served to the guests. The riders quickly parked their bikes, and within a few short minutes, everyone found seats at the tables or spread blankets on the grass and dug into barbecued chicken, potato salad and beans.

Sinking down to the blanket Wiley had pulled from the storage compartment of his bike and spread out under a tree, Josie deliberately sat with her back to where Sanchez sat at a table thirty feet away. Wiley had gotten them each a plate of food, but Josie's stomach was knotted with nerves. She ate a few bites, but that was all she could manage.

"Something wrong with your food?" Wiley asked, frowning.

"I'm just nervous," she said quietly. "I thought you said Sanchez wouldn't stick around long."

"He won't," he replied. "In fact, it looks like something's going on now. He's about to make a speech."

The words were hardly out of his mouth when Sanchez addressed the crowd. "I want to thank everyone for coming. Carlos would have been touched by today's turnout. He was a good man."

Carlos Trevino was, in fact, a drug dealer who had been killed in a collision trying to outrun the police. Everyone there knew it, but Wiley wasn't surprised when no one said a word. After all, the majority of the people there were probably on the shady side of the law, too.

The direction of his gaze hidden behind the dark lenses of his sunglasses, Wiley never took his eyes off Sanchez as he finished his speech. The mafia kingpin, with his date at his side, moved among the tables, exchanging hugs with friends. Obviously, they were making their goodbyes.

That was all Wiley needed to see. Leaning across the blanket toward Josie, he murmured, "They're getting ready to leave. Follow my lead." And with no other warning than that, he kissed the side of her neck.

Josie's heart turned over in her breast. "Wiley..."

"We're going to get up and walk toward the trees behind me," he said huskily. "I want anyone who happens to notice to think we're going off to make love. Okay?"

Her blood heating and her head spinning, she wanted to ask him why he wanted all the people on the ride to think such a thing, but this obviously wasn't the time or place to ask any questions. When he rose to his feet and held out a hand to her, she followed his lead, just as he'd requested, and let him help her to her feet.

"Good girl," he murmured, smiling directly into her eyes. Grabbing the blanket, he threw it over his shoulder, then slipped an arm around her waist and pulled her snug against his side. "Let's go."

Heat climbing in her cheeks, Josephine didn't dare look back. "Do you think anyone is watching?" she whispered.

"I hope so," he growled. "Hang in there, sweetheart. Just until we get into the trees."

"What happens in the trees?"

"Just a little further," he urged, picking up the pace. "We're almost there."

Three steps later, they were in the trees. Another four, and they were completely hidden from view of the other riders. Wiley threw the blanket to the ground and grabbed her hand. "C'mon!"

Surprised, Josie stumbled, but he caught her without ever breaking stride. "Where are we going?" she panted.

"To the truck," he retorted, and pulled her with him further into the trees.

"The truck?" she huffed, puzzled. "What truck?"

The words were barely out of her mouth when they burst into a clearing and she stopped in amazement at the sight of the road she hadn't even known was there. And parked on the shoulder was a faded red pickup truck that looked like it had seen better days.

Confused, she frowned. "Is this yours? How—"

"The announcement on the Internet said the picnic would be here," he said as he jerked open the passenger door for her. "There are some things for you to change into," he added with a nod toward the items in the floorboard.

He hurried around to the driver's side and started the truck before he was completely in his seat. A heartbeat later, he put the truck in gear and took off. "I knew Sanchez would spot us if we followed him on the bike," he explained as he picked up speed, "so I borrowed the truck from the same friend who gave me the clothes. He followed me out here early this morning so I could drop the truck off."

Her heart pounding, Josephine hurriedly pulled off her wig, then shed her leather jacket. Reaching into the bag of goodies at her feet, she pulled out a long blond wig, a cowboy hat and sunglasses. "Yee-haw," she laughed, and quickly donned the entire disguise. "How do I look?"

"Like a different woman," he chuckled. Reaching behind her seat to the gunrack across the window, he grabbed his own cowboy hat, plopped it on his head at a rakish angle, then pushed on sunglasses. Very carefully, he peeled off the fake mustache, then took his eyes from the road long enough to arch a brow at Josie. "Well? What do you think?"

"Ride 'em, cowboy," she said with a chuckle. "I just can't get over how good you are at this. Now, would you mind telling me where we're going?"

"We're tailing Sanchez, of course. This road intersects the road that fronts the polo field. If our timing's right, Sanchez should be a quarter of a mile ahead of us when we reach the stop sign. Keep your eyes peeled— we're coming up on it."

The words were hardly out of his mouth when they saw the stop sign in the distance. Just as it came into view, a motorcycle zoomed by on the cross street.

Pleased, Wiley grinned. "There's our guy. He's a little ahead of schedule, but that's okay. We'll just take our time."

Reaching the stop sign, he turned right and casually picked up speed. If Sanchez happened to notice the pickup far behind him, he would see exactly what Wiley wanted him to see—a cowboy and his girlfriend out for a casual drive in their old pickup.

Other vehicles joined them on the road, passing them, turning off, but Wiley was content to keep Sanchez in sight. And when the motorcycle turned down a residential street fifteen minutes later, Wiley was far enough behind Sanchez that it was several long minutes later before he and Josie drove down the same street. By that time, there was no sign of Sanchez and the blonde, but the motorcycle was parked in the driveway of a small brick house.

Driving past, Wiley didn't slow down. "Did you get the address?" he asked Josie.

"Seven thirty-six," she said.

"Good job," he replied. "Now we'll go back to the office and check it out. If we're lucky, we'll have the name of at least one of Sanchez's girlfriends within the hour."

It didn't take that long. Fifteen minutes later, they arrived at the office and rushed inside. Seated at his computer, Wiley immediately went to the Bexar Appraisal Website and typed in the address of the little brick house.

When the name of the owner of the property popped up a few moments later, Josephine frowned. "Valencia Enterprises. A *company* owns the house?"

Far from worried, he only laughed. "Valencia Enterprises' parent company is J.R. Sanchez, Incorporated. Juan *Roberto* Sanchez. He owns the house, just as I thought he did. We've got him, sweetheart. We've got him!"

Chapter 8

"Let's go out to dinner to celebrate!"

Dazed that they'd been able to get so much incriminating evidence against Sanchez in just two days, Josie said, "Shouldn't we wait until we've tracked down all the women Sanchez is involved with before we celebrate?"

Grinning, Wiley said, "Are you kidding? We may never track down all the women he's got on a string."

"But he's a drug lord!"

"The world is full of people who couldn't care less how someone makes their money as long as they can get their hands on some of it," Wiley retorted. "We'll spend a couple of more days on Sanchez and come up with an impressive list of names for Mrs. Sanchez. Trust me, she'll be satisfied."

"And if she's not? We just pick up the case again and get more pictures of her husband's paramours?"

"Exactly. So we're halfway home. Let's celebrate. You haven't seen the Riverwalk yet—not at night. Let's go out to eat, then go dancing. It'll be fun."

Josephine didn't doubt that. Whenever she was with Wiley, life was full of surprises…and fun. He made her laugh…and attracted her in a way no man ever had. For no other reason than that, she should have restricted her time with him to just work. But pain squeezed her heart just at the thought of turning down his invitation. It was just dinner and a little dancing, she reasoned. Surely she could handle that without losing her head. She just had to remember that he was one of those men who liked to flirt. If she didn't take him too seriously, she would be fine.

"I *would* like to see the Riverwalk at night…"

"Good! I'll pick you up at seven."

Her heart thumped in excitement. "I'll be ready," she promised huskily.

At five minutes to seven, Josephine studied herself in the mirror and wondered what had possessed her to buy, let alone wear, the outfit she had bought that afternoon at a small, eclectic dress shop around the corner from Boonie's house. The pencil-slim skirt was a black-and-white zebra print that molded her hips and thighs, and she'd topped it with an off-the-shoulder summer sweater in blood red. Cashmere soft, it had a feathery brooch at the neck that tickled her every time she looked to her left. She'd never worn red before…or anything that was dipped so low in front that it showed the curve of her breast. She felt feminine, sexy, nervous.

"Lady in red!" Ethel called out from her perch. "I like it!"

"Maybe I should change into something more conservative," Josephine said worriedly.

That, however, was as far as she got. The doorbell rang, and just that quickly, she ran out of time. Ethel called out, "Come in!" and Wiley stepped through the front door.

He took one look at her and stopped dead. "Wow! You look gorgeous!"

She blushed. "Actually, I was thinking about changing."

"Are you kidding? You can't! You're beautiful! I can't wait to show you off on the dance floor."

For the first time since she'd met him, he was completely sincere, without a glint of humor or teasing in his eyes. Her insecurities dissolving, she smiled. "You look pretty fantastic yourself."

His lips twitched, fascinating her. "We're going to create quite a stir tonight. Shall we go?"

When he held out his hand, they both knew that he wasn't just asking her to go out with him for the evening. He was asking her to step with him into the night and change their relationship forever. Her heart threatening to pound right out of her chest, she placed her hand in his.

If she was dreaming, Josephine didn't want ever to wake up. It was a beautiful summer evening, warm, but not too hot, with a breeze that stirred her hair and whispered through the ancient cypress trees that towered over the Riverwalk. And right from the beginning, Wiley let her know that their time together had nothing to do with work. He took her hand and twined his fingers with hers. His eyes met hers, and sparks jumped between them. The world could have stopped turning, and Josephine would have never noticed.

They had dinner at a little French restaurant located on a secluded section on the river. They were shown to a candlelit table for two under the stars, and the night turned magical. The food was delicious, but later, Josephine couldn't have said what she ate. All she remembered was the touch of Wiley's foot under the table as he played footsy with her and the almost physical stroke of his eyes as they wandered over her.

"Dance with me," he said huskily when they'd finished eating and the waiter had taken their plates away.

Surprised, she looked around. "Here? There's no band."

"There is across the river," he said, nodding to the bar across the river, where couples swayed to the romantic song the live band was playing. Rising to his feet, he held out his hand and smiled.

She could no more resist him than she could convince her heart to stop pounding when he smiled at her as if she was the only woman in the world. Placing her hand in his, she let him gently tug her to her feet and into his arms. Their waiter smiled, as did the other patrons seated around the restaurant, but Josephine never noticed. She was in his arms. Nothing else mattered.

When she melted against him as if there was nowhere else on earth she would rather be, Wiley swallowed a groan. He should have taken her home right then and there and ended this madness before it went any further, but he couldn't bring himself to let her go. When Boonie had told him she was leaving her half of the business to her great-niece, the librarian, he'd never expected his new partner to be anything but a prim and proper pain in the neck. Instead, she'd turned out to be the most fascinating woman he'd ever met.

Josie moved with him to the sounds of the old Frank Sinatra number being played by the band across the river, and the soft, subtle scent of her perfume drifted between them, teasing his senses. Urging her closer, he knew he was playing with fire, but he couldn't seem to stop himself. Over the course of the last two days, he'd pretended to be her lover for the sake of work, but he didn't want to pretend any more. And that shook him to the core. What had she done to him?

He was, he realized, getting in too deep, too fast. If he'd had a brain in his head, he would have ended things right then and there and taken the lady home. But he only had so much willpower, dammit, and when she was in his arms, there was no way in hell he could make himself let her go. Kissing her ear, the side of her neck, he took her from one dance to another.

Lost in the feel and heat and softness of her, he never noticed the passage of time until their waiter appeared and discreetly cleared his throat. When he pointed to his watch, Wiley realized with a start that the rest of the diners had left and the restaurant was about to close.

Shocked, he started to laugh. "It's time to get out of here," he told Josie, grinning.

Blinking as though she was coming out of a daze, she lifted her head from where it rested against his shoulder and frowned. "Why?"

"Because they can't lock up until we leave," he said with a chuckle. "It's after ten, sweetheart. We've been here all evening."

"Are you kidding? It can't be!"

When she glanced at her watch and blushed, Wiley wanted to pull her right back into his arms. After he paid their bill, however, he had to be content with taking her hand, instead, and walking her back home.

On her perch in the living room, Ethel stirred and observed them with what looked like irritation in her eyes. "Turn out the light!"

Chuckling, Wiley did just that. In the darkness, Josie grinned up at him. "I guess she told us."

"She's cranky when she doesn't get enough sleep," he said. "Boonie was the same way."

In the darkness, Ethel grumbled under her breath, then settled down to sleep. Wiley knew he should have taken that as his sign to leave, but when he stared down at Josie in the dark shadows of the night, leaving was the last thought in his head. He'd been waiting all night for a chance to kiss her, and this time, it would be for himself, not because some lowlife might be watching and he couldn't take the chance that either one of them might be recognized.

"I had a great time tonight," he said huskily. "I loved dancing with you."

She smiled and had no idea how she glowed. "It was wonderful. I didn't want it to end."

"It doesn't have to," he rasped, and reached for her.

A kiss, he told himself. Be content with just a kiss.

He should have been. It seemed as if they'd known each other for years, but it was only a matter of days since she'd first stepped into the office and introduced herself. Considering that—and the heat she stirred in him just by breathing—it was way too soon to jump into anything other than a kiss.

So why couldn't he let her go?

Because she lifted her mouth to his before he even touched her. Because she kissed him back hungrily, sweetly, and slipped her arms around his neck as if she would never let him go. Because just that easily, she made him want her so badly that he burned.

"You're driving me crazy," he rasped, kissing her again and again. "I've been wanting to do this all evening."

"Me, too," she said with a groan as his hands slid over her caressingly. "I don't want you to leave."

"Good," he growled. "Because I'm not."

Crazy about her, insane with need, he swung her up into his arms and carried her into her darkened bedroom. A few short minutes later, he laid her on the bed and reached for the zipper of her skirt. He was still struggling with it in the dark when she unbuttoned his shirt and slid it off his shoulders.

When her hands moved over his shoulders, tracing every muscle, he abandoned her skirt to snatch her sweater over her head. An instant later, he pulled her back in his arms for a scorching kiss. When he finally let her up for air, he was stretched out on the bed and his legs were twined with hers. When he reached for her zipper again, it slid down easily. A heartbeat later, the rest of their clothes went flying.

Gathering her close, skin against skin, he moved against her and Josie gasped softly. How long had she wanted him so badly? It seemed like forever. He stroked and teased and kissed his way up and down her body, and she forgot to think, forgot to breathe. He filled her senses, filled her, and she'd never felt so wonderful in her life.

When she came apart in his arms, Wiley very nearly lost what was left of his control. Groaning, he fought to hold on, to savor her release, to draw out the pleasure until they were both out of their mind with need, but he was fighting a losing battle. She was so sweet, so hot, and when she tightened her arms around him, urging him closer, she destroyed him. With a groan, he gave himself up to the need that tightened around him like a fist and lost himself in her.

She was falling in love with him.

Lying in his arms, feeling more complete than she'd ever felt in her life, she was almost asleep when the thought came out of the darkness to jerk her wide awake. Wiley never noticed. With his arms around her, her head on his bare chest, he soothed her with his stroking hands and slowly drifted to sleep.

Her heart slamming against her ribs, Josie didn't understand how he could possibly sleep at a time like this. Didn't he realize she was falling in love with him? She'd never loved anyone before. Did he love her? Should she ask him? She felt like a teenager suffering from her first crush, and she didn't know what to do. There were no books she knew of that she could study, no standard rules of procedure for falling in love for the first time in her life. She felt wonderful, on top of the world, terrified. All she needed in order for her world to be perfect was for him to tell her he loved her, too.

He didn't, unfortunately, say a word.

Chapter 9

The next morning, she drove him back to the old polo field to get his motorcycle. Relaxed, he teased her just as he always did and didn't say a word about the previous night. Pain squeezing her heart, Josephine followed his lead, but it wasn't easy. She couldn't pretend that nothing had happened between them. She was falling irrevocably in love with him, and he didn't seem to notice—or return her feelings. And that hurt. All she wanted to do was drop him off, then go back home so she could cry.

"You're going to go back to the office and work on the report for Olivia Sanchez?" he asked as she pulled up to his motorcycle.

It's Sunday—I need the day off, she almost told him, only to bite back the words just in time. Work would, she realized, distract her, and right then, she needed to think about anything other than the fact that Wiley wasn't in love with her.

All business, she said quietly, "I was going to drop the film off for development, then work on the report. What about you? What do you have to do today?"

"Paperwork," he said with a grimace. "I got behind when Boonie died and I haven't caught up yet. So I guess I'll see you back at the office."

When he pushed open the passenger door, then hesitated, she thought he was going to say something. His eyes searched hers, and Josie actually felt her heart skip a beat. Holding her breath, she waited for him to say something, anything, but he'd already thought better of it. "See you later," he said huskily, and stepped out of the car.

Fighting tears, she didn't dare look at him or she would have cried. As soon as he slammed the car door, she drove off and told herself not to look back. He'd given her directions to a camera shop where she could have the photos developed in an hour, so when she turned right at the next corner, the opposite direction he was going, he was lost to view. Only then did she let the tears flow.

Caught up in her misery, she didn't realize she had a low tire until it suddenly went completely flat. Alarmed, she quickly pulled over onto the shoulder and cut the engine. "Well, this is just great!" she said aloud, swiping at the tears that trailed down her cheeks. "Wiley's headed back to the office and I get to change a flat. It must be my lucky day."

Feeling sorry for herself, she reached for her cell phone and punched in the number of her road service.

She knew how to change a flat, of course, but she just didn't feel like getting her hands dirty. Not when all she wanted to do was cry.

When she hung up a few minutes later, however, she was tempted to call the road service back and cancel. It would be fifteen to thirty minutes before anyone could arrive to help her, and by that time, she could have the flat changed and be halfway to the tire store to have it fixed.

The decision made, she reached for her cell phone again, but before she could make the call, a vehicle pulled up behind her. Help, at last, she thought with a smile, and pushed open her door. "Thank you for stopping—"

The rest of her words died in her throat at the sight of the man stepping from the black SUV parked directly behind her. Roberto Sanchez. Horrified, she didn't believe for a minute that he had come across her by chance.

His first words confirmed it. "You've been following me," he said coldly. "Who the hell are you?"

The office seemed empty without her, and that surprised the hell out of Wiley. It wasn't like they'd worked together for years. And even if they had, he'd just left her. How could he possibly miss her so soon? He didn't even know her that well.

You know her well enough to know her smile, a voice in his head pointed out. *And what about her taste? Her scent? Out of all the women in the world, you would know her kiss even if you were blindfolded and on the dark side of the moon. What do you mean…you don't know her that well? Your heart recognized her the second she walked into the office. What else is there to know?*

Stunned, he sat at his desk as if turned to stone, unable to deny the truth when it hit him right in the face. He was falling in love with her! And he didn't even know how it had happened. He played the field—he always had. Everyone in his family was divorced and miserable, so he'd decided a long time ago that he wanted nothing to do with marriage. But Josie made him think of wedding bells and kids and holding her hand when she was in labor. He wanted to go to church with her and sleep with her in his arms for the rest of his life. He didn't care that they hardly knew each other. He'd been hers from the first moment his eyes met hers. And he had to tell her. Now!

Suddenly noticing how late it was, he frowned. Where the hell was she? She'd told him she was dropping the film off, but even then, she should have made it to the office twenty minutes ago. Had she decided to run some other errands? She didn't have to answer to him, of course, but she could have at least called to let him know that she'd be back later than expected. After all, they were partners, and keeping in touch was just common courtesy. Maybe he'd just call her and tell her that.

But when he punched in the numbers of her cell phone, she didn't answer. He tried to tell himself that she was probably caught in traffic and didn't want to take her hands off the wheel to answer the phone, but he had a sinking feeling in his gut that something was wrong. And he'd learned a long time ago to trust his gut.

Maybe she'd had car trouble, he thought worriedly. Was she all right? For all he knew, she didn't even have her cell phone with her. He'd just retrace the route she took and see what had happened to her. If nothing was wrong, then she could rib him the rest of their lives about being a worry wart. He could handle that. What he couldn't handle was something happening to her.

Jumping onto his motorcycle, he quickly retraced the route to where she'd dropped him off at the old polo field, then followed the directions he'd given Josie to the camera store where he usually had film developed. The second he turned the first corner, his heart stopped dead at the sight of her car parked on the side of the road, the rear right tire flat as a pancake. And parked right behind her was Roberto Sanchez's Mercedes SUV. His vehicle, like Josie's, was empty.

Sanchez had her.

Wiley couldn't ever remember tasting pure fear before, but he tasted it then. Swearing, he braked to a stop behind the SUV. Across the street was the entrance to a subdivision. Sanchez wouldn't have taken her there—if he was going to hurt her, he'd take her some place isolated, some place where there were no witnesses…some place like the woods right next to where the vehicles were parked on the side of the road.

Quickly reaching for his cell phone, he punched in 911. "He's taken her into the woods on the north side of the polo field," he told the dispatcher after giving a quick summary of the situation. "Get someone over here quickly. I'm going in after them."

"I'll have someone there in a matter of minutes, sir," the dispatcher said disapprovingly. "Please wait and let the officers do their job."

"The hell I will," he growled, and hung up. A split second later, he rushed into the woods.

Roberto Sanchez wasn't a man who wore his rage on his sleeve. He didn't rant and rave or cuss her out, he just grabbed her by the arm with a control that was frightening and forcibly marched her into the woods before she could do anything but gasp.

Hurrying to keep up with his long strides, Josie had never been more terrified in her life. He hadn't made a single threat, but he hadn't had to. His cold black eyes had spoken volumes. He was livid and someone was going to pay. She was that someone.

"There's no reason for force," she said as he jerked to a stop and his long fingers bit into her arm like talons. "If you'll give me a chance to explain—"

Lightning-quick, he jerked her arm up behind her back. "Who hired you?"

Hot fire streaked from her shoulder to her elbow. Crying out in pain, she gasped, "No one!"

"Don't make the mistake of thinking I'm an idiot," he warned. "You'll die regretting it. Now I'm going to ask you one more time. Who hired you to follow me?"

Fear clutching her by the throat, she almost blurted out, "Your wife!" But the words wouldn't come. How could she tell him Olivia had hired her? For all she knew, he'd go home and kill her…or have someone do it for him. Just the thought of that chilled her to the bone.

"I'm a librarian from Seattle," she blurted out. "I don't know what you're talking about."

For a moment, she thought he believed her. Surprise flaring in his eyes, he dropped his hand. Relieved, she released her breath in a rush…and never even saw the backhanded slap that knocked her off her feet.

Her scream echoed through the trees.

A hundred yards away and closing fast, Wiley felt his heart stop cold. Sanchez had hurt her! Enraged, he ran like a man possessed through the trees, bursting into the small clearing where Sanchez held Josie just as the man jerked her to her feet and drew back his clenched fist. Growling low in his throat, Wiley launched himself at Sanchez.

He hit him hard from the side and wrapped his arms around him, dragging him to the ground and away from Josie. Caught off guard, the older man grunted as he landed on a sharp rock, but it took more than that to bring down a bully like Sanchez. Swearing, he was back on his feet almost instantly and throwing punches like a heavyweight.

Wiley took the first one with a grunt. The second one sent his temper, which was already boiling, over the edge. He was quicker and younger than Sanchez, and, snarling he landed three hard shots before the older man knew what hit him. Staggering, Sanchez started to sink to his knees, but he wasn't done yet. He muttered a curse, clenched his jaw, and forced himself to his feet. Before he was fully erect, he lunged at Wiley.

In the distance, the whine of sirens cut through the silence of the woods, but Wiley hardly noticed. His eyes locking with the older man's, he waited for his next move. He didn't have to wait long. With the last of his energy, Sanchez swung at him.

In the time it took to blink, it was over. Wiley jumped to the side at the last second and gave him a shove. Caught off guard, Sanchez lost his balance and fell on his face in the dirt. Instantly, Wiley was on him, jerking his arms behind his back and slapping handcuffs on him before he could draw a breath to curse him.

The police arrived then, running through the woods to burst upon the scene just as Wiley rose to his feet, leaving Sanchez hogtied on the ground, cursing a blue streak. "I don't think I have to introduce you gentlemen to Roberto Sanchez. He was in the process of slapping the lady around when I arrived on the scene."

"I had a flat," Josie added huskily. "I had just called my road service when he pulled up behind me and accused me of following him. Then he grabbed me and dragged me into the woods."

The officer eyed the bruise on her cheek. "Are you all right, ma'am? Do you want me to call an ambulance?"

"Oh, no," she said quickly, horrified. "It'll be fine once I put some ice on it."

Satisfied, the officer pulled out a small notebook and began taking notes. "I'll need your name and address, ma'am, and a statement."

Wiley pulled out his ID and flashed it for the officer. "We were hired to investigate him," he said quietly. "I want the lady protected at all cost, so let's do this over there." He nodded to a fallen tree twenty feet away where Josie could sit and almost be out of earshot of Sanchez.

"No problem," the officer replied easily, and moved with them through the trees, away from where Sanchez was being read his rights. "He's a nasty character. I don't blame you for being concerned."

"His wife hired us to see if we could discover if he was having an affair," Josephine explained after giving her name and address, then sinking down to the log. "I think she was afraid to confront him without proof. Now I can see why."

"I have a right to know who hired you!" Sanchez yelled after them as two of the other officers moved to restrain him. "You can't keep it from me. Tell me, damn you!"

Ignoring him, Wiley said, "Throw the book at him. I'm going to take the lady home, if that's okay."

Quickly going over his notes, the officer nodded. "I've got everything. If something comes up and I need more information, I'll call you."

Helping Josie to her feet, Wiley slipped his arm around her and urged her back through the trees to where he'd left his motorcycle and her car. "C'mon, sweetheart. You're safe now. He can't hurt you any more. He wouldn't dare!"

"We have to tell his wife," she said huskily. "If he figures out that she hired us, she could be in danger."

"I'll call her later. You rest while I change this flat— you're too upset to ride the motorcycle right now."

"No, I'm not. The road service is on the way to change the tire. We can take the bike and go to Mrs. Sanchez's," she insisted. "She has to know what her husband's capable of."

"She's been married to the man for twenty years, sweetheart," he said dryly. "Trust me, she knows."

When Josie just looked at him, the bruise on her cheek a badge of courage, Wiley realized he could deny her nothing. "All right," he sighed, pulling her close for a fierce hug. "We'll go by and talk to her. But then you're going home and you're going to let me take care of you. Okay?"

Relieved, she pressed a quick kiss to his mouth. "I think I can suffer through that. Let's go."

Chapter 10

In spite of the fact that Roberto Sanchez was the notorious head of the Mexican mafia, he lived in one of the most exclusive gated communities in the city. There was a reason for that. When Wiley pulled up at the front gates and told the guard they were there to see Mrs. Sanchez, the guard just looked at him.

"It's business," Wiley told the man easily, refusing to accept no for an answer. "We work for her."

"Yeah, right," he growled, making no move to lift the cross bar that blocked their entrance.

Wiley's eyes narrowed at the guard. "What you're going to be is out of a job if you don't change your tone. I'm sure Mrs. Sanchez wouldn't appreciate you being rude to a guest."

Not the least impressed with the threat, the guard

smiled snidely. "If you were a guest, you won't need me to get through the gate—you'd know the code."

Wiley wanted to bust him, but Josie had other ideas. Grabbing her cell phone, she punched in Olivia Sanchez's phone number. When she answered on the second ring, she said, "Olivia? This is Josephine London. My partner and I are at the gate, but the guard won't let us in. In fact, he's been quite rude. Would you care to speak to him? I know this is short notice, but it's very important that we talk to you as soon as possible."

Wiley couldn't hear the other woman's response, but he didn't need to. Seated behind him on the bike, Josie held out her cell phone to the guard. "Mrs. Sanchez would like to speak to you."

Whatever Olivia Sanchez said to the guard, he obviously didn't like it. His face turned red, his jaw clenched, and his mouth pressed tight into a thin white line. He didn't, however, say anything disrespectful. Instead, he growled, "Yes, ma'am," and handed the phone to Josie. Without another word, he pushed the button that lifted the cross bar that blocked their access to the gated community.

Five minutes later, Wiley pulled up before Roberto Sanchez's home and cut the engine. When he helped Josie off the bike, his jaw clenched at the sight of the darkening bruise on her cheek. "Are you sure you want to do this now? You've had a rough day. Why don't you let me take you home and you can deal with Olivia Sanchez tomorrow?"

"We're here," she said stubbornly. "And she needs to know what kind of man she's married to."

Resigned, he reached out to gently cup her bruised

cheek in the palm of his hand. "It's your call, sweetheart. And you're right. Maybe this is better. Once you tell her about Sanchez, you'll be done with her, and I won't have to worry about her low-life husband coming after you any more."

Relieved, Josie covered his hand with hers. "Thank you for understanding. I guess we'd better get this over with."

She wasn't looking forward to it. Even though Olivia Sanchez already suspected that her husband was playing around on her and had hired them to prove just that, Josephine couldn't believe that she really wanted her suspicions verified. What woman would? How would she react to the truth? Would she hate her for being the bearer of bad news?

"Don't worry," Wiley said as they started up the front walk. "If she kills the messenger, I'll take care of Ethel for you. And see that you get a decent funeral, of course."

Surprised that he'd read her thoughts, she looked up to find him grinning down at her knowingly. "Gee, thanks," she said dryly. "I feel so much better."

"That's what I'm here for, sweetheart." Reaching the door, he stepped back and motioned for her to precede him. "It's showtime. Go for it."

Dragging a calming breath, she stepped up to the door and rang the doorbell. When Olivia Sanchez answered the door a few seconds later, Josephine greeted her with a cool smile. "Thank you so much for seeing us so quickly, Mrs. Sanchez. This is my partner, Wiley Valentine."

"Mr. Valentine," she said, shaking his hand. "Please…come in."

She showed them into the living room, which had been formally and expensively decorated in antique French imports, and motioned them to take a seat on the couch. Once they were side by side, she settled into a delicate armchair across from them and frowned at the bruise on Josephine's check. "Are you all right, my dear? That's quite a nasty bruise."

"I'm fine," she assured her. Touching her cheek, she added, "This is one of the reasons I'm here, though. Your husband hit me."

"What?"

"Somehow, he realized I was following him and demanded to know who I was working for."

"Did you tell him?"

"No, but it's only a matter of time before he figures it out," she replied. "That's why I had to see you. Once he knows you're behind the investigation, he's going to come after you."

Olivia Sanchez didn't seem the least bit concerned with that. Instead, she said, "Were you able to find out anything? Is he seeing someone behind my back?"

When Josie hesitated, Wiley said, "It's only been two days, Mrs. Sanchez."

"But you discovered something, didn't you?" she replied, her shrewd eyes noting Josie's hesitation. "You don't have to spare my feelings. If I didn't want the truth, I wouldn't have gone to the trouble of hiring you."

"Your husband appears to be seeing at least two different women," Josie said grimly.

Surprised, she blinked. "Two?"

"There could be more," she warned her. "We've been

on the job two days, and he's been with a different woman every day."

"Who are these women? What are their names?"

"We're still working on that," Wiley said. "One of them lives in a house owned by one of his companies."

"We'll have a full report for you in several days," Josie assured her. "I just wanted to warn you that you're in danger. Your husband was furious when he discovered we were following him. I'm afraid he's going to turn all that anger on you when he figures out that you're the one who hired us."

"He was arrested for assault," Wily told the older woman flatly. "If I hadn't come on the scene when I had, he would have seriously hurt Josie. He'll do the same to you—or worse—if he gets the chance."

"Why don't you come with us?" Josie asked impulsively. "We'll find you somewhere safe to stay where Roberto won't be able to find you. You should get a restraining order. After what he did to me, I'm sure you won't have any trouble—"

"That won't be necessary," Olivia said with a faint smile as she rose to her feet. "My husband would never hit me."

"But—"

"I want to thank you for doing your job so quickly," she added as she strode over to a delicate French writing desk and sat down to write out a check. "I know we agreed to an hourly rate, but I added a bonus for your promptness and concern. I never expected you to have anything for me so quickly."

"But we don't have the women's names yet," Josie said in confusion as Olivia returned to where she and

Wiley sat and held out a check. "And I didn't bring the pictures. I can send them with the report, of course, but we haven't finished the investigation. Don't you want us to finish?"

"You have finished," she simply. "Thanks to you, I know what I needed to know. I thought I wanted the details, but now I've decided I don't. And the last I heard, it was a woman's prerogative to change her mind."

Put that way, there was nothing Josephine could say. Helpless, she looked at Wiley, who rose to his feet and pulled her up beside him. "Then we thank you for your business," he told Mrs. Sanchez, offering his hand as Josie dazedly accepted the check. "If there's anything else we can do for you, just let us know."

Taking Josie's arm, he escorted her outside with him and hustled her onto the back of his bike. Still reeling from the turn of events, Josie held her tongue all the way back to her house. The second they walked through her front door, however, she turned on him. "Can you believe that?" she exploded. "We gave her what she wanted—proof that he was playing around on her, even that he was violent! And what did she do? Write us a check and say thank you very much!"

"Check the check," he said. "How much of a bonus did she give us? The way I figure it, at $350 an hour and a minimum of ten hours' work, she owed us $3,500, at the least."

"How can you think about money at a time like this?" she asked, shocked, as she pulled out the check. "She could be in danger—"

Wiley grinned when she gasped in shock at the sum. "That good, huh? I figured as much."

Her eyes wide, she looked up at him in confusion. "Wiley, it's for $25,000! Has she lost her mind?"

"Not at all," he said easily. "The woman knows exactly what she's doing. We gave her proof of her husband's infidelity, and she plans to use that to get what she wants out of Sanchez. Trust me, 25K is a small price to pay for that kind of power."

"You think she's going to blackmail him? But that's crazy! Doesn't she realize how dangerous he is?"

"Of course she does. And still she stays with him. What does that tell you about her?"

"That she's as ruthless as he is," she replied, stunned. "I can't believe I didn't see that. She seemed so nice."

"I'm not saying she's not nice," he said. "She's just got a different set of values than you and I. She lives in an expensive house, drives a Mercedes, and no doubt, has a closet full of designer clothes. Obviously, those things are more important to her than having not only a faithful husband, but a law-abiding one."

"I guess so. I just can't understand that kind of reasoning. She's sold her soul to the devil for a fancy zip code and diamonds, and she thinks she has respectability."

Stepping into the kitchen to wrap some ice in a towel, he returned to press it to her bruised cheek. "This has really gotten to you, hasn't it? What's going on? Why do you care?"

"Because it's such a waste. You saw her. She's sophisticated, beautiful, pleasant. And she's married to a drug lord who apparently makes a mockery of their marriage every time he leaves the house. And she's okay with that."

"Like I said, she has a different set of priorities."

"Then they deserve each other."

"My feelings exactly. How's the cheek?"

"I'm all right. Really," she insisted when he studied her with a frown. "It's just a bruise."

"And the Grand Canyon is just a hole in the ground," he retorted. "Sanchez hurt you, and that's my fault."

Shocked, she blinked. "How do you figure that? It's not your fault I had car trouble."

"No, but I should have made sure you made it home safely. All of this is new to you, and I knew Sanchez was sharp as a tack. He probably nailed us both the second we walked in that bar the other night."

"You don't know that for sure," she said as he began to pace. "He never even glanced our way."

"Then I made a mistake later…"

Her bruise forgotten, she tossed the ice aside and stepped into his path to confront him with a scowl. "Will you stop? None of this was your fault. Why are you doing this?"

Standing toe to toe with her, his eyes locked with hers. "I don't want you to hate me."

"Hate you? Why would I hate you?"

"I can think of any number of women who want nothing to do with what I do for a living. After everything that's happened, I thought you would feel the same way."

Just a month ago, she would have had a difficult time stepping out on a limb and telling a man how she felt about him. Thanks to Boonie, however, she wasn't the same woman who'd spent most of her adult life hiding in the narrow aisles of the library. She couldn't retreat back into her shell. Not when the happiness she'd always longed for but was afraid to go in search of was right in front of her.

The thunder of her heart loud in her ears, she faced him with her heart in her eyes. "I could never hate you," she said huskily. "I…"

When she hesitated, his smile faded. "What?" he asked softly, stepping closer. "How do you feel, sweetheart? Tell me. Put me out of my misery. Am I the only one falling in love here?"

Searching for the right words, it was a long moment before his last sentence registered. Startled, she gasped, "What did you say?"

"Throw me a lifeline because I'm sinking fast," he urged huskily, lifting a hand to gently trace the curve of her cheek. "I never expected to fall in love with you, but the second you walked into the office, I felt like I'd been waiting for you my entire life. And it scared the hell out of me. Didn't you notice? Why do you think I offered to buy you out?"

"I just thought you didn't want to work with a stranger," she replied, unable to stop smiling. "I guess this is the time to admit that when I first decided to check out my inheritance, I told myself I *would* sell out if things didn't work out. Then I met you."

Grinning, he slipped his arms around her waist. "And?"

"And I decided I wasn't going anywhere," she said with twinkling eyes. "I didn't realize I was the kind of woman who could fall in love at first sight—"

He moved so fast, she spoke the last few words against his mouth. Then he was kissing her as though they were the only two people on earth.

Standing on her perch, Ethel sang out, "When's the

wedding? Make him buy you a diamond. A big pretty one. Because *diamonds are a girl's best friend.*"

"You always did like the shiny stuff," Wiley told the parrot, laughing. "Don't worry—she'll have a diamond and something old and something new and something borrowed and something blue. And I'm going to do everything in my power to make sure that she has stars in her eyes for the rest of her life."

When he swept her up in his arms, Josie felt as if she was going to cry. "Oh, Wiley. I can't even remember what my life was like before I met you."

"You ain't seen nothing yet," he said huskily, and sealed the promise with a kiss.

Not concerned that she was being ignored, Ethel quietly hummed, "I'm getting married in the morning." And somewhere up in heaven, Boonie Jones grinned happily and hummed along.

Dear Reader,

When I get an idea for a story, it's often hard for me
to tell whether it began with a plot that demanded the
characters, or whether the characters led to the plot, but
with "The Man in the Shadows," it was neither. This story
started with chocolate.

No, I don't mean I consumed chocolate to kick-start my
little gray cells, although come to think of it, there likely was
a Hershey's bar involved somewhere along the line. That
plus coffee are vital inducements to my muse. In fact, it's
rumored that Juan Valdez had to ditch the donkey and hire
a mule train just to get my daily requirement of beans down
the mountain. Coffee and chocolate to me are the equivalent
of diesel fuel to a long-haul trucker. Without it, neither of us
would get far, no matter how compelling the cargo might be,
even if we got out and pushed.

But the chocolate that inspired this story wasn't mine, it was
Erika Balough's, the intrepid female sleuth who tracks down
"The Man in the Shadows." When I discovered that this
woman loves chocolate as much as I do, everything about
her fell into place. The matter of who she was, where she
came from and how she would get to where she wanted
to go unfolded so vividly, I could, well, taste it.

Enjoy!

Ingrid Weaver

THE MAN IN THE SHADOWS
Ingrid Weaver

Chapter 1

Erika Balough was thinking about chocolate when she saw her lover's ghost.

Neither event was unusual. Chocolate was Erika's one remaining indulgence. She'd sworn off alcohol four months ago when she'd awakened in her car at the side of the Jersey Turnpike with no memory of leaving her uncle's bar in Queens. She'd kicked her nicotine habit long before that because she didn't like the smell of cigarette smoke and hated doing laundry. She'd even given up taping her soaps two weeks ago when the rubber bone she'd lobbed for Rufus had bounced off the floor and broken her VCR, but give up chocolate? No way.

So she was thinking about the Hershey's bar that she'd stashed in the glove compartment, debating whether to break off another square now or to ration it so it would last to the end of the stakeout, when Sloan Morrissey flickered on the edge of her vision.

But as she'd realized, seeing Sloan wasn't unusual. Over the past year, it had become an all-too-common occurrence. Erika understood it was a natural step in the grieving process, that reluctance to let go, the refusal to accept that a man as vital as Sloan could possibly be gone.

For weeks after the funeral, she'd seen him everywhere. In passing cars, in the crowd at a Jets game, in elevators just before the doors closed. He appeared each time a tall man on the subway platform shoved his hands into his pockets and angled his shoulders a certain way as he looked for the train. Or when some man cocked his thumb to push a lock of black hair from his forehead or chewed the inside of his cheek when he wasn't sure what to say. Sometimes when she jogged through the park she caught snatches of Sloan's laughter, or an echo of his footsteps just out of sight.

Damn, it was embarrassing.

At least with practice she was getting better at restraining herself from actually chasing the ghost. Experience had taught her that most men got nervous when they spotted a sobbing woman running toward them while screaming another man's name.

Yet Erika had never learned how to get used to that first raw instant, when her senses trumped her logic and her breath caught and her pulse spiked and her heart shouted that the man she saw was real.

Oh God, yes. Please, let it all be a mistake. How could Sloan be dead when she still held him in her soul? How was it possible that she would never feel his body fit so perfectly with hers again? It couldn't be over. She'd never had the chance to say goodbye.

Or to say that she was sorry.

Maybe, just maybe, he had managed to come back. What if…?

Exactly. The two most powerful words in the English language—*what if.*

She fumbled her can of root beer into the cupholder and snatched her camera from the passenger seat, adjusting the focus for maximum zoom.

Of course, it wasn't Sloan. It was a shadow from the sign that overhung the doorway of the warehouse across the road. A gust of wind had set it swaying, giving the illusion of a large figure moving in the darkness. It was a trick of the poor lighting combined with the distortion from the rain that streamed down the windshield.

Erika lowered the camera and wiped her eyes on her sleeve. She held out for almost five seconds before she leaned over to open the glove compartment and took out the Hershey's bar.

Her teeth sank into the chocolate, setting off a tingling rush of saliva. Comfort, sugar, pleasure and familiarity. She breathed slowly through her nose, holding the sensations on her tongue, waiting as the chocolate melted and the taste seeped into the emptiness that always followed a Sloan sighting.

Okay. This was reality. She wasn't ready for the rubber room yet.

Good thing, since few people wanted to trust a PI who saw ghosts. Before that Jersey Turnpike incident had made her go on the wagon, her clients had been surprisingly tolerant about her descent into booze—it tended to fit right in with the whole hard-boiled private-eye schtick—but yes indeed, they got twitchy about cold-sober hallucinations.

She folded the wrapper over what was left of the chocolate bar and slipped it into the pocket of her raincoat, then checked her watch and picked up her tape recorder.

"November seventeenth, 12:35 a.m." She had to blot her eyes on her sleeve again as she said the date. "Have observed no activity in the area for the past hour. Possibly due to the weather." She squinted at the warehouse. "Advise client to install better lighting over the door beside the loading dock. What he's got now wouldn't discourage thieves, it would only annoy them."

She paused the tape while she took a tissue out of her pocket and blew her nose. Hartwell, the owner of the small appliances in the warehouse she was staking out and her current client, was phenomenally tight with his money. That was probably why one of his employees had decided to help himself to a few fringe benefits in the form of toasters and blenders. It would be cheaper in the long run to give everyone a raise to keep them happy instead of hiring Erika after the fact, but she wasn't about to give Hartwell that piece of advice. A girl had to make a living.

She reactivated the recorder. "Recommend client hire Adeel to install video surveillance at all entrances. Note to self: call Adeel to negotiate possible finder's fee if client follows recommendation to buy equipment from him. Second note to self: pick up dog food on way home—"

The recorder slipped from her grasp, clunked against the stick shift and thudded onto the floor mat. That shadow wasn't from any sign, it was moving along the front of the building. Erika grabbed her camera again and aimed it at the figure approaching through the rain.

It was a man, and he was moving fast. The hem of his black raincoat billowed behind his calves with each long stride. He didn't appear to be interested in Hartwell's warehouse. He had his head down, with his chin tucked inside his upturned collar and his hands shoved into his pockets. Rain gleamed from his black hair and from the ridge of his bold hawk nose as he passed in front of the light above the door.

And for the second time in five minutes, a fist of hope slammed into Erika's gut. Her pulse spiked, her breath caught. *Sloan!*

Before she could capture the image with her camera, he reached the corner of the building, turned into the alley and disappeared.

Erika thumped the back of her head against the headrest. "No," she muttered. "Get a grip, Balough. It wasn't him."

Sure. She knew that. It had been months since she'd had a sighting this vivid. It was because of the date, that was all. The date and the spooky weather.

Okay, so what legitimate business could Raincoat Man have in this neighborhood after midnight in a storm? He very well could be Hartwell's thief. And if he was, he could be planning to access the warehouse by some other entrance while she was sitting on her butt, obsessing about a dead man.

There. She hadn't lost her mind yet. She had perfectly rational reasons to follow him. It would be staying put that would be crazy. She stuffed her camera into her bag, slung the strap over her shoulder and slipped out of the car.

The rain drove into her face like pebbles, making her gasp and duck her head. She pulled up her hood and sprinted across the road to the entrance of the alley. A mini river was snaking down the center of it, carrying cigarette butts and the kind of mushy autumn debris typical of most paved surfaces in Brooklyn. Discarded crates, some soggy cardboard boxes and a heap of old tires huddled near the walls, but there was no sign of movement.

She jogged along the edge of the puddle, warily scanning the sides of both buildings as she went. There was a button factory beside Hartwell's warehouse, but she couldn't imagine Raincoat Man or anyone else being interested in breaking in there. The market for stolen buttons was even smaller than the market for hot food processors.

Wind funneled through the alley, bringing with it the distinctive fishy, oily smell of the East River. Erika reached the fence that ran behind the warehouse, but she could see no one there, either. She stopped to listen. Although it was tough to hear anything over the constant applause of the rain, she detected the rhythmic splash of footsteps to her right, heading away from her. She peered around the corner of the button factory just in time to see a tall, dark figure step into the next street.

He wasn't heading for Hartwell's warehouse, he was heading for the docks.

Sloan had always liked boats. He'd loved to sail. That was one of the things they hadn't had in common. Erika got seasick the instant she stepped on the ferry. She didn't care for the water and had never learned to swim, yet not Sloan. He adored his sloop. He'd named it after her, hoping to entice her on board, but she'd always refused.

Maybe things would have turned out differently if she'd made more of an effort. What if she'd swallowed a bunch of Dramamine and strapped on a life jacket and gone with him that last time? What if…

Oh, God. He was heading for the docks, for a boat, for the water. It was happening all over again.

But this wasn't Sloan.

Yes, of course, she knew that.

Erika took a step forward. That one was the hardest. The rest got easier, especially once she hiked up her skirt and broke into a run.

She wasn't insane. She did have logical reasons for this. It was because of the way the man had moved, head down and shoulders hunched, his body tensed and his strides eating up the distance. He might not be Sloan, but whoever he was, he was up to something.

And she always felt better when she was busy. She was good at her job. Through the rough patches, it had been the constant that had kept her grounded. Tonight, of all nights, she needed this.

So she blocked out everything else, the blisters that were forming on her heels from her new leather boots, the increasingly heavy yards of wet wool skirt that sloshed against her shins and the aching cold in that hollow place inside her chest. She concentrated on tracking the man who definitely, positively couldn't be her lover.

It wasn't easy. He changed direction twice before he got to the river, as if he were checking for a tail, causing Erika to dive behind a garbage bin the first time and duck beside a parked truck the second. She lost sight of him as a curtain of rain descended between them, then spotted his silhouette flit past the gaping doorway of a lit storage shed.

The shed was directly across from a moored freighter. Unlike the other buildings she'd passed, this one was filled with activity. A forklift hummed inside, moving long wooden crates from a stack. Men milled about just inside the entrance where they could keep dry. No, their movements were too deliberate to say they milled. They patrolled.

Erika slowed her pace. Her instinct for self-preservation had been pretty quiet for the past year, but now it was screaming out a warning. This seemed as good a time as any for it to reassert itself. What was in those crates, and why were people guarding them? Whatever was going on in there likely had nothing to do with Hartwell's stolen toaster ovens. The body language of those guys by the door told her they were probably armed.

She stepped into the lee of a building beside the shed and did a survey of the area. The man she'd been following had disappeared again. He hadn't gone inside, but how could he have passed those guards without being seen?

Unless he hadn't been there to begin with.

Erika shivered. She had to consider the possibility that Raincoat Man had been a figment of her imagination after all.

Wonderful. Maybe she truly was cracking up.

But if someone was going insane, would they be rational enough to realize it?

Sloan's ghost hadn't appeared to anyone else. He'd been close to his family, but he hadn't seen fit to haunt his mother or his sisters. None of his buddies on the NYPD had admitted to catching sight of him, either.

If he was going to haunt anyone, it should have been the guys on the force. Erika had never known a cop as totally dedicated to his job as Sloan. Coming from the other side, as it were, he could have given a whole different perspective when it came to informants. Who better to know where the bodies were buried? Dead men might tell all kinds of interesting tales.

And that's what Sloan was. Dead. As long as she was aware of and accepted that fact, she had to be sane, didn't she?

Yes. That sounded reasonable, she decided.

Headlights slashed through the rain. Erika hunkered down quickly, taking cover behind a stack of wooden pallets as the beams swept along the side of the building where she had been standing. A truck turned into the shed. As soon as it cleared the entrance, the overhead door lowered, cutting off her view of the interior, but not before she got a good look at the truck.

It was olive green, with large tires and a canvas back. That, plus the sign on the side of the door, led her to conclude it belonged to the U.S. army.

The army? Were those guards soldiers? Exactly what had she stumbled across?

Or had she been led here? Maybe Sloan's ghost was trying to give her a tip…

Stop it!

She tilted her head back, letting the cold water pummel her face for a moment to clear her brain, then dug into her bag for her phone. Returning her gaze to the closed door of the storage shed, she fitted her phone under her jacket hood and thumbed the speed dial for her uncle's bar.

Four rings, then a burst of rock music and male laughter in the background. A gravelly voice came through the receiver. "Cherry on Top. Hector speaking."

"Uncle Hector, it's Erika."

"Hey, Riki, where have you been? The guys gave up on you half an hour ago."

Her uncle was referring to the men from Sloan's precinct. The Cherry on Top, with the vintage red patrol car light that flashed in the front window, was primarily a cop bar. Sloan's friends had arranged to meet there tonight to toast his life. "I already told them, I had to work," she said.

"You're working too hard, Riki."

"It runs in the family, Uncle Hector. Is Ken still there?"

"Hang on, I'll check." The phone was muffled, probably against Hector's stomach, but Erika could hear him bellow Ken's name. Detective Ken Latimer had been Sloan's partner, a bond that made him feel some residual responsibility for Erika, so he helped her out with information when he could.

Half a minute later, Hector came back on. "Sorry, Ken already left. His kids have chicken pox and his wife's going nu—" He caught himself before he could complete the word. "He went home to help. What's up?"

"I'm not sure. I just wanted some info."

"About what?"

She hesitated. "Have you heard any talk around the bar about an undercover government operation near the docks? Something involving the army?"

"No, nothing like that. Why?"

"I was following a suspect and I found something that looks suspicious."

There was a pause. "Erika, have you been drinking again?"

"No, Uncle Hector. Nothing stronger than a can of root beer."

"There's no shame in it if you did, what with today marking—"

"I haven't touched a drop of alcohol in more than four months."

Another pause. "What kind of suspect were you following?"

"That really doesn't matter."

"Tall, dark-haired guy who walks too fast for you to catch up to him?"

She recognized the sympathy in his voice and hated it. Just as she hated the way he avoided saying *nuts* to her. "Uncle Hector…"

"Was this the same guy who appears out of nowhere and disappears into thin air?"

She wiped her wet face with her free hand. "It's different this time. I swear. I'm not hallucinating."

"Riki, go home. Sleep it off."

"I did see someone."

"On second thought, I better pick you up. Tell me where you are."

She terminated the connection and put the phone back in her bag. He meant well. Sloan's mother and Erika's friends meant well, too, but that didn't make the situation any less frustrating.

Then again, why should they believe her when she had difficulty believing herself?

Another set of headlights glared along the pier. Two more army trucks drove up to the shed. Before they could come to a stop, the overhead door in the front of the shed was already lifting. Erika squinted against the sudden light, trying to peer inside, then belatedly remembered her camera. She pulled it out of her bag and went down on one knee, steadying the camera on the edge of the pallets as she zoomed in on the interior.

She spotted the rear of the first truck. The canvas had been pulled aside and men were unloading crates from the back of it, the same long, wooden ones that she'd seen on the forklift. Whatever was inside the crates must be heavy—it took three men on each side to maneuver one of them out of the truck.

None of the men wore army uniforms, though. Instead, they wore jeans and plaid shirts or denim jackets. Several had long hair and scraggy beards, and a few sported substantial beer bellies. They looked more like the type of people who would belong to a biker gang than to the military.

She managed to shoot a few frames before the door lowered and cut off her view again. What on earth had she stumbled into?

Whatever it was, it was more trouble than she was being paid to investigate. The smart thing—the sane thing—to do right now would be to beat a strategic retreat and call the cops from her car. She could phone anonymously. That way the credibility issue wouldn't come up.

See? She wasn't nuts, she decided, backing further into the sheltering pile of pallets. Her problem-solving and self-preservation skills were both still functioning. Dr. Goldstein would be proud of her. She pulled the hood of her jacket closed at her throat and twisted to look behind her, trying to assess the best route to take to get out of there without being seen.

And because she was looking away, she never saw the blow coming. Pain exploded across the back of her skull. Mercifully, she was out cold before her face hit the puddle.

Chapter 2

She was going to barf. The realization dragged Erika back to consciousness. She could feel the bile rise, burning the back of her throat. Next, she registered the pain. It throbbed psychedelic patterns through her head, like one of the pressure headaches she got when the weather changed. She clenched her jaw and tried to lift her hands to make sure her head was still the same size.

Only, she couldn't lift her hands. They were stuck together in front of her, with her arms pinned to her sides. She couldn't move her jaw, either. She couldn't even open her mouth.

Panic surged through her. Was she paralyzed? Was she dead?

No, she couldn't be dead. She didn't remember any tunnel with a white light at the end. No floating around the ceiling while looking down at her body, either. And for a headache this bad, her heart had to be pumping and her nerves working overtime.

Okay. Great. Dead wasn't an option, so what about paralyzed? She experimentally tried to move her hand again and felt something pull across the skin of her wrists. She tried puffing out her cheeks and felt the same stretching sensation. Tape. Someone had taped her mouth and her wrists. Cautiously, she tried flexing other body parts, but except for her arms, she felt no further resistance, so she had to conclude the rest of her was unfettered. She was lying on her side on a hard, cold surface that smelled like rust.

Her brain moved sluggishly into gear, like a film running backward in slow motion. She remembered the pain in her skull, the army trucks in the warehouse, the rain, Sloan.

No, not Sloan. He was dead, she wasn't. Even if he really had tried coming to visit her from the Other Side, no way was she going to join him.

Well, that was easy. After a year of skirting around the issue, first with denial, then with alcohol, Erika was surprised by how firmly that point had been settled, but there it was.

Yes, she loved Sloan, loved him so much it hurt. His absence was a gaping hole in her life, but she wasn't ready to follow him. She was alive and planned to stay that way.

Of course, this was a fine time for a realization like that. Why couldn't she have figured that out during one of her therapy sessions? Or at the very least, before she'd left her car?

But she'd never been that great with timing, had she? Take that last fight with Sloan. Terrific moment to fling words at him such as, *It's over,* and *I never want to see you again.* He'd known she hadn't meant it, hadn't he? Oh, please. She hoped he'd known.

Their relationship had been intense—they'd been opposites, two halves of one whole. He'd been passion and impulse, she'd been practicality and logic. The sparks they had struck together had powered her days and lit up her nights. How could she have driven him away?

Her eyes tingled as they began to fill. She inhaled fast and hard through her nose. She couldn't cry now. With tape over her mouth, if her nose plugged, she'd suffocate. The same thing would happen if she threw up. Regrets were a luxury she could no longer afford. In order to live, her first priority was controlling the tears and the nausea.

So she thought about chocolate. Instead of the bitter tang of guilt or the acid taste of bile, she imagined the smooth slide of a melted Godiva, with a hint of almonds coating her tongue. Thick, sensuous indulgence glazing the roof of her mouth. She drew on the memory of the taste, letting the phantom pleasure fill her throat and her nose until her tears receded and her stomach calmed.

Then a millimeter at a time, she cracked open her eyelids.

Everything was a hazy gray blur, except for a pale strip at the bottom of her vision. She must be blindfolded. Closing one eye at a time, she could make out the contour of her nose. Looking past the curve of her cheeks, she glimpsed gray duct tape wrapping her wrists. More gray tape looped around her jacket, pinning her arms to her sides above her elbows. Beyond that she saw nothing but a metal floor and a swirl of moss-green wool where the fabric of her skirt pooled like a blanket around her legs.

In a way, the blindfold was a good sign. If they had taken the trouble to blindfold her, that meant they assumed she would regain consciousness and they didn't want her to identify them later. Which meant they also assumed there would be a "later."

So who were "they?"

That was a no-brainer, which was fortunate, since her brain was still throbbing and not yet functioning at full steam. Someone from that storage shed must have spotted her. Guys who patrolled the docks after midnight in a storm wouldn't have taken kindly to anyone snapping pictures.

So where had they brought her?

The light had a dim, yellow tinge, the kind that came from a low-wattage bare bulb overhead. She strained to listen for clues to her surroundings, but she couldn't hear warehouse or street sounds. No voices, no rustle of movement or hum of a forklift, only a deep, rumbling vibration that transmitted through the rusty-smelling surface she was lying on. She sniffed. The air was damp and tinged with a hint of mildew, likely from the rag that covered her eyes. Beneath that, she caught the fishy, oily scent of the river…

She swallowed fast, suddenly recognizing the source of her nausea. Oh, hell. She was on a boat.

There was a scrape of metal and a loud creak. A puff of cool air blew past her face as heavy footsteps thudded along the floor. "See if she's awake yet," someone said.

For a split second, Erika thought about playing possum, but one glimpse of the large leather work boots that moved into the narrow slit of vision below her blindfold made her reconsider. She didn't want to find out precisely how these people would determine whether or not she was awake. She lifted her head and made an interrogatory grunt.

The toe of one of the boots connected hard with her shin anyway. "Yeah, Leavish. She's awake."

Erika rolled to her knees and ducked her head between her shoulders, curling her body into a defensive ball. With her wrists and arms immobilized, it was the only way she could protect her face and chest.

"Quit fooling around, Dick," the first voice said. "Wates wants to talk to her."

"Get up, woman." The man who had kicked her grabbed her by one arm and hauled her upright.

Erika fought to suppress her moan. For a second she thought her arm was about to be wrenched from the socket, but she managed to get her feet underneath her and the pain eased. It was just as well that her mouth was duct-taped. That prevented her from telling this Dick what she thought about men who got off on abusing defenseless women.

Then again, by taping her mouth they had neutralized her best defense. She might not have that firm a grip on reality sometimes, but she harbored no illusions that she'd be able to win a physical confrontation with two adult males as long as her arms were bound and her eyes were covered. Her only hope right now was to talk her way out of this.

They led her out of the metal room into a metal corridor. Although the blindfold was disorienting, being upright eased her headache. She tried to absorb as much of her surroundings as she could, counting the number of steps they took, keeping track of direction changes, listening for more voices or background noises. She felt a spurt of hope when she heard the distant bleat of a siren.

If she could hear a siren, they couldn't be at sea. Otherwise, she likely wouldn't have been able to control her nausea. The boat was a large one, which was another reason the nausea wasn't as severe as it might have been. There was a good possibility they were on the freighter that she'd noticed moored across from the shed with the trucks.

They went up a steep staircase. Erika had to concentrate hard to maintain her balance as her heels kept catching in the metal grating that formed the steps. She thought about the damage those heels could do if she kicked backward, especially when Dick crudely moved his hand to her buttocks and gave her a squeezing grope to keep her climbing, but this wasn't the time to attempt an escape. She likely wouldn't get far if she did.

Finally, her footing leveled out and she could feel fresh air on her face—they must be on the boat's deck. There was a film of water on the deck plating. The rain had been replaced by a thick mist that curled around her boots. It was still dark. That, plus the fact her skirt hadn't dried out completely, led her to believe she couldn't have been unconscious for more than a few hours. Another turn, a second, shorter staircase, a narrow corridor and she was pushed through a doorway. White light seeped through the fabric of her blindfold. This room evidently rated more than a few bare bulbs.

The first man, Leavish, announced their arrival. "Here she is, Mr. Wates."

"Take her to the table."

Dick squeezed her upper arm and dragged her a few steps into the room. "Sit," he ordered, shoving her sideways into what felt like a straight-backed wooden chair.

"Remove the tape from her mouth."

Erika tensed her lips and braced herself as Dick dug a fingernail under one edge of the tape and gave it a yank. Stars burst across her vision. She was grateful she was already sitting down.

Chair legs scraped across the floor in front of her. Wood creaked. "All right, who sent you?"

She turned her head toward the voice of the man she deduced was Wates. He spoke with the fast, flattened-vowel accent of a Bronx native. At a guess, she would put him in his mid-fifties, but if the wear on his voice had come from cigarettes and not age, he could be in his late thirties or forties. He did seem to be the one in charge, so the more information she could glean about him, the better. She coughed, feigning more discomfort than she felt. "Let me go," she croaked. "I haven't done anything to you. Why—"

"Shoulda let me throw her in the river when I found her," Dick muttered. "This is a waste of time."

Wates snapped his fingers. "That's enough, Richard. Go back to the hold and tell Tanner she's awake. I'll send word if I need you again."

Dick gave her chair a parting shove before his footsteps gritted across the floor and into the corridor.

The men she had glimpsed in the warehouse might not have looked like military, Erika thought, but this Wates character acted as if he were accustomed to being in command.

"All right, Miss Balough," Wates said. "Tell me who you're working for."

They knew her name. That threw her for an instant before she remembered she'd had her bag with her. They would have seen her driver's permit as well as her P.I. license. She moistened her lips and tasted the gummy residue from the tape. Drawing her lower lip be-

tween her teeth, she gnawed at the gum, stalling for time
as she tried to figure out the best approach to use.

Wates wanted to know who had sent her. He had to
be worried that someone else was aware of whatever action he had going with those army trucks. That explained the blindfold and the duct tape. It was probably
why Dick hadn't been allowed to throw her into the
river.

If she told the truth, Wates would have no reason to
keep her alive.

His knuckles rapped hard on the table between them,
startling her into jerking backward. "Miss Balough, I'm
waiting. Who hired you to take those pictures?"

Her camera had been in the bag, too. Wates must
have checked through the digital files and had seen the
images she had captured of the trucks. She couldn't
plead ignorance. Her only choice was to lie. It was just
a matter of deciding which lie would keep her alive the
longest.

"You have five seconds, Miss Balough," Wates said.
"Then I'll give you back to Richard. Five. Four—"

His countdown was cut off by a gurgling scream from
somewhere beyond the door. It was followed by a thud.

The sound made the hair on the back of Erika's arms
rise. The way it had echoed was like something out of
a slasher movie. Voices outside swirled in confusion.
Wates's chair scraped. He stood and walked toward the
entrance of the room. "Leavish," Wates said. "Get me
a report."

"Right away, Mr. Wates."

Erika tipped her head back, trying to get a glimpse
of what was happening from beneath her blindfold but
all she could see was the edge of a wooden table in front
of her and a pair of polished shoes. Expensive-looking

leather shoes the red-brown color that was called ox-blood. Above them she saw the tailored hems of trousers the color of wet sand.

There were more raised voices and the sound of running feet. Erika angled her chin higher to increase her range of vision but at the movement, her chair teetered backward. She jerked herself forward, bringing the front chair legs down to the floor. A minute later, Leavish returned. "Dick fell over the railing, Mr. Wates."

"How?"

"Nobody saw. This fog is too thick."

"Damn idiot. He probably slipped. How badly is he hurt?"

"He split open his head on a hatch cover. He's dead."

Wates muttered an oath. "That's going to leave Floyd short on the loading detail."

"He said we're eighty percent done."

"Good. We have to keep on schedule. We'll dispose of Dick once we're at sea. And where's Tanner?"

"I heard he was on his way."

Dick was dead? Erika felt a spurt of relief that he wouldn't have the chance to abuse her again. Strange that he could fall over a railing, though, no matter how thick the fog was. And that scream had been so eerie.

So was the lack of compassion displayed by Wates. If he had this little regard for an accomplice, he would have no mercy for her.

She didn't have time to dwell on it further. Wates and his oxblood shoes were returning from the doorway.

"All right, Miss Balough." Wates paused beside her chair. "Time's up. Who sent you?"

She heard a metallic click—a safety sliding off? Her guess was confirmed when she felt the cold tip of a gun barrel press into the skin beneath her ear.

Her mind blanked. Simply erased. Another example of her knack for excellent timing. Now that she'd decided unequivocally that she wanted to live, the whole major breakthrough in her mourning could be moot. One twitch of this man's trigger finger could send a bullet into her neck.

It would be quicker than drinking herself to death, or playing DWI roulette, or escaping into a fantasy world. It would be faster than falling off a sloop and drowning in Long Island Sound like…

Sloan.

It had happened one year ago tonight. It had been raining then, too. The water would have been cold enough to numb flesh and cramp muscles within minutes. Had he struggled for long? Had he suffered?

Had he called out her name the way she'd awakened alone in her bed that night and whispered his?

Sloan!

"Who?" Wates slid the gun muzzle around her neck to push into the underside of her chin. "Speak up."

She could see the black gleam of the barrel beneath the edge of her blindfold. It was an older model Heckler & Koch military pistol, likely a 9 mm. There would be no second chances with this one.

"Who's Sloan, Miss Balough?"

Good God, had she spoken aloud? Erika tipped her head away from the gun. It was a futile gesture, and it made her chair wobble again, but it relieved the pressure enough to allow her to swallow. "Sloan," she said. "Detective Sloan Morrisey. He's with the NYPD and he knows all about your operation."

"You're bluffing."

"Am I? How else would I have known you were expecting that shipment tonight?"

"The cops don't work with P.I.s."

"Sloan does. He's my fiancé."

"This is bull."

She couldn't move her hands against the tape so she wiggled her fingers. "Didn't you notice the ring?"

Wates seized her left hand. She could see his fingers were short and blunt-tipped. His touch was rough, the skin of his palm dry and thick like that of someone accustomed to manual labor, but the sleeves of the cashmere sweater she glimpsed looked soft as silk.

He twisted her wrist as far as the duct tape allowed, then dropped her hand and returned the gun to the side of her neck. "That doesn't prove anything."

Oh damn, she could feel tears again. No, the diamond engagement ring didn't prove anything. Those were more words she'd flung at Sloan during their final weeks together. He'd wanted her to wear the ring, but she'd found one excuse after another not to. It caught on her clothes. It drew too much attention when she was playing out a cover. It was an outdated, chauvinistic symbol of male ownership.

Sloan had laughed at that last excuse. Then he had kissed her senseless and told her she'd had it backward, that she was the one who owned him, body and soul. He would be hers forever.

Forever, Erika. I swear it.

"You're lying," Wates said. "No cop would bring his girlfriend into an investigation."

"No? That would depend on the cop, the girlfriend and the investigation." She had nothing to lose, so she decided to try a gambit. "Police protocol isn't as strict as the military protocol you would have learned in the service, Mr. Wates."

Wates was standing close enough for her to hear the

soft hiss of his breath. She caught a whiff of his deodorant, a pungent, musky scent that reminded her of the taste of the duct tape.

If he was sweating, her stab in the dark about the military must have found its target. She expanded on the bluff. "You didn't think the military had forgotten you after you left, did you, Mr. Wates? The authorities have been cooperating to track your activities."

"Tell me what you know."

She paused. "Why should I? It will come out at your trial."

"Then there's no reason I shouldn't kill you now."

"Killing me won't help you, it will only make things worse. Your men made a mistake by abducting me. Sloan knows I'm here."

"A cop doesn't worry me in the least, Miss Balough."

"That's another mistake. Sloan Morrisey isn't an ordinary cop. He's the best there is."

"Then why did he let my men take you?"

"That's another detail that will come out at your trial. Your time is running out."

Wates pressed the muzzle of the gun upward into her ear hard enough to fold the lobe over on itself. "It's your time that is limited unless you start talking."

"If you hurt me—"

There was a rumbling clank. It seemed to come from deep within the hull of the ship. Erika felt it vibrate through the floor and into the soles of her boots. Someone shouted in alarm but the words were muffled by distance and by the fog.

Wates withdrew the gun from her ear. There was another gush of deodorant-scented sweat. He moved two steps away. "Leavish?"

"I'm on it, Mr. Wates."

Erika stretched her neck and rolled her head from side to side. She didn't know how long the respite would last, but she had to make use of every second. The mention of the military had hit a nerve. She could buy a few more minutes of life by expanding on that, try bluffing about the size of the investigation Sloan had supposedly brought her in on.

The irony of it was that Sloan never would have encouraged her to become involved with something this dangerous. It was the other way around. He had even wanted her to cut back on the cases she took because of the risk the jobs often entailed.

She understood why he'd been wired like that. He hadn't been much more than a kid when his father had been shot. It had happened here at the waterfront, and the perp had never been caught. Sloan had coped with his loss by assuming the role of the man of his family. He'd grown up believing it was his responsibility to protect all the people in his care.

He was at his worst when he got worried. His mouth would go tight, the bones at the corners of his jaw would stand out and the blue of his eyes would turn icy. His voice would drop to the low, velvety rasp that had reminded her of the sharp edge of a Toblerone bar—it was sweet when it melted, yet it could hurt when it rubbed the wrong way.

Sure, at times Sloan could act like an overbearing, macho throwback to caveman days, but deep inside he was a pushover. She had seen tears trickle into the corners of his grin when his youngest sister had graduated college. Each time one of his other sisters produced a new niece or nephew, he was among the first to show up at the hospital, his arms filled with giant teddy bears and miniature football cleats.

Erika couldn't pin down the moment when she'd first realized she loved him. It might have been the night she'd come home from a stakeout to find her kitchen floor strewn with newspaper and Sloan sitting cross-legged in the middle of it, with the scraggly puppy he'd just rescued from a crack house curled up asleep on his lap.

What else could she have done but let them both stay?

God, what she wouldn't give for one more chance…

Running footsteps sounded in the corridor. Someone skidded to a halt at the door. "A cable on the main winch snapped." It was Leavish's voice, high-pitched and out of breath. "Two of the crates dropped into the hold."

"We have to repair that winch."

"Floyd sent some men for a spare cable."

"Were the contents of the crates damaged?"

"There were some scratches. Nothing the buyer will notice."

"How long before we can recommence the loading?"

Leavish hesitated. "Tanner said to tell you at least forty minutes."

"Tanner? What was he doing there?"

"He was checking on the merchandise. I passed him on my way back."

Erika soaked in as much of their conversation as she could hear. The pieces were beginning to move into place. If Wates was a former member of the military, he could have used his old connections to get whatever had been in those army trucks.

Her first guess would be weapons. She doubted whether crates of uniforms or freeze-dried rations would elicit this much interest from anyone. A crate of combat boots wouldn't be heavy enough to require six men to lift it out of a truck, but a crate of machine guns likely would. Wates and his gang must be dealing with stolen army ordnance of some kind.

It was a lucky break for her that the loading had been delayed. Once the cargo was on board this ship, who knew where they would end up? Her chances for escape at sea would be dismal.

Actually, the snapped winch cable was the second lucky break. The first one had been when that thug Dick had fallen to his death.

Or had it been luck?

Maybe there had been some other force at work. Maybe her bluff wasn't totally a bluff. What if Sloan had found some way to come back and watch over her?

It was the anniversary of his death. It was a dark and stormy night. They were on the water. What more opportune time for a drowned man...

She curled her fingers, squeezing hard enough to drive her nails into her palms. Stop it right there, she told herself. There were no such things as ghosts.

She couldn't crack up now. God, talk about the worst possible timing. Her wits were her only weapon—if she lost them, she'd be left with nothing. She was done with the ghost thing. She wanted to live.

Erika, hang on!

The voice in her mind was so vivid, she lifted her head toward the sound. It was Sloan. She could feel him. All those other times hadn't come close to this. Like the sun just before it rose over the horizon, like the thunder that inevitably followed a flash of lightning, he was coming. He was almost here. *She could sense his presence.*

No. Stop it. This was crazy.

Footsteps approached in the corridor. This set seemed different from the others she'd heard. They weren't light—the metal floor rang beneath solid boot heels. Those steps didn't belong to a phantom, they were being made by a large man. He walked with a controlled stride, unhurried yet deliberate, confident.

Sloan used to walk like that, his strides long and sure, a cross between a strut and a prowl. It had something to do with his lanky frame and his daily workouts at the gym. He'd had a distinctive way of moving, one Erika had always been able to recognize, whether he was jogging through the park or strolling along a subway platform.

Or walking past a kitchen appliance warehouse in the rain?

She ground her teeth hard enough to send pain shooting through the roots of her molars. For God's sake, not now!

The footsteps stopped. The conversation in the doorway halted. "Mr. Tanner," Leavish said.

"It's about time, Max," Wates muttered.

"Did she tell you anything yet, John?"

At the deep, velvety rasp, Erika's heart stopped. Simply froze between one beat and the next. Her lungs emptied. Light streaked across her vision.

Logic be damned, that was Sloan!

Chapter 3

Erika rocked forward, using the momentum of her upper body to lever herself upright. The chair toppled to its back behind her, the legs tangling with her feet. She lurched sideways, trying to regain her balance and her hip struck the edge of the table.

"Get her, Leavish!" Wates ordered.

"Sloan!" she screamed. She was grabbed by the arm before she had gone two steps. She threw her weight to the side and wriggled free of Leavish's hold. "Sloan!"

Firm footsteps crossed the floor. There was a whiff of fresh air and damp fabric, then Erika was caught from behind. One arm fastened around her waist and a palm flattened over her mouth.

She had fainted only once in her life. It had been during that endless search last November. She had been banned from the command center by the third day because she'd taken a swing at the captain of a Coast

Guard cutter when he had suggested it was time to scale down their efforts. She hadn't wanted to go back to her apartment, so she'd joined Sloan's mother in their church. Mrs. Morrissey had gone home after a few hours to have dinner with her family, but Erika had remained on her knees and had prayed through the night until she'd fainted from exhaustion.

So she knew the warning signs. The lightheadedness, the cold that spread from her fingertips and worked its way into her body, the loss of sensation in her legs, the peculiar echoing quality to the sounds around her, as if she were being pulled backward into a bell.

It was happening again now. The light that had streaked her vision moments ago contracted to pinpricks. Her senses were folding in on themselves, a defensive reaction to a reality that was too much for her mind to accept.

Sloan. He was here. *And he was touching her!*

He flexed the arm he held around her waist, pulling her back against his body. "Take it easy, sweet cheeks." His breath stirred the hair over her ear. "Don't make me bruise those freckles."

She sucked in deep breaths through her nose, charging her blood with oxygen, determined to stay conscious. The scent of damp fabric intensified. Along with it was a hint of male skin and the clove-and-ginger tang of Old Spice. Sloan's favorite aftershave.

She started to tremble. This was Sloan's smell. And Sloan's body. She recognized the fit. She could feel the solid breadth of his chest behind her, the strength in the arm he held around her waist, the warmth of his palm against her lips. She could see the blur of his knuckles.

"Do you want more duct tape, Mr. Tanner?" Leavish asked.

Tanner? Erika thought wildly. No, this was Sloan. She twisted, trying to dislodge his palm from her mouth as she called his name.

He curled his little finger under her jaw and hung on, muffling her cry. "If you keep that up, we'll have to gag you again." He slid his arm above the tape that wrapped around her jacket and boldly cupped his other hand over her breast. "Or do you like it rough, baby?"

The touch was cheap and crude, but with her arms taped to her sides, she had no way to avoid it. She blinked furiously to stem the tears.

Which was worse, to realize she was losing her mind, or to wish that she already had? It would be so much easier if she could believe the illusion...

But she had to trust her brain, not her senses.

He wasn't Sloan. He couldn't be. It was because of the walk, that was all. She'd been picturing the way Sloan had walked and her heart had projected the rest.

So think, she ordered herself. Use your head and not your heart.

This man was one of Wates' henchmen, possibly a partner, judging by his use of Wates's first name. This was the Tanner person Wates had been asking about. Max Tanner. The Old Spice aftershave was just a coincidence. So was his build—there must be zillions of men in the world who were six-foot-two and moved like an athlete. His voice might be similar to Sloan's, but it wasn't the same. The cadence was different. This man's words had the trace of a Western drawl.

And Sloan would never have called her "sweet cheeks" or "baby," nor would he have touched her that demeaning way in plain view of two other men.

And Sloan was dead.

Erika stopped struggling.

"Too bad," Max murmured. He returned his hand to her waist. "Playing rough can be fun, and I've always liked redheads."

"We're wasting time, Max," Wates said. "She still hasn't told us anything."

"Who was she shouting for?" Max asked.

"Her boyfriend. Some cop by the name of Sloan Morrissey."

His grip tightened. "A cop?"

"She claims she's working with him," Wates said. "But I don't believe her."

"We have an extra forty minutes before we can move, John. It won't cost us anything to check out her story."

"I already sent Abrams to look for her car. He'll get rid of it."

"That won't be enough. There's too much riding on this to take chances. What if she is telling the truth?"

Wates swore.

"Exactly," Max said. "Come on, Red. We're going to have a little chat."

Max swung her against his hip, lifted her off the floor and carried her back toward the table. He waited while Leavish righted the chair she'd knocked over, then took his hand from her mouth, set her on her feet and guided her to sit. Leavish returned to his post beside the door while Wates resumed his seat across the table.

Erika caught a swirl of black on the bottom edge of her vision as Max moved away.

It was the hem of a long, black raincoat.

"So, tell me about this cop friend of yours, baby," Max said.

Erika tipped back her head and focused on what she could see of him. Beneath the raincoat, faded blue jeans topped a pair of scuffed cowboy boots. Wood creaked, as if he had leaned against a corner of the table.

She fought to get her thoughts back on track. That was easier now that Max was no longer touching her, but her senses were still on overload. "Sloan is my fiancé," she said.

"Oh, yeah?"

"He gave me this ring."

Max crossed one ankle over the other, resting the toe of one boot against the floor. Patches of dampness mottled the tan leather. "Uh-huh. How did he afford a rock like that on a cop's salary? He's probably working both sides."

"You're wrong. Sloan is as straight as they come. And the longer you keep me here, the worse it's going to be for you."

"You trying to scare me, Red?"

"I'm simply giving you a warning."

"You and your big spender Prince Charming must be into some kinky stuff if he brings you down to the docks for a date."

"We're working together."

"Isn't he any good as a cop?"

"He's the best there is."

"Then why would he need your help?"

"He doesn't need my help." She thought fast. "Sloan is letting me in on this investigation so I can collect the reward. A girl's got to make a living."

"What reward?"

"The Department of Homeland Security has a standing reward for any information that leads to the arrest of people like Mr. Wates."

"Your bluffs are getting tiresome, Miss Balough," Wates commented.

Erika didn't know whether or not Homeland Security actually did offer rewards, but it sounded reasonable to her. "The FBI and the ATF want a piece of this, too," she said, embroidering the lie. "Smuggling stolen weapons out of the country gets a lot of people very excited."

There was a pause. Someone, probably Leavish, cleared his throat.

Another hit, Erika thought. "They know everything I do," she said. "If you hurt me—"

"Leavish, did you search her?" Wates demanded.

"Uh, Dick said he did."

"That idiot," Wates said. "Did he check her for a wire?"

"I don't know."

Erika realized the next logical step at the same time Max apparently did. He pushed away from the table and moved in front of her. "Stay where you are, Leavish," he said. "I'll do it."

She heard the slithering hiss of a switchblade locking into place. Sucking in her breath, she got her feet under her and tried to rise from the chair but Max caught her shoulder to keep her where she was.

"Relax, Red. I'll be gentle. This time, anyway."

She saw the flash of metal near her ribs and jerked her chin down. "No!" she gasped. "Please!"

"Hold still." The blade of Max's knife was razor sharp—it sliced through the duct tape that bound her arms as if the layers were no more than paper. He peeled the tape from the front of her jacket, then used his grip on her shoulder to lean her forward and ripped the rest of it from around her back. Before she could register the relief of being able to draw a full breath, he unzipped her jacket, thumbed open the top four buttons of her blouse and thrust his hand inside.

The shock of his palm against the bare skin of her chest sent more lights dancing across her vision. She knew he couldn't be Sloan, but oh *man,* how was it possible that the touch of any two men could feel so much alike?

Max skimmed his fingertips along the ridge of her collarbone, over her bra and down the side of her ribcage. "Nothing so far," he said.

Erika knew what he was doing. He was making sure she wasn't wearing a hidden microphone. Considering her bluff, she should have expected this. Struggling against Max's search would gain her nothing. She had no hope of overpowering him—her arms might be free but her wrists were still taped and he outweighed her by at least eighty pounds. Resisting would probably make things worse. It might result in Wates and Leavish joining the search.

At least no one else was aware of the real source of her distress. Max couldn't guess how each brush of his fingers was awakening nerve endings that had been dormant for a year. He wouldn't know how the smell of his Old Spice and the scent of his skin were jabbing tiny, insidious holes in her wall of sanity.

He ran his palm along her midriff, and her breath hitched on a sob. This was sick, she told herself. The ghost thing was bad enough, but feeling anything other than revulsion at this stranger's touch under these circumstances really was crazy. Wasn't there a psychological syndrome that dealt with being attracted to your captor? Something else to talk to Dr. Goldstein about if she ever got back to his couch.

"Well?" Wates asked.

"Still nothing," Max said. His voice sounded strained, like stiffened velvet. "Where are you hiding it, Red?"

Erika spoke through her teeth. "I'm not hiding anything. I'm not wearing a mike."

He tugged her blouse from her skirt and slipped his hand around to the small of her back.

Longing, sharp and hopeless, broke through her reason.

Sloan had loved to rub his cheek along the dip at the base of her spine. Sometimes when he hadn't shaved, the rasp of his beard would make her skin tingle on the edge between pleasure and pain. Then he would smooth his fingertips along the rise of her buttocks, just the way Max was doing now, except Sloan would follow the caress with a kiss...

"How about that?" Max muttered. "It looks like you're telling the truth." He withdrew his hand from her blouse. He hesitated for a beat, then refastened her buttons.

Erika exhaled slowly. Considering the way Max had grabbed her breast before, she was surprised he hadn't lingered. With his body blocking the view of the other men in the room, he could have taken advantage of the situation by copping a few more cheap feels.

Wait. Was that why he hadn't? Because the others *couldn't* see? It was almost as if his initial crudeness had been for show...

She frowned. What was she doing? Trying to make excuses for him so she could justify this mindless response of her body?

Max's knuckles skimmed the side of her neck as he brushed a lock of hair behind her shoulder. He stroked the pad of his thumb over the place where Wates had jammed his pistol. "This boyfriend of yours can't be much of a cop if he sent you here without a wire."

"I didn't need one. He knows where I am."

"How?"

"Sloan and I are a team. We share everything."

"Uh-huh. So where is he now?"

"Closer than you think."

He snorted. "Screaming his name when I came in was another bluff, wasn't it? Great performance, Red."

"You'd better check her for weapons, too, Max," Wates said. "Dick might have missed something."

"Sure." The sides of his raincoat folded against the floor as he squatted in front of her. He ran his hands down her jacket sleeves, squeezing lightly every few inches. "Are you packing heat, baby?"

"I'm not armed."

Max skimmed his palms along her hips. "What's this?" he asked, patting the side of her jacket. He fumbled at her pocket. "Was this your lunch?"

He must have found what was left of the Hershey's bar, she thought. "There're some used tissues in the other pocket," she said. "Want to check them out too?"

He progressed to her thighs. Instead of pushing up her skirt, he explored the contours of her legs through the fabric. He moved more quickly than before, as if he didn't want to prolong this additional search any more than she did.

"If I had a weapon and had been able to reach it," she muttered, "don't you think I would have used it already?"

"Aw, you said you didn't like it rough." He slid his hands over her knees to her shins. "Sexy boots, Red. You got a whip to go with them?"

Angling her head to one side, she was able to see his hands as he felt her calves through the supple leather of her boots. His fingers were long and had the same shape as Sloan's. Dark hair sprinkled the backs of his hands, shifting as his skin stretched over his lean tendons, also like Sloan's. He wore no rings, but the gold band of a watch glinted from his left wrist where the sleeve of his raincoat had pulled back. He wore the watch with the face turned to the underside of his wrist the same way Sloan used to.

Great. More coincidences to mess with her mind.

Max reached the blisters that had formed on her heels. She tried to mask her start of pain by jerking her feet out of his grasp.

Max unfolded from his crouch and backed up. "She's clean, John. No wire, no weapons."

"No cops, then," Wates said.

"We still can't be sure." Max resumed his perch on the corner of the table. "Did she have anything with her besides that bag, Leavish?"

"No, Mr. Tanner," he replied.

Max's legs shifted, as if he twisted to look behind him. There was the sound of something being dragged across the table. A moment later, several objects clattered to its surface. He must have emptied her bag.

"That camera had some shots of us," Wates said. "I erased them. Her ID's in that yellow folder."

"What about that phone?"

"The last number she dialed was just some bar. It's closed. All I got was a recording."

"Which bar?"

"The Cherry on Top."

"I've heard of the place," Max said. "It's a cop hangout in Queens. That supports her story, John."

Erika wondered fleetingly how Max would have known about her uncle's bar. Then again, criminals probably made it their business to know where they would be more likely to run into cops.

Wates drummed his fingers on the table. "Fine. I'll

send someone to check out the addresses on her ID. They'll see if there's anything at her home or her office to confirm what she told us."

"Good idea," Max commented. "If she's on the level, we might be able to use her as a hostage."

The tension in Erika's shoulders went down a notch. Okay. She'd bought another few minutes. Now all she had to do was figure a way out of this before—

"What's that paper?" Wates asked suddenly. His chair creaked. "It fell out of the folder with her ID."

Erika did a mental inventory of her bag. What could he be talking about? A receipt? A business card?

"It looks like a newspaper clipping," Max said.

Oh, no. Why had she saved that? She should have gotten rid of it long ago.

She could only hope that the clipping was too tattered to read by now. Maybe the tear stains had made the ink run. She didn't know what kind of condition it was in, since she hadn't unfolded it for months. She took it out mainly to touch it, to have a concrete focus for the grief that had no other outlet.

It was a link to Sloan that she hadn't been able to bring herself to break. Throwing it away would have seemed too final.

Paper crackled. Max whistled softly and got to his feet. "Hey, sweet cheeks. You and that boyfriend must be kinkier than I thought. You always go on dates with dead guys?"

It was no use. It looked as if everyone was right after all: her inability to let go of the past might wind up costing her her future.

"What are you talking about?" Wates demanded.

"This is an obituary," Max said. "For Detective Sloan Patrick Morrissey."

Chapter 4

The funeral had been a blur. Erika hadn't wanted to attend—how could they bury Sloan without his body? Yet everyone had agreed that there was no hope of recovering him alive. The *Riki B.* had been found drifting off Montauk, her hold awash from the waves that had broken over the deck and flowed through the sloop's open hatch. There had been empty beer cans on the floor of the cabin and an open bag of Doritos on the bunk, along with the running shoes Sloan had been wearing when he'd slammed out of the apartment.

That final fight had been a bad one.

But Erika had never dealt well with ultimatums. That was one way in which she and Sloan were too much alike.

I'm sorry, Sloan. You know I'll always love you, don't you? I would take every word back if I could.

Yet she couldn't take back the words. They were chiseled into her memory like dates on granite.

"You're analyzing everything to death, Riki. Let's just get married."

"We've got a good thing going between us, Sloan. We need more time to be sure we want to take the next step."

"Time isn't going to change how I feel about you."

"I'm trying to be practical. Right now I've got too many cases on the go. Wait a few more months until things settle down and—"

"That's what you said last month and the month before. You're using your work as an excuse. What are you so scared of?"

"You're the one who's scared. You want to wrap me up in cotton and keep me safe on a shelf somewhere."

"I can't help worrying about you, Riki. I don't want to lose you to some punk with a gun."

"I don't want to lose you either, Sloan, but I wouldn't expect you to walk away from any of your investigations just to prove your feelings for me."

"I'm not asking you to do that."

"Yes, you are."

"What I'm asking for is a reason to stay."

"Are you threatening to leave?"

"If that's what it takes. We've been dancing around this for three years and I'm out of patience. I want it all."

"Sloan—"

"All or nothing, Riki. You decide."

It had taken her almost three weeks to find the ring again. She'd thrown it at him so hard before he'd left, it had bounced off his chest, ricocheted from the wall behind the bed and rolled beneath the dresser.

After the funeral, she'd gone over every inch of the bedroom and had been starting to fear that Rufus had sniffed out the ring and swallowed it, but she'd been determined not to give up. It had been on the nineteenth day when she'd been flat on her belly, with her chin on the floor and a flashlight gripped in her hand, that she'd finally spotted the glint of the diamond. Somehow it had become wedged into the crack between the floor and the baseboard.

Her hands had been shaking so hard, it had taken an hour to slip the ring on her finger. She hadn't removed it since.

It had been forty-three days before she'd changed the sheets. Her reluctance hadn't been because of her dislike of doing laundry, it was because Sloan's pillowcase had smelled like the back of his neck. Burying her face in his pillow had been the only way she'd been able to fall asleep alone. After she'd washed his scent out, she'd had to resort to liquor.

They had said that Sloan had been drunk the night he'd died. The empty beer cans in the *Riki B.*'s cabin had borne only his prints. He'd gone out on his boat to drink beer, eat chips and sulk about the argument. Not prudent, not sensible, but exactly what a stubborn, proud guy's guy like Sloan would do.

The official police report had called it an accident. A combination of tragic circumstances. Sloan had likely been too annoyed to remember that the head in the sloop had been out of commission when he'd set sail, so after he'd downed his beers and started into his chips, he'd gone out on the pitching deck in his sock feet in the rain to answer nature's call. Then he'd slipped and fallen overboard.

That was the theory, anyway. In honor of his memory, Sloan's colleagues had kept those particular details away from the public. They had decided that for a detective who had survived the worst that the streets of

New York could throw at him for twelve years, it would have been the ultimate humiliation if news got around that he'd bought it when he'd been taking a leak.

But Sloan would have appreciated the absurdity of it all. He probably would have curved his lips into that lopsided grin that brought out his dimple and remarked that he didn't give a damn what anyone thought. Sometimes a man had to do what a man had to do.

"It says here he died in a boating accident," Max said. "A year ago tonight."

"The cop is dead?" Wates asked.

"Left a grieving mother, four younger sisters and a fiancée," Max continued. "Father was a cop, too. Sounds like a good Irish Catholic boy. How did he hook up with a hot babe like you, Red?"

How? At the Cherry on Top. Her uncle had introduced them at the bar's annual St. Patrick's Day party.

"The important question here, Max, is why did she lie?" Wates's chair scraped. He paced around the table and grabbed Erika by the back of her head, twisting her hair along with the knot of the blindfold. He gave her a shake that made her eyes water. "Do you think I'm a fool, Miss Balough?"

"Whoa, John." Max stepped forward. The pressure on Erika's scalp immediately eased. "I'll handle this."

"Take your hands off me, Tanner."

"Sure, as soon as you put away that gun."

"Don't you give me orders."

"I'll do whatever the hell I have to." Max's voice hardened. "We have a deal, John. I've got as much invested in this as you do, so I'm not going to stand by and watch you screw it up by getting trigger-happy."

For a moment, neither man spoke. Tension coiled between them, with Erika caught smack in the middle.

She tried to remain as motionless as possible, in spite of the moisture that was trickling from the corners of her eyes. Wates's rough treatment had ripped out the hair at her temples by its roots, but there was more than pain behind these tears. There was stark, edge-of-panic fear.

Wates had taken out his gun. Erika hadn't seen it or felt it since the last time he'd jammed it under her ear, but she knew instinctively that the 9 mm Heckler & Koch was pointed at her head.

Part of her, the sane and logical part, realized that her odds of seeing another day were next to nothing. But the rest of her, that stubborn, irrational core that for weeks had kept clinging to the possibility that Sloan had survived, wasn't ready to accept her own death, either. No matter how hopeless the situation seemed, she couldn't give up yet. Dear God, she wanted to live.

"Damn it, Max," Wates muttered. "We can't afford complications like this woman."

"I couldn't agree more. But we still need to find out who sent her."

"Well, it wasn't Sloan Morrissey…." Wates paused. "Morrissey," he repeated. "That obituary said his father was a cop, too."

"That's right. Why?"

Wates stepped back. "Never mind," he snapped. "Ancient history. It's got nothing to do with the Stingers."

Stingers? Erika thought. Oh, God. He meant Stinger missiles. *That's* what was in those long, heavy crates. She'd guessed they contained weapons, but this was far worse than she'd imagined. Her mind reeled as she thought of the destruction that could be done if just one of those missiles got into the wrong hands.

And they had truckloads. A ship full.

"Give me until we're ready to weigh anchor," Max said. "I'll get the truth from her."

"You'd better. I don't want any surprises when we meet your people."

"You see to your end and get the cargo on board. I'll make sure nothing interferes with the rendezvous." Max moved beside Erika and put his hand under her elbow. "We're going back to the hold, sweet cheeks. And then we're going to finish our chat."

Her stomach knotted at the ice in his tone. She didn't want to think about how he intended to "get the truth" from her. She couldn't let Max's resemblance to Sloan cloud her judgment—the switchblade he carried would be just as deadly as Wates's pistol.

Still, she didn't resist as he helped her to her feet. One-on-one gave her better odds of escape than three-on-one.

"Leavish, keep an eye on them," Wates said, snapping his fingers. "We wouldn't want Mr. Tanner to lose his way and slip over a railing the way Dick did."

Max's fingers manacled Erika's upper arm. "Absolutely, John," he drawled. "Another accident is the last thing I'd want."

The fog had thickened since the last time Erika had been outside. She could feel drops of water burst on her cheeks as she moved through the mist. Cold air prickled against her nose and the back of her throat, helping to clear her head and focus her thoughts.

It wasn't that difficult, because there was only one thought. Survive. That was it. Amazing how simple things got when it came down to the crunch.

A foghorn droned somewhere to her right, the mournful tone raising goose bumps on her arms. Good.

Since the foghorn was to her right, the shore must be to her left. At least she knew which way to run if she got the chance.

Not if. When. She had heard Wates dispatch someone to check out her office and her apartment. No matter what kind of lie she tried to spin for Max in the meantime, he and Wates would eventually realize her only open case was her search for Hartwell's appliance thief. She had to make use of this opportunity. Once she was back in the hold, she probably wouldn't leave it alive.

She replayed the route she had memorized on the way up. So far, they had followed it exactly. Any second now they would get to the first of the staircases she had noted. That would take them to the main deck. There would have to be a way to get off the ship from there, right?

As he had when he'd brought her to Wates, Leavish was leading the way. He stayed no more than two steps in front of her, close enough for her to glimpse the backs of his heels. Like the late Dick, he wore work boots, but they were several sizes smaller than Dick's had been, so he was likely shorter than the other men she'd encountered.

Erika decided that if she kicked out when they were on the staircase, she should be able to knock Leavish down the steps. She was in better shape for an escape attempt now that the tape that had bound her arms was gone—although her wrists were still stuck together, her balance was less impeded and she did have some use of her hands. She would have the element of surprise in her favor, plus the cover of the fog, so with the right timing, she might be able to make a break for it while Max was still caught on the stairs behind her.

As plans went, it sucked big-time, but Erika didn't have any other options. It would be better to go down swinging than to be led like a lamb to the slaughter. And there was no telling how many other people would be slaughtered if this load of missiles wasn't stopped. She had to get away and warn someone.

It wouldn't be easy. Max's grip on her arm was like a set of handcuffs, not pressing into her flesh but enclosing her in a circle of steel. He would have to shift his grip when they started down the stairs. She had to be ready to move when he did.

She was vividly conscious of how close he walked. She could also smell his aftershave and hear the solid thud of his boots, both of which kept setting off jabs of recognition and adrenaline and stupid, pathetic spurts of longing. All those dormant nerve endings in her skin that he'd awakened when he'd searched her continued to spark. Try as she might, she couldn't quell the reaction.

Yet these reminders of Sloan were good. They energized her. They were something familiar to hang on to in this nightmare, as comforting as the taste of chocolate.

On her next step, she intentionally caught her heel on a rivet in the deck plating. Stumbling sideways, she ducked her head and lifted her hands, as if bracing for a fall. She had just hooked one thumb under the edge of her blindfold when Max pulled her back.

"Hey, careful, Red." He stepped behind her, his chest brushing against her shoulders as he steadied her.

Another jab of recognition, another spurt of adrenaline. It was astounding how much this criminal reminded her of Sloan. He was precisely the same height Sloan had been. Her body wanted to soften and lean into his. They had always fitted together so perfectly.

She gritted her teeth and raised her head. She had managed to slide the blindfold upward an inch on one side before Max had stopped her, so she did a quick scan through one eye. They were on a railed-in walkway about forty feet above the deck. The fog was like gauze, spinning a fuzzy halo around the floodlight that was fixed to one corner of the bridge. More light shone from below, where a group of men worked on some machinery beside huge, horizontal doors that angled outward from a cavernous space.

Were those what Leavish had meant by hatch covers? Was this where Dick had fallen?

She flicked her gaze in front of her and saw a gap in the railing. Her memory of the route had served her well—they were only a few steps from the staircase. She also saw that Leavish was indeed short. He had the buzz cut of a marine recruit and a baby-face profile. She ducked her head again as he glanced back at her so he wouldn't notice her crooked blindfold.

Erika's pulse tripped with anticipation as she watched Leavish's work boots move to the head of the stairs. She inhaled carefully, tensing her muscles, preparing to break for freedom the instant Max loosened his hold.

Max dipped his head next to hers. "Don't even think about it, Riki," he whispered.

She jerked, as much from the shock of his breath on her ear as from his words.

"Wates has guards at the gangplank and on the pier," he continued, still in a whisper. He pinched the edge of her blindfold and tugged it back into place. "Stay with me if you want to stay alive."

Damn, how had he guessed?

Then again, if she had figured out this was the best

spot for an escape attempt, Max had probably figured it out, too. So much for the element of surprise—

Good God.

He had called her Riki.

"Problems, Mr. Tanner?" Leavish asked, pausing on the stairs.

"No," Max replied. "Lead on."

Erika's knees wobbled as she moved forward. She couldn't have heard him right. Only three people in the world had ever called her Riki. Her mother, Uncle Hector and…

Sloan.

How would some switchblade-packing arms smuggler know Riki was one of her nicknames?

Simple. The name of Sloan's boat had been mentioned in his obituary.

But why had Max whispered that warning at all?

It was a head game. Classic good cop/bad cop technique. He wanted to put her off guard before he questioned her by pretending he was on her side. Not that he was a cop, but anyone who watched *Law and Order* would know about how they worked. Or maybe Max had learned the technique because it had been used on him.

After all, what other explanation could there be?

Oh boy, was that the wrong question. Erika's heart clamored with alternative answers to it, but she had to use her head.

She placed her foot on the first step.

"The new boots might be sexy, Red," Max said. "But they look lethal." He grasped her by the waist, turned her to face him and bent down to slip one arm behind her legs.

"What are you doing?"

He flipped her over his shoulder and straightened up. "Making sure we all get down that staircase in one piece. Keep clear of her feet, Leavish," he said. "Those heels could do serious damage to your head."

"I've got her covered."

"Yeah, great, but point that somewhere else. Wates said he didn't want any more accidents, so he wouldn't want you hitting me by mistake, would he?"

"Sorry, Mr. Tanner."

Locking his arm around her thighs to hold her in place, Max started down the staircase.

Erika gasped and clutched the back of his raincoat between her hands. Blood rushed into her head, along with a flood of memories.

Sloan had carried her like this the last time they'd been at the beach. They'd had less clothes on then, but they'd both been laughing too hard to concentrate on all the naked contact. She had lost a bet—she couldn't remember now what it had been about—and her penalty had been a dunk in the surf. It was the only time she had actually enjoyed going in the water.

She'd known that Sloan wouldn't have let her go under. She trusted him completely.

Max carried her to the bottom of the stairs and shifted her smoothly to her feet.

Erika leaned over, braced her joined wrists on her thighs and fought to catch her breath. She could still feel the slide of Sloan's skin against hers and the jouncing from his laughter against her stomach.

Max resumed his handcuff-hold on her arm. "You're heavier than you look, baby." He tugged her upright. "You must have been hitting the chocolate pretty hard."

Leavish snickered and started off once more.

Erika shoved aside the memories and focused on

keeping her footing on the wet deck as Max guided her forward. His comment hadn't made sense. He had picked her up and carried her effortlessly—even through his clothes, she had felt the easy play of his muscles. And she'd never been heavy. She'd been blessed with a metabolism that burned off whatever she ate. During the past year, she had eaten less than usual and had ended up dropping ten pounds. Why had he remarked on her weight unless…?

Unless he'd deliberately wanted to bring up the subject of chocolate.

Sloan knew how she loved it. He used to kid her about how easy she was to shop for. Every birthday, Christmas and Valentine's Day he'd never failed to bring her something decadently rich and delicious. Not that he waited for a special occasion to indulge her. There had been one weekend morning that final October together when his idea of breakfast in bed had been a jar of chocolate sauce. He had shared it with her in the most creative way.

Erika realized with a start that she had lost track of how far they had come. Had that been Max's intention? Had he been trying to distract her so she wouldn't think of attempting an escape?

Yes, that must be it. He was trying to distract her. He must have realized she had a fondness for chocolate because he'd found the Hershey's bar in her coat pocket.

And he'd carried her to be sure she didn't have the chance to kick Leavish or to get away from him on the stairs.

And he'd called her Riki to mess with her mind.

The deck rang with the tread of several pairs of boots. Someone called out to Max as the group passed, something about installing the new winch cable. She heard other voices from her left, in the direction she'd assumed led to the shore. Those voices probably belonged to the guards Max had cautioned her about.

She hadn't seen that Leavish was carrying a weapon, but from what Max had said, she had to conclude Leavish was armed, too. She wouldn't have gotten far if she had made a break for it. She might even have been killed.

Stay with me if you want to stay alive.

Okay. Whatever his motives, Max didn't want her dead right away, and he was already proving to be her best bet for staying alive.

Good. Fine. Max was prolonging her survival, which was essential if she wanted to escape. That explained why she no longer wanted to run from him. It was why she didn't protest when he did the caveman toss-over-the-shoulder thing again and carried her down the next staircase.

Yet could she explain why her pulse was continuing to accelerate at his touch, his smell and the sound of his walk? Was there a reason for this mad spurt of hope and the sudden lightness she felt in her chest and the growing excitement that was battering at her senses?

Once again, Erika's heart shouted the answers.

Well, certainly. There was another way to put together the clues: Max had carried her down the stairs because he hadn't wanted her to catch her heel in the grating and break her neck. He'd mentioned chocolate because he'd wanted to give her a private signal. If she thought about it, he'd been trying to give her signals since he'd shown up. And he'd called her Riki because he'd realized no one else could hear him and he'd known that would get her attention.

Sure, believing her lover's ghost had come back from

the dead to help her was insane. It was right 'round the bend, nutso, loony-tunes crazy.

But this Sloan sighting wasn't anything like the others. He hadn't disappeared into thin air when she'd chased him past the warehouse, he'd come on board this ship. This was no shadow or hallucination or figment of her imagination. The man who held her arm and walked behind her was solid flesh and blood.

Max wasn't Sloan's ghost.

Max was Sloan.

Chapter 5

In a way, allowing herself to acknowledge what her heart had been telling her all along was a relief. It was like the one and only time Erika had gone skydiving. The worst part had been standing in the doorway of the plane, feeling the wind on her face, watching the earth scroll past beneath the wing, wondering if she was about to do the stupidest thing in her life.

Regarded logically, voluntarily jumping out of a plane was insane. Nothing was ever a hundred-percent certain. There was always the chance of an error that could quickly turn deadly, and yet…

And yet there was nothing quite as invigorating as that moment when the decision was made. The point of no return. One instant her fingers had been gripping the solid sides of the hatch and her feet planted firmly on the floor of the fuselage. The next instant, she had launched herself into the air with nothing for certain except gravity.

She had screamed all the way down.

Her instructor had refused to take her up again when he'd heard rumors about her hallucinations and had found out that she was in grief counseling. Understandably, he'd been worried about his liability if she chose not to pull the rip cord the next time.

Yet those reckless, terrifying, exhilarating seconds had been worth every shriek. They were moments out of time, a taste of total freedom. An affirmation of her ability to face her fear and win.

To take a leap of faith.

But skydiving was a stroll through the park compared to what she was contemplating now.

Then again, what did she have to lose? Jumping from a plane that was about to crash anyway wasn't crazy at all, was it?

Erika took stock of her surroundings. Judging by the echo of their footsteps and from what she could see of the floor, they were progressing along a narrow corridor deep in the hold, close to the room where she'd awakened. Any moment now they might stop moving. This was as good a time as any to test her parachute. She jerked her hands to her face, shoved up her blindfold and twisted to look behind her.

He must have been expecting it. Before she could glimpse more than the blur of a square jaw, Max grabbed the back of her head and pushed her face into his shoulder.

Yet she didn't need to see his face, did she? She'd already recognized him in a hundred other ways. "Sloan," she whispered. She leaned against him, letting her body soak in the feel of his.

Oh, yes. This had to be him. She drew in his scent on a sob. More nerve endings sparked. The reaction was overwhelming now that she was no longer fighting her instincts. "Sloan, I know—"

"Take it easy, sweet cheeks." His voice drowned out her whisper. "If you want to dance, I'd prefer to do it in private. Hey, Leavish."

"Yes, Mr. Tanner?"

"Do you still have that duct tape?"

Erika tried to push away from his chest but his hand held her fast.

"It's in my pocket," Leavish replied. "Do you need some?"

Max yanked her blindfold into place, spun her away from him and gripped her upper arms. "Yeah. Red's getting feisty."

Had he heard her whisper? She couldn't be sure. She had to find some way to communicate that she had understood his earlier message. "I know who you are," Erika said aloud. "The blindfold isn't necessary."

"More bluffs, Red?"

"I'm not bluffing. I've been telling the truth all along."

Leavish's footsteps moved in front of her. There was a hollow, ripping sound. "Want me to do her arms again?"

"Yeah," Max said. "Around the elbows like before so she can't use her hands."

Erika jerked against Max's grip. "No! I'm going to cooperate."

"Yeah, right. You would do or say anything if you thought it would give you an advantage. I know you were thinking about making a break for it back there. We don't want you getting yourself into more trouble. Watch out for her feet, Leavish."

She kicked and felt her toe connect with Leavish's shin. "Don't you dare put more tape on me."

Max gave her a quick shake. "Are you going to be-have?"

"Why won't you listen? I did tell the truth. My fi-ancé knows I'm here."

"The dead guy?" Max asked.

"He's not dead."

"So you carry his obituary around for a joke?"

"He's a cop. He used the reports of his death to dis-appear so he could work undercover."

Erika's words dropped into a sudden silence. She hadn't realized she was going to say them until they were out. She hadn't even realized until now that she'd thought them, but it was the only explanation possible.

Sloan was the most dedicated cop she knew. He was also the most protective man she knew. If he hadn't re-ally drowned the last time he'd taken out the *Riki B.*, then he would have to have a good reason to let every-one think he had.

A shipload of stolen Stinger missiles would be a damn good reason. If Sloan had assumed the identity of Max Tanner in order to stop a criminal like Wates, he would have needed to immerse himself in his role completely. Contacting anyone from his former life would have put them as well as himself in danger.

And he would have known that if he'd told Erika what he'd been doing, she wouldn't have been content to sit on the sidelines. She would have insisted on help-ing him.

Yes! The theory wasn't merely possible, it was plausible. He'd let her believe he was dead for her own protection.

But it had been a year. She'd been through hell. Couldn't he have given her some hint?

Max laughed. It was sharp and sardonic, nothing

like Sloan's deep rumble. "You had all this time to dream up a new story. Is that the best you could do?"

Leavish cleared his throat. "Do you still want the extra tape?"

"Forget it." Max cupped her shoulders and propelled her forward. "I think she got the message."

"Maybe I should tell Mr. Wates what she said about the cop," Leavish said, falling into step behind them. "He'd want to know if someone infiltrated our operation."

Max reached past her and opened a door. It swung into complete darkness. "John wouldn't believe that any more than I do."

"But—"

"Leavish, if her boyfriend really *was* alive and working undercover with us, do you think she would volunteer that piece of information so easily?" He moved his hand to the small of Erika's back and guided her over the raised threshold. "She'd have to know that would be signing his death warrant."

Erika bit her lip. Dear God, she was right! Max had to be Sloan. He'd just given her a warning that was as clear as glass.

He knew that she knew. Yet he had to play his role as long as there was someone else around. So did she. Their lives depended on it.

But she didn't want to play a role. Sloan was here and he was alive and oh, God, she wanted to wrap herself around him, fit her body to his and press her lips to that special place at the base of his throat that she loved to kiss, the spot where she could feel his pulse beat beneath his skin.

"On the other hand," Max said. "Maybe they had a fight and she wants us to off him for her. Leavish, where's the light switch?"

"It's out here. I'll get it."

Thin, yellow light glowed through her blindfold. A familiar rusty, fishy smell permeated the air. Erika swallowed fast. She'd managed to stay on top of the nausea. She didn't want it coming back now. She had to concentrate.

As long as they weren't alone, she couldn't touch Sloan. Yet she'd prayed every night for a year to have another chance to talk to him.

Against all odds, here it was.

"Sloan and I are a perfect match," she said. "We rarely argue."

"Sure. With that hair?" Max led her to a low wooden crate and pressed on her shoulders until she sat. "I never met a redhead who didn't have a mean temper."

"I love him," she said. "He knows that."

Max stood in front of her, his feet braced apart. "Babe, give it up. The guy's dead."

"It makes no difference. I still love him. I never stopped."

"Terrific. So he was a paragon."

"Hardly," she said. "Sloan had plenty of faults. He was stubborn and overprotective and short on patience. He had trouble compromising and he hogged the blankets and he left the toilet seat up but I wouldn't want him any other way. We fit. He was the other half of me." She felt a lump in her throat. "He never really left me. I see him everywhere."

"Skip the sob fest, Red," Max muttered. "This isn't *Oprah*."

She heard a faint thread of voices float through the doorway. Leavish's boots scuffed on the floor near the threshold. Any minute they could be interrupted, but there was so much more she wanted to say. *Needed* to say. "That's why I still wear his ring. It's a symbol of my faith in our love. Sloan and I—"

"You're getting way off topic," Max said.

"You told your friend upstairs you were going to get the truth out of me. That's what I'm giving you."

"Baby, there are plenty of things I'd like you to give me." He took a step closer and reached out to stroke his knuckles along the edge of her jaw. "But we have some business to take care of first, for me and my friend upstairs. Quit stalling."

This was Sloan, so it was all right to feel the thrill that followed his touch. Erika moistened her lips and ever so slightly leaned into his hand. He'd mentioned stalling. That must be another message. Of course, he'd want her to stall because he knew this interrogation was a farce. He was doing it for Leavish's benefit.

But these words were meant just for Sloan. She was giving him a message of her own. For all she knew, there wouldn't be another chance. "I tried to stall Sloan. He wanted to get married more than I did. I'm not the domestic type, but he wanted it all: the house with the yard, the kids and the dog. He liked kids. He would have been a great father. He practically raised his sisters."

"Poor guy's lucky he drowned."

"I've taken good care of Rufus. That's Sloan's dog. We get along great now, but he howled for the first week after the funeral. He almost got us evicted. When Sloan's buddies from the precinct heard about it, they paid a visit to my landlord. They made his unpaid parking tickets disappear, and he changed his mind about Rufus."

Max moved around the crate she was sitting on and spoke from behind her. "Come on, Red. Try to focus."

She shuddered when she realized how close he stood.

He was only a deep breath away. "I've visited Sloan's family a lot since the funeral," she said. "They took some getting used to. I never had a large family around when I was growing up. After my parents died it was just my uncle and me."

She felt a light brush on her back between her shoulder blades, as if Max had picked up a lock of her hair. The gesture was familiar. Sloan had liked to rub her hair between his fingers, especially when they were in bed. He would often tickle her neck with the ends.

"That's why I didn't want to get married." She spoke more quickly, seized with an urgency to get the rest of it out. "Not because I didn't love Sloan but because I was afraid of the whole family thing. I've been independent most of my life, and I wasn't sure I could handle total commitment."

"Geez, Red. You're putting us to sleep."

"But that changed after Sloan died. Taking care of his dog and spending so much time with Sloan's relatives made me realize he'd been right. I was overanalyzing everything. There was nothing to be afraid of after all." Her words wound down as she marveled at how simple it sounded now. Too bad it had taken her a year to figure it out. "Wherever Sloan is, I hope he knows that."

"He's fish food, baby. Fast forward a bit here. Get to the part where you went for a stroll in the rain with your camera."

She paused, drawing in the scent of Old Spice. "I was working."

"Okay, now we're getting somewhere. Why were you working?"

"Because I'm good at my job."

"So am I," Max said. "Maybe you should keep that in mind and stop trying to jerk me around."

"And what exactly is your job, Mr. Tanner?"

"Nuh-uh, Red. I'm the one who asks the questions. You already know everything about me that you need to."

Something soft tickled the side of her neck. It was one of her curls.

She blinked back a wave of tears at the caress. *Sloan, my love, I can't keep this up much longer. I need to touch you.*

The thread of voices she'd been hearing in the background strengthened. Footsteps approached rapidly. "Hey, Leavish," someone called. "Is Tanner around?"

"He's in here, Floyd."

Max squeezed her shoulder. "Stay put," he ordered. His voice had dropped to a low rasp, exactly the way Sloan sounded when he was worried. "Or I'll tape your feet together and tie you to this crate. Understand?"

She nodded.

He brushed past her, his strides long and sure as he stepped through the doorway and into the corridor.

Erika inhaled slowly through her nose. This man had to be Sloan. He was letting her know in subtle ways, but the messages were there. She wasn't imagining them.

On the other hand, everything he had said and done was also consistent with the character of Max Tanner.

What if she had finally cracked from the stress? Her heart had cried wolf so many times, how could she be sure she wasn't deluding herself again?

"Mr. Tanner, Abrams found her car."

"Where?" Max asked.

"A few blocks over. It was parked in front of a warehouse."

"What kind of warehouse?"

"It was full of kitchen stuff. There was a button factory beside it."

"Do you know if he got rid of the car, Floyd?"

"He dumped it off the pier, Mr. Tanner. This was inside. He said you'd want to hear it."

"Thanks. How are the repairs to the winch coming along?"

"It's up and running. We'll be finished loading in ten minutes."

"Good work."

Erika strained to listen, but she could detect only one set of footsteps retreating down the corridor. Max still wasn't alone. She heard a soft whirring sound from the doorway, followed by a click. She tilted her head, trying to picture what the noise could be from.

"November seventeenth, 12:35 a.m."

It was her voice.

"Have observed no activity in the area for the past hour. Possibly due to the weather."

Oh, no. She had forgotten about the tape recorder. She had dropped it on the floor of the car when she'd first seen Sloan.

"Advise client to install better lighting over the door beside the loading dock. What he's got now wouldn't discourage thieves, it would only annoy them. Recommend client hire Adeel to install video surveillance at all entrances. Note to self: call Adeel to negotiate possible finder's fee if client follows recommendation to buy equipment from him. Second note to self: pick up dog food on way home—"

The recording clicked off. She angled her head back and saw the tips of Max's cowboy boots just inside the doorway.

"Well, Leavish," He crossed one ankle over the other,

as if he leaned a shoulder on the doorframe. "It appears our conversation with Red is over."

"Let me explain," she said.

"If you were expecting a reward from Homeland Security, you wouldn't be thinking up ways to milk your client. You weren't looking for us, baby, you were staking out that warehouse where Abrams found your car."

This was Sloan, she told herself. He wasn't going to hurt her. "What difference does it make whether I was looking for you or not? I found you."

"No one knows you're here."

"Wrong. The authorities know."

Max laughed again. The harsh sound grated on her nerves. It was so wrong, so unlike Sloan. "Too late, sweet cheeks," he drawled. "It was a gutsy bet, but your bluff just got called. Game's over."

"Wait. Give me some more time to—"

"Time isn't going to change anything."

The words were familiar. They were some of the last Sloan had said to her.

Time isn't going to change how I feel about you.

"Take the recorder to Wates, Leavish," Max continued. "Tell him I'll meet him on the bridge."

"I'll wait for you to finish up first, Mr. Tanner. He ordered me to stay with you."

Finish up? Erika's pulse kicked with a spurt of adrenaline that had nothing to do with recognition. Wates would expect Max to kill her. Once they were underway, they would dispose of her remains along with Dick's. Oh, God. If she'd made a mistake…

No. She was going to trust her heart. She clasped her hands and leaned forward. "All right. I admit it. I lied. But please, don't hurt me. I don't want to die. I'll do anything you say."

"Anything?" Max asked.

She rocked to her feet. "Yes." She walked toward his voice. "Tell me what you want."

"Whoa, Red. You're getting me all excited."

This was Sloan. And this was the best way to give him an excuse to be alone with her without blowing his cover. She stopped walking and bent her elbows to bring her joined hands to her blouse buttons. "You said you liked redheads."

"Baby, as tempting as this is, I've got business to take care of."

She caught the flash of her engagement ring from beneath her blindfold. Her tears made the stone sparkle as if it had a life of its own. She undid the first button. "I'll do whatever it takes to stay alive."

Max grunted and pushed away from the door frame. "On the other hand," he said, "you're giving me some good reasons to stay."

What I'm asking for is a reason to stay.

Another echo from that final night. Erika's fingers trembled as she opened three more buttons and pulled the edges of her blouse apart. "I'll give you as many reasons as you can handle for as long as you want. You've already seen what I have to offer. You can have it all. You decide."

The moment spun out. Voices drifted in the distance. A low hum of machinery rumbled through the floor. She could hear harsh breathing and her own heartbeat and Sloan's voice in her memory.

Did he realize what she'd said? Had the way they had parted haunted Sloan as much as it had haunted her?

Or had she just bared her soul—and her body—to a complete stranger?

"Get out of here, Leavish," Max said.

"Mr. Tanner—"

"Sweet cheeks just asked me to dance." There was a slithering click that sounded like his switchblade. "And I like it rough."

Erika fought to keep her whimper inside. Sloan was putting on an act. A very convincing act. There was no reason to be scared.

But the ground was coming up fast and the parachute hadn't opened.

The light went out. The door to the room slammed shut.

She hadn't been able to see much beneath the blindfold to begin with, but this sudden, total blackness that enveloped her was terrifying. She had never felt so completely defenseless in her life. She extended her arms, her fingers touching nothing but shadows. "Sloan," she whispered.

Boots thudded across the floor to where she stood. Cold steel pressed against the back of her hand. "Scream," Max muttered.

Her breath caught on a sob. "Sloan?"

"Damn it, Riki, scream. Leavish is listening."

He didn't have to tell her again. She parted her lips and let loose with everything that had been building inside for a year. The regret, the guilt, the anger and the grief. She emptied her lungs, pouring out the emotions that words alone could never express.

She screamed just as she had when she'd jumped from that plane, the last time she'd taken a leap of faith.

Max slit the tape that bound her wrists and dropped his knife to the floor.

Then he caught Erika's face in his hands and ended her scream with a kiss.

Chapter 6

It was hot fudge, dark and rich and honest, sizzling through her senses with a power that left her breathless. It was too intense to be pleasurable. It burned, it stung. It tore away what was left of her reason and sent her soaring to a realm of pure sensation.

Erika's legs buckled. She clutched his shoulders. Sloan slid one hand behind her waist and clamped his other hand at the nape of her neck, holding her mouth to his as he turned in a circle, whirling her in a dizzying, jubilant dance.

Yes, he was Sloan. He was here, he was real. His breath warmed her cheek, his taste filled her mouth. *Sloan!*

They sank to their knees together on the floor. With her body sealed to his, she touched her fingertips to his jaw and felt the square corners. She followed the lines that bracketed his lips and skimmed her thumbs upward to the bridge of his bold, hawk nose. There was the bump where he'd broken it as a kid, that wonderful, one-of-a-kind bump.

He splayed his hand over her back, crushing her breasts to his chest so hard she gasped. He swept his tongue over her lips in a sweet, wet demand that she answered with a moan and a tilt of her head.

No one could kiss like Sloan. There was no halfway with him, and he was throwing himself into this one full-throttle. It was making her giddy. After a year of denial, she was drunk on the joy that careened through her soul.

Sloan, her lover, her other half. He was real and alive and kissing her.

She traced his features greedily, seeing his beloved face in her mind. She stroked his eyebrows, pushed back the lock of hair that fell over his forehead and felt the smooth line of scar tissue that curved along his left temple. That was a souvenir from a perp who had swung a bottle at him. She ran her little finger around the curve of his right ear and felt the tiny raised bump in the lobe where he'd had it pierced for a cover.

She wasn't looking for proof—she already had more than she needed—yet any doubts that might have been lurking on the edges of her mind were shattered the instant she touched his cheeks.

They were wet.

Erika grabbed her blindfold and yanked it off. She scarcely registered the pain at the strands of hair that got ripped out along with it. She flung the cloth into the blackness and returned her hands to Sloan's face. Something broke loose deep inside her heart as she wiped the tracks of his tears with her fingertips.

How was it possible to love this man more?

His chest rumbled with a groan that tingled through her breasts and down to her thighs. He spoke against her lips, his voice barely above a whisper. "Riki, are you okay? Did they hurt you?"

"I'm fine."

"What about your head?"

"It's fine."

"What's wrong with your feet? You winced when I touched your heels."

She smiled. Oh, yes. This was Sloan. "My boots are too tight, that's all."

"What the hell were you doing snooping around here anyway? Of all the reckless stunts…" He plunged his hand into her hair, brought it to his face and inhaled hard. "It damn near killed me when I saw what the jerks had done to you."

"It was a bit of a shock to see you, too."

"I know. I'm sorry I couldn't warn you. I'll get you out of this. I promise."

She didn't want to stop and think how he would be able to keep that promise. The odds hadn't improved by much. Now they were two instead of only one against a ship full of armed men. This time with Sloan might be all that she would get.

Still, it was more than she'd ever dreamed of having, and she would savor every second of it. "I love you, Sloan. Whatever happens to us, I want you to know that."

"And you, my precious Riki, are the love of my life." He cupped her buttocks, dragging her up to straddle his lap as he sat back on his heels. "You are also one brave, clever, magnificent woman."

"I meant everything I said tonight, Sloan. About the ring, about us."

He buried his face against her neck. His silent laugh puffed across her skin. "That was a hell of a way you decided to tell me. Do you have any idea how close I came to blowing my cover?"

"I'm sorry it took me so long to figure everything out."

"Hey, you held it together great once you caught on. The way you let me know you knew was downright brilliant."

"Not that. I meant I'm sorry I didn't figure things out about us before that last fight."

"No, Erika, it was my fault. I was an idiot for leaving like I did." He moved his hands over her back to her shoulders and down her arms, kneading and stroking, as if he needed to reassure himself as much as she did that this was really happening. "It was only supposed to last two weeks."

Her skirt bunched at her thighs as she wrapped her legs around his hips. She had to get closer. She would crawl inside him if she could. "Two weeks?"

"The case. Two weeks tops. I had no idea I was going to get in this deep. It was because of the accident."

"You mean you didn't fake falling off your boat?"

"No, I didn't fake that. It happened exactly as everyone said. All of it. That's when things got complicated."

"But how did you survive?"

"It would take too long to explain now. We don't have much time."

"But—"

"I always planned to come back to you, Riki. I never thought I'd be gone this long." He nuzzled aside her hair and kissed his way to her ear. "I missed you so much, I thought I'd go crazy."

"Crazy?" She choked on a bubble of pure mirth.

"You're not the only one. You have no idea what I went through."

His breath tickled her neck. "Actually, I do. You chased me at least five times."

"What?"

"Once in Central Park. Twice at Penn Station."

"You were there? Really there?"

"I shouldn't have been, but I couldn't go on without seeing you, even if it was only from a distance. After the close call in the subway, I got better at keeping out of sight."

"You…" She hiccupped as a laugh turned into a sob. "I thought I was losing my mind."

"I was worried about you."

"Couldn't you have said something?"

"I was tempted, but it was for your own good. I know how persistent you are." He nipped her earlobe. "And you had the nerve to call me stubborn."

"Don't forget overprotective."

He looped his arms around her back. "I did everything in my power to take care of you, Riki, but you didn't make it easy. Thank God you quit drinking."

"How did you know about that?"

"I drove you to Jersey that night last July when you got wasted at the Cherry."

She pulled her head back. She couldn't see him, but she could swear she heard his mouth move into his lopsided grin. "Wait. You mean *you* left me on the side of the turnpike? I'd thought I'd driven there drunk."

"You had passed out before you started your car. I wanted to shock you into taking better care of yourself."

She smacked his chest. "Damn it, Sloan. That scared me half to death."

"That was the idea."

"All those times I saw you, I thought I was seeing your ghost."

"Do you still think I'm a ghost?"

She pushed aside his coat and slid her palms over his chest. Thin cotton, likely a T-shirt, stretched across the contours she knew so well. She centered her hand over his heart, then curled forward and pressed her mouth to the hollow at the base of his throat.

His pulse throbbed against her lips.

And the nightmare of the past year simply collapsed. She touched her tongue to his skin and laughed softly. "That would be crazy, Sloan. You're the man I love. I would know you anywhere."

The hum of machinery that had been droning in the background abruptly stopped. A low rumble resonated through the floor. Was that the ship's engines starting up?

Erika felt Sloan tense. Her laughter quickly died. She slid higher on his lap, folding her arms behind his neck as she locked her ankles behind his back. One nightmare had ended, but there was another that was far from over. "Don't go yet," she whispered. "Please."

"I have to."

"Sloan—"

"I need to play this through. It's the only way out for either of us."

"But what will you do?"

He leaned to one side and patted the floor with his hand, as if he were searching for something. Metal scraped on metal. There was the soft snick of his switch-blade closing. "You'll be safe here as long as you keep quiet," he said. "I'll say you're dead. No one except Wates would think of questioning my word, but I'll secure the door behind me to make sure no one comes in."

"You're not answering me. We're setting off, aren't we? What's going to happen once we're out at sea?"

"Trust me, Riki. I'll handle it." He grasped her arms and tried to pull them from around his neck.

She laced her fingers together and hung on. "You're posing as the middle man, aren't you? Between Wates and his customers. That's what it sounded like."

"Riki—"

"Do you have backup?"

He reached behind his back to tug at her ankles. "I've been working this for a year. It's all arranged."

"Who are you working with? Is it the NYPD? The FBI? They know about the Stingers, right?"

"Same old Riki," he muttered. "Why couldn't your uncle have owned a deli or a flower shop instead of raising you around cops?"

"I can help you, Sloan. I'll keep out of sight, but I can still watch your back."

He gave up trying to pry her loose, put his arms around her and rose to his feet. He carried her a few steps until his toe thudded against the wooden crate where she'd sat earlier. "I don't have time to explain. The best way for you to help me is to stay here and keep quiet, okay?"

"Sloan—"

"If I don't go, we'll both be dead."

Logically, she knew that, yet she had just found him. How could she possibly survive if she lost him again?

"Riki, you have to let me go."

Let him go? That's what everyone had been telling her to do for a year.

There was a sharp rap on the door, as if someone had struck the metal with the butt of a gun. "Mr. Tanner?"

"Get lost, Leavish," he called.

"Mr. Wates needs you on the bridge."

"Yeah. I'll be there when I'm done."

"Mr. Tanner—"

"Hell, Leavish. You want to come in here and watch me zip up?"

Erika unhooked her legs from around Sloan's hips. Her knees buckled again when her feet touched the floor. She caught his sleeves to keep from falling. It was jarring how easily Sloan could slip back into the role of Max.

Fabric rustled as he reached inside his coat. He took her hand and pressed something vaguely square into her right palm. "I don't have any Dramamine, but nibble on this if you start feeling seasick. It might help."

She closed her fingers and felt the crinkle of foil. He'd returned the Hershey's bar he'd taken from her pocket. "Same old Sloan," she murmured, her voice breaking.

He took her other hand, lifted it to his lips and brushed a kiss across her knuckles. "Wait for me, Riki B. It'll be over before you know it."

"I'll wait for you forever if I have to, Sloan." She turned her hand over and touched her fingertips to his face, memorizing the lines, the angles and the dips. "As long as you promise to come back."

He cradled her face in his palms and spoke against her lips. "I will, Riki. I swear it on my love for you. Nothing on this earth is going to keep us apart again."

The first kiss had made her giddy. This one left her weak. It was swift and savage and bittersweet. She could taste the goodbye.

No, not yet. Please.

The rumble in the floor got louder. There was another series of raps on the door.

And suddenly, Erika was holding nothing but shadows.

* * *

The ship stopped moving after five hours. Erika assumed it was five hours. She was usually good at estimating time, but it felt as if they'd been moving for five years. Cautiously, she lifted her head from between her knees and blotted her forehead on her sleeve.

How far had they traveled? The fact that they had gone anywhere without colliding with something was beyond her, but perhaps the fog had burned off with the sunrise. It would have to be late morning by now. She deduced the storm of the night before must have cleared, since the sea was relatively calm, apart from the occasional swell that treated her to a slow-motion, gut-churning, roller-coaster shrug.

The crate she was sitting on shifted uphill. Erika sank her nails into the wooden sides and inhaled shallowly through her nose until the floor and her stomach settled back into place. The Hershey's bar was long gone, but it had served its purpose. She'd kept it down through sheer stubbornness—she didn't want to waste perfectly good chocolate.

She pushed herself to her feet. She wavered a little until she got her balance, then inched her way to the door and groped for the wheel that served as its handle.

During the lulls in the swells, she'd explored every inch of this storeroom. She hadn't found a porthole or any other exit. There was a grate in the ceiling beside the left wall that probably led to the ventilation system, but it would have been too small for her to get through, even if she'd had some tool to unfasten the screws. She hadn't found a light switch, either. It had to be outside the door.

Damn the man. Couldn't Sloan have turned on the light before he'd left? Okay, it might have been hard to explain to Leavish why a corpse would need a light. But would it have killed him to have given her some straight answers about what was going on? It wasn't as if she was about to rush out there and try to interfere...

She leaned her shoulder against the door. Well, yes, that was exactly what she would do if she could. She would be out of this room like a shot if Sloan hadn't locked her in. That was the primary reason he'd done it.

Sloan knew she couldn't help being wired this way. She'd been an impressionable ten-year-old when she'd gone to live with her Uncle Hector. He'd put her to work polishing glasses at the Cherry on Top so that he could keep an eye on her after school. From her seat behind the bar, she'd grown up listening to the stories of men like Sloan and his friends. That's what had inspired her to become a P.I., so she could have the challenge of solving crimes without having to put up with the police department bureaucracy the cops always complained about.

But whether the investigating was private or tax-payer-funded, nothing was ever a hundred-percent certain. No matter how much planning went into an undercover sting, stuff often went wrong. It never hurt to have an ace in the hole. She could have been Sloan's ace. Instead, he was still pulling this super-macho protectiveness thing that had always driven her nuts.

She rubbed her hand over her face, muffling her laugh against her palm. What was she doing? How could she be annoyed with him? She loved him. She was overjoyed to know he was alive. Her heart was still staggering from the emotions he'd released.

Yet now that the emotions were out, it was impossible to cram them back inside. All this time, she'd tortured herself with guilt. She'd believed her final argument with Sloan and her inability to commit had precipitated his death. But no, he'd been alive all along and had stayed away by choice. By *choice*. She wanted an explanation. He owed her that much, didn't he?

She gave the door handle a twist, but naturally it didn't move. Muttering a curse, she flattened her palms against the door and dropped her forehead to the back of her hand.

Damn, she was a mess. It wasn't only the ship that had been giving her a roller-coaster ride. Her mood had been swinging from one extreme to another.

What she and Sloan had between them was solid. She had absolute faith in their love.

But the euphoria of their reunion had dimmed somewhat beneath the misery she'd endured over the past five hours. Sure, she was in love. She was also exhausted, seasick and worried out of her mind, so it was understandable that she would be getting a tad cranky.

A man's voice drifted from somewhere down the corridor. Erika quickly put her ear to the door. The voice had sounded like Leavish's.

"I still can't see why Tanner couldn't clean up his own mess."

"Quit whining, Leavish." Footsteps rang through the floor, approaching fast. "Wates wants us to get rid of the loose ends now before the transfer."

"Well, you better do the lifting, Floyd. I threw my back out getting Dick overboard."

Erika grasped the situation instantly. Wates must have sent Leavish and that other man, Floyd, to get rid of her body.

Well, she'd wanted to get out of this room. One way or another, that was about to happen.

She moved to the side of the door that had the hinges and flattened herself against the wall. This time, she would definitely have the element of surprise in her favor. These men expected to find a corpse, not a desperate, pissed-off woman with ten years of self-defense training.

Something clunked against the door handle. "Why'd Tanner padlock it?"

"I think it got messy," Leavish said. "He used his knife."

"Ah, hell."

"Yeah. These are new jeans."

"Move over, I've got a key." There was a scraping creak as the door swung inward.

Erika held her breath as the door came within a millimeter of striking her breasts. Shifting her weight to the balls of her feet, she blinked at the light that came in from the corridor, praying her eyes would adjust fast. She knew she would only have one crack at this. She had to make it count.

"I can't see anything. Where's the light switch?"

"I'll get it," Leavish said.

Yellow light flooded from a bulb in the ceiling. An instant later, a stocky blond man in a plaid shirt walked into the room.

Erika slipped out from behind the door, pivoted on one foot and whipped her trailing foot directly at the blond man's head. She shifted her balance just before she made contact, straightening her leg to deliver her entire momentum into the kick. The sole of her boot hit the side of his jaw with a dull crunch.

She didn't wait to watch him fall. From the corner of her eye she saw movement in the doorway. She dove to the side, grabbed the edge of the door and slammed it shut.

The thick metal panel caught Leavish full in the face and bounced open again. He screamed and lifted his hands to his nose. Erika lunged past him to the corridor, whirled and delivered a kick to the back of his knees.

Leavish tripped over the raised threshold and tumbled into the room, clearing the doorway by less than an inch.

Erika caught the door and yanked it shut, then rehooked the padlock and snapped it closed.

Then she braced her hands on her thighs, leaned over and gulped in a few lungfuls of air. Real fights weren't anything like the drawn-out slugfests in the movies. That whole brutal encounter couldn't have taken more than four seconds. Nevertheless, she felt totally drained. It hadn't done her blisters any good, either.

But she was alive and had just reduced the odds against her and Sloan by two.

The door vibrated with a sudden thud. At first she thought Leavish or his companion had managed to crawl over to hit it, but then she realized the vibration had come from the hull of the ship. There was a second, deeper clunk, a lull, and then a distant, popping sound.

Gunfire?

She straightened up and scanned the corridor. Yes, that was gunfire. Whatever sting Sloan had arranged must be going down right now. Where was he? Was he safe? Something must have already gone wrong if he'd let these men come down here to get her.

"Open the door!"

Erika jumped backward. She spotted a switch on the wall beside the doorframe and flicked it off.

"Hey!"

There was another string of pops. The sensible, rational thing to do would be to find a safe place to hide until it was all over, but Sloan was out there, so she wasn't about to stay here. She closed her eyes, picturing the route that would lead to the deck. Without further thought, she hiked up her skirt and ran.

She didn't get there as fast as she would have liked. Twice she had to duck behind bulkheads to avoid being seen. By the time she saw daylight, the gunfire had tapered off. Fresh air swept through the hold, carrying with it the chugging roar of helicopters. A voice shouted commands through a loudspeaker, the words distorted by volume and distance, yet still recognizable.

"Put down your weapons. You are surrounded."

Erika raced up the staircase. Her first view of the deck brought tears to her eyes. Some of it was a reaction to the sunshine that glared from every metal surface, dazzling her light-deprived retinas. Yet the bulk of the tears were from relief. Great, sobbing hunks of it.

Men and women in Coast Guard uniforms were everywhere. So were people in dark-blue windbreakers with FBI emblazoned across the backs. Flack-jacketed sharpshooters were poised in the open doorway of a helicopter that hovered above the main hatch. At least two more helicopters hung in the air beyond the sides of the ship. Past the railing at the edge of the deck she glimpsed the shape of another ship bobbing on the swells, smaller than this freighter yet crawling with more uniforms.

It was going to be all right. It was over. Thank God.

"Stop right there, ma'am," someone shouted from behind her. "Hands above your head."

"Don't shoot!" Erika clasped her hands on top of her head and turned around. "I'm on your side."

One of the FBI men was pointing a pistol at her chest. With his eyes hidden behind sunglasses, his expression was the blank game face of any on-duty cop. He spoke into a transmitter that curved around his jaw. "It looks like I found the hostage."

Hostage? Sloan must have been able to get a message out. Erika started forward. "Where's Sloan? Detective Sloan Morrissey? Is he all right?"

He motioned with the gun. "Stay where you are, ma'am."

She stopped and glanced around fast, still struggling to cope with the influx of light. She spotted several men lying facedown on the deck near a large funnel-shaped air shaft, their hands fastened behind their backs with plastic bundling ties. She didn't recognize any of them, but judging by the way they were dressed, they could have been some of the men she'd seen inside the storage shed.

"What's your name?"

"Erika Balough," she said, returning her gaze to the FBI agent. "I'm a private investigator. I was knocked out and brought here against my will and for God's sake, point that pistol at someone who needs it."

He spoke into the microphone again, his gun not wavering. "The description matches, but Hutchison isn't with her. Ma'am, where is Special Agent Hutchison?"

"Who?"

"Floyd Hutchison. Five-ten. Blond hair. He was sent to secure your safety."

"Floyd…" She dropped her hands. "Oh, my God. Was he working with you, too? I knocked him out. He's locked in the hold with—"

Her words caught in her throat. Past the FBI agent's

head, she saw two figures running along the opposite side of the deck. The one in front was a gray-haired man wearing a cashmere sweater and tan slacks. That had to be Wates. A tall, raven-haired man was pursuing him, his black raincoat flapping behind him with each stride like the wings of a dark angel. "Sloan," she whispered.

The helicopter with the sharpshooters that had been hovering above the open hatch swooped past her head and angled toward the running men. The loudspeaker beneath its fuselage crackled above the din. "Stop where you are!"

Erika sprang forward. "No!"

The FBI agent caught her arm before she could go past him. "Ma'am, the area isn't secured. For your own safety, you have to—"

"Tell them not to shoot!" she yelled. "Don't you see who that is?"

From the front of the ship, a second helicopter veered toward Wates and Sloan. A spate of automatic weapon fire struck a hatch cover, ricocheting from the metal in a trail of sparks.

"No!" Erika snatched the agent's headset from his head and shouted into the microphone. "Hold your fire! That's Detective Morrissey!"

It happened with the slow-motion horror of a nightmare that just wouldn't end. Wates reached the railing at the edge of the deck and turned, his black pistol in his hands, at the same moment Sloan dove for him. The two men grappled for the weapon. Gunfire tracked across the deck at their feet, sending up more sparks and a orange-red haze of rust.

Erika threw away the headset. The racket from the helicopters would have drowned out a cannon.

Wates jerked from the impact as bullets slammed

into his back. He let go of Sloan and crumpled like a deflating balloon.

Sloan staggered backward. His hips hit the railing. The ship rolled into a swell and he went over the side.

"*No!*" Erika screamed. She sprinted across the deck. "*Sloan!*"

But she was too late.

Sloan was gone.

Again.

Chapter 7

Music throbbed from the speakers in the corners of the bar. Hector was playing his Rolling Stones collection tonight. The vintage red patrol-car light in the window was keeping the beat as Mick sang about time being on his side. Erika found the song ironically fitting. "He is coming back to me, Uncle Hector."

"Riki, he's gone. He was never there in the first place."

"Oh, he was there, all right. Sloan promised he would come back, and he will."

Hector Balough smoothed a hand over his fringe of red hair, a gesture of pained patience that Erika recognized all too well. "Honey, it doesn't make sense. The FBI said there was only one man working undercover. That Floyd character. Why would they lie?"

"Besides the fact that I broke their guy's jaw?" she asked. "Technically, Sloan's NYPD, so they weren't really lying when they said he wasn't working for them."

Hector reached beneath the bar and brought out a can of root beer to refill her glass. "Maybe you should talk to someone about this."

She hooked her heels onto the bar stool. "Thanks, but all I've done is talk for the past week and the only person who doesn't think I'm crazy is Rufus."

"We don't think you're crazy, Erika." Ken Latimer patted her shoulder as he took the stool beside her. "You just need a rest."

She sipped her root beer. "I still haven't caught Hartwell's appliance thief."

"Seriously, you should relax. That was a major bust last week. Wates is dead, his weapons-smuggling ring is smashed and all the Stingers are accounted for. Isn't that enough excitement?"

Erika glanced at the mirror that hung behind the bar. Some of Sloan's buddies were gathered near the pool table in the far corner. They were watching her uneasily while trying to pretend they were interested in their game. Evidently, they had sent Ken to test the waters since he had been Sloan's partner. She saluted them with her root-beer glass and turned to Ken. "I'm just getting warmed up. Did you get me the information I asked for about Sloan's father?"

Ken ran his index finger beneath the neck of his NYPD sweatshirt and cleared his throat. "Are you sure you want to do this now?"

"Absolutely. What did you find?"

"Your hunch was right. The slug that killed Patrick Morrissey came from a 9 mm Heckler and Koch."

She put down her glass and smacked her palm on the

bar. "I knew it! Is ballistics running a comparison with Wates's gun?"

"That's the strange part. I found the file, but the box of evidence was signed out of the property room more than a year ago."

"By Sloan, right?"

"Yes. He never told me he was looking into it. How did you guess?"

"It was something Wates said after Sloan read that obituary I used to keep in my bag. He reacted to the Morrissey name and the fact that Sloan's father had been a cop. At the time I had other things to worry about, but it got me thinking. Ken, what do you believe Sloan would have done if he had discovered who had killed his father?"

"Geez, that ate at him since he was a kid. He thought the world of his family. He would have done whatever it took to nail the killer."

"Uh-huh. Including going undercover as a criminal named Max Tanner?"

Ken turned his head and actually met her gaze straight on for a change. "Possibly. He always was impulsive."

"And what if, once Sloan started poking around as Max, he discovered the man who murdered his father twenty years ago was now involved in smuggling arms that could lead to the deaths of thousands of innocent people?"

"Same thing. He would have done whatever it took to stop him." Ken furrowed his forehead. "I checked out Patrick Morrissey's last case. He was investigating a smuggling ring when he was killed."

Erika nodded. "See? It fits, doesn't it?"

"You know, this has possibilities."

"And what if, in the middle of all this, Sloan happened to accidentally fall off his sloop and was picked up by the Coast Guard, who were working with the FBI who were also investigating Wates?"

"That would get complicated."

She smacked the bar again. "That's exactly what Sloan said. The feds would have jumped at the chance to get a man deep undercover, and Sloan had loads of incentive. They probably promised him it would be over in a matter of weeks."

"Honey," Hector said, sliding his hand over hers. "You know the FBI said Max Tanner was the genuine article. He had a record that went back to his teens. You saw his mug shot. He wasn't Sloan."

Oh, the doubts were always there, gnawing at the edges of her mind, but she refused to succumb to them. Yes, she had seen Max Tanner's photograph. He had black hair, and his height and weight were close to Sloan's, but his face had been completely different.

And there had been the matter of Max Tanner's rap sheet. Theft, extortion, aggravated assault and manslaughter. His prowess with a switchblade was well known in his home town of Dallas. "They never found Tanner's body," she said.

"Well, no, but—"

"Sounds familiar, doesn't it?"

"Riki…"

"And we all know records can be faked." She pulled back her hand and rubbed the underside of her ring with her thumb. "The Max Tanner I met on the ship was Sloan. He'll be able to explain the rest when you see him."

The door of the bar swept open, letting in a rush of cold air. Erika's pulse leapt, as it always did whenever a door opened. Or a phone rang. Or someone called her name or she saw a dark-haired man on the subway platform tilt his head a certain way. She twisted to look behind her.

The man who had entered the bar was plump and bearded.

"Dr. Goldstein," Erika murmured. "What's he doing here?" She returned her gaze to her uncle. "Uncle Hector?"

He rubbed his fringe again. "I called him, Riki. I thought you might like to talk."

She glanced at Ken and then at Sloan's friends. Everyone suddenly looked the other way. "What's going on? Is this some kind of intervention?"

"Good evening, Erika." Dr. Goldstein pulled off his gloves, used them to brush off the seat of the barstool to her left and sat. "How are you feeling?"

"I am not crazy," she said through her teeth.

"No one is saying you are, Erika. We're all your friends and we're concerned."

"Well, sure," she said. "You think I was hallucinating again, but those times I ran after Sloan, he really had been there. He told me. He loves me as much as I love him, and that's something that never dies." She pointed to her heart. "The truth is in here, not in my head. It was there all along, but I'd been too afraid to listen to it. Not anymore."

"Erika—"

"Nothing on this earth is going to keep us apart." The room wavered. She choked back her tears. "One way or another, we'll find each other again."

The front door opened. Erika's pulse spiked as it always did. She wiped her eyes with the back of her hand and glanced in the mirror behind the bar.

A tall, raven-haired man stared back at her, his gaze the pure blue of an August sky. Shadows of exhaustion tinged the skin beneath his eyes and a week's growth of beard darkened his cheeks. He moved slowly, his progress hampered by the crutches he balanced on. A cast enclosed his right leg from above the knee to his ankle.

Of course, she thought. The deck of the freighter was as high as a house. He must have broken his leg when he'd hit the water.

Her heartbeat tripped into a sprint. "Sloan," she whispered.

He hobbled forward. The lines beside his mouth deepened with his lopsided grin. "Hello, Riki."

She spun off the stool and leapt across the room.

Sloan's crutches clattered to the floor as he opened his arms. "Sorry I took so long, but those damn feds and their paperwork—"

She caught his face in her hands, stopping his words. She no longer needed explanations. There would be time for those later. Besides, some things you had to take on faith. She lifted herself on her toes and smiled. "Welcome home, Sloan."

He wasn't a ghost or an illusion. He was solid flesh and blood, as real as the love that glowed from his face. His arms locked around her back, his lips sealed to hers, and joy exploded through her soul.

Sloan's name rippled around the room. Chair legs scraped. Glasses shattered as a table toppled over.

On some level, Erika was aware of the commotion. She heard the whoops from Sloan's friends as they crowded around them. She felt Ken slap his partner on the back. She glimpsed her uncle vault over the bar.

Yet right now, she was busy getting reacquainted with the taste of her lover.

And this was one indulgence she would never give up.

Dear Reader,

During the fifteen years I spent as an English teacher, I was often surprised by the stereotypes that some folks would have about me. Spinster schoolmarm. Mean old battle-ax. Having to use perfect grammar around me or else I'd call them on it. (Okay, I still correct my son sometimes—but then teaching is in my blood and he's the most important student in my world.)

Every now and then I run across someone who insists on calling me "Miss" instead of "Mrs." And more than once I've reassured acquaintances that after hours and on summer break, I'm off-duty, and they can relax and speak in whatever sentence fragments and with whatever pronoun references make them comfortable around me. And I always loved the students who were surprised enough to tell me I was nice, occasionally eccentric and usually fun—and that they learned a lot from me, anyway.

I tried to bring some of those same sensibilities to my story in *Cornered*. English teachers can be very nice people—they can be as normal as the next guy—funny, shy, smart, resourceful, sexy, caring. You name it. As with any stereotype, sometimes it just takes a better awareness—a chance to get to know that person before truly realizing what a treasure he or she is. Rafe, my hero, has some definite stereotypes to overcome if he intends to survive this mission. But Hannah is the go-to woman to debunk his misconceptions about spinster schoolmarms—and teach the rugged mountain man a thing or two about love, as well.

And to all you fellow English teachers out there—you rock!

Enjoy,

Julie Miller

A MIDSUMMER NIGHT'S
MURDER
Julie Miller

While the Teton Mountains are a real location for this adventure, many of the place names for encampments and natural features on Mt. Moran are fictitious.

I'd like to thank my parents, my hubby and the University of Missouri for taking me to the Tetons time and again. It truly is God's country.

Thanks to my eighth-grade English students for letting me make grammar a fun class to teach! And for one young man, in particular, you're welcome. I'm glad my methods helped you "actually get it now!"

Chapter 1

"Oh. my God."

Hannah Greene gaped at the scene inside the tent. Her blood seemed to rush to her feet, leaving her light-headed.

"Breathe deeply, girl," she coached herself. "Keep it together. You can handle this."

A good Greene woman would.

She squeezed her eyes shut, wished the ugliness away, then slowly re-opened them. She swallowed back the bile rising in her throat as her resolve failed her. "No, I can't."

Glancing over her shoulder, she groaned at the deserted campsite. It was too early for anyone else to be stirring yet. So much for Randolph College's fractured English department turning over a new leaf, learning to bond and help each other instead of hindering goals and careers. She was on her own.

What should she do? What would her father do? Her mother? Her sister?

Hannah peeked back inside the tent. She swallowed hard. Somebody had to go inside. That somebody was going to be her.

In a minute.

"Frank?"

Maybe he'd answer. Or not.

She crushed the edges of the tent's nylon flap in her shaking fists and stared at the gruesome scene. There was so much blood. Too much for this scene to be natural.

Nature. Hannah shook her head, silently cursed her track record with Mother Nature.

What was a near-sighted English professor doing up here in the boonies of Wyoming's Teton Mountains, treading through patches of high-altitude snow on what should have been her summer vacation? Camping with nine people she barely liked and didn't trust? Pushing her plump body to new extremes of physical exertion and thin-aired endurance? How had she gotten so far away from the security of her books and research?

And how the hell would she ever get back to them without their mountain-climbing and survival guide to lead the way?

Hannah forced herself to take another look at the man on the cot. Frank Brooks, the taciturn mountaineer from Extreme, Inc., Adventures who'd been so patient with her and her inexperienced cohorts as he led them up Mount Moran on this week-long wilderness-bonding retreat, was truly and completely dead.

"Now what are we supposed to do?" she fretted out loud.

Oh, how she longed for the normalcy of a classroom. Or some improperly punctuated sentences to grade.

Or a cop.

"Dude. That guy's dead."

"Rowdy!"

Hannah jumped inside her boots, startled by Rowdy Trent, the young man who'd sneaked up behind her. Where had he come from?

Pressing a hand to her thumping heart, she spared a withering glance for the graduate assistant who preferred surfer lingo to iambic pentameter and who, fortunately, wasn't going to be *her* assistant and create more work for her. But, incompetent as Rowdy could be, Frank's death was shocking, and Rowdy did have feelings.

Inhaling a steadying breath, she reached out and gave Rowdy's arm a reassuring squeeze before entering the tent ahead of him. She could do this. She was a Greene. If she chewed the inside of her lip hard enough, she could stem the panic that threatened to make her run screaming from the tent, and remain calm enough for the both of them. If. "We'd better wake up Dr. Copperfield and let him know what's happened."

Not that the new president of the college—and self-appointed leader of this misguided expedition—would know anything more about handling dead bodies and hiking down mountains than she did. But Dick Copperfield was in charge. And from the time she was a child, Hannah had been trained to defer politely to status and authority.

Or rather, she'd been given little opportunity to do otherwise. After all, she'd inherited the recessive genes of the Greene pool—she was the shyer one, the plainer one, the less ambitious one. Not that her parents didn't love her, but they just didn't expect the same things from their brilliant, book-loving daughter as they did from her older sister.

But her mother and father weren't here. And Piper wouldn't be caught dead on a mountain in her Jimmy Choos.

Dead on a mountain. What a lousy train of thought.

Buzzing her lips with a dismissive sigh, Hannah squatted beside the body on the cot. She needed to fully assess the situation. She needed to help.

She breathed deeply, wishing that a lungful of crisp, mountain-morning air could alter the image of their guide's blank, staring eyes and bloody chest. She didn't know whether to cover him up or try to administer CPR in an impossible attempt to revive him. But one brush of her hand across his cold, stiff knuckles had her reaching for the blanket still tied to his backpack.

"Dude, is that a climbing piton?" Rowdy leaned over her shoulder and fingered the metal stake that skewered the left side of Frank's chest.

"Don't touch that!" Hannah swatted the air in lieu of his hand. "It could be evidence."

"Of what?"

She adjusted her narrow-framed, tortoiseshell glasses on the bridge of her nose and glared her shaggy-haired colleague back a step. "Murder."

Rowdy's blue eyes blanched. "You don't think this is an accident?"

Hannah visually inspected the pistol-like device used to fire stakes into a sheer rock face to anchor rappelling lines and climbing gear. Frank had demonstrated how to use the device yesterday in a training session before taking them up thirty feet of a vertical cliff.

Mentally gauging the distance between the equipment on the opposite side of the tent and Frank's body—and remembering that it had taken the muscles in both hands for her to fire that thing yesterday—Hannah was doubtful it could have gone off accidentally. Besides, Frank would have cried out or cursed, awakening the rest of them in the night. Unless he'd died instantly. In which case, he wouldn't have been able to get back to his cot and lay himself out so neatly in a supine position.

Hannah was no expert in mountain-climbing, but she'd read plenty of Agatha Christie and true-crime books over the years. She taught an elective writing class on how to structure a mystery novel. The clues were evident to her observant eyes. She shook her head. "This was no accident."

"Crap." Rowdy was already shuffling toward the exit. "You mean there's somebody up here on the mountain with us? Killing people?"

"I don't—"

"I'm gettin' the hell out of here."

"Rowdy." They needed a plan. They needed to think rationally. Hannah pushed to her feet and tried to calm him. "We need to keep our wits—"

"One of us could be next."

"I doubt—"

But the tall man with the shaggy, sun-bleached hair had already bolted, leaving Hannah alone with the corpse.

Swallowing her worry, Hannah planted her hands on her hips and glanced back at the blank brown eyes that had smiled so kindly at her last night when Frank had promised to show her how to forage for edible foods among the trees and rocks this morning. With a silent prayer, she closed his eyes and pulled the blanket up to cover his face.

Maybe it was a good thing that Rowdy had run off. It probably wouldn't have reassured him to hear that the killer didn't need to return to camp. Hannah had understood the dire nature of their situation almost immediately.

By stranding them up on the mountain, more than two days away from civilization—without a clue or a compass to guide them—the killer had already sentenced them to death.

"A little help, please?"

"Yeesh."

Hannah stood in the morning sunshine that, even at the end of June, was cool enough to raise chill bumps beneath her long flannel sleeves. Or maybe the chill had more to do with the dead man inside the tent behind her. Fighting off guilt and an unexpected sorrow for the man she'd known for only a few short days, Hannah surveyed the quiet tents nestled among crags of granite outcroppings. Bordered on two sides by a forest of Douglas fir trees, and on a third by a drop-off only mountain goats could climb, the camp was eerily silent. Without the bustle of Frank building a fire and preparing breakfast, the others must have slept in.

Except for Rowdy, of course. His stomach kept a regular schedule that even an alarm clock would envy. He must have slipped back into the tent he shared with retired professor emeritus William Hawthorne.

Why hadn't Rowdy awakened Dr. Copperfield? Or anyone else?

This place was called Targhee Meadow, according to Frank. Though to Hannah's way of thinking, it barely qualified as a clearing. True, there were shoots of grasses and wildflowers springing up anywhere enough dirt could cling to the rock. But there was no real path among the patches of lingering snow and clumps of vegetation. No landing pad for a helicopter to rescue them. No phone booth where she could even call for help.

Her *phone*. Duh.

Shaking her head at her own incompetence, Hannah hurriedly scaled the slope up to her tent. Maybe if she'd been more assertive about finding out why Frank had stood her up this morning, and gone to his tent sooner to investigate why he was a no-show, she could have saved him. Instead, she'd watched an amazing sunrise, and told herself she didn't care that Frank had forgotten her. He wasn't the first man to overlook her or conveniently forget a promise to her; he wouldn't be the last.

"Damn pity pot." She concentrated on the cold stone beneath her palms as she slipped on a patch of snow and caught herself. At thirty years of age, she'd long ago learned that being shy or plain or wrapped up in her books was no excuse for not taking action when action was needed. Those traits made it hard for her to come out of her shell at times, to assert herself. But they were no excuse.

She wasn't the medical doctor in the family, but she could have done something to help Frank. The Greene name demanded that she try.

Correction. The Greene name demanded that she succeed, thrive, shine. There was no *try* in her family's book. Somehow, she should have saved Frank Brooks's life.

"Irene?" Hannah announced herself to her tent-mate before unzipping the flap.

A monotone of ohs and ums greeted Hannah as she ducked inside and nearly tripped over her roommate. The forty-something woman, with a pink floral scarf tied turban-style around her head, sat in the middle of the floor, her body twisted into a yoga position that made Hannah's back hurt just to look at her.

Irene Sharp was the team-building consultant who'd been hired to help Randolph's once-reknowned English faculty and staff bond with each other and formulate a plan of action. With her daily quotes, trust games and meditation exercises, she was supposed to motivate them to return to Kansas ready to raise funds, win awards and attract the best students.

"Good morn-ing, Han-nah," Irene chanted in the same tuneless drawl.

Though Hannah liked the woman well enough, there was something practical lacking from the consultant's training techniques. She definitely didn't count Irene as much of an ally when it came to helping out in the crisis-management department. But she offered a polite "Good morning" before climbing over her cot to grab her backpack and dig through the contents.

"Prob-lem?"

Hannah's fingers wrapped around the reassuring plastic and metal of her tiny cell phone. She pulled it out, clutched it to her heart and sighed with relief. "Yeah." She scooted around Irene again. "I just found Frank Brooks dead in his tent. I'm calling for help."

Outside in the cool morning light, Hannah opened her phone and turned on the power. "Damn."

Out of range.

That unsettling chill of isolation was back.

"Does anyone have a cell phone that works?" she called out across the camp. As usual, her voice wasn't loud or authoritative enough to snag anyone's attention.

A rustle of nylon alerted her to Irene coming out beside her. "Did you say dead?"

Hannah tucked her phone into the back pocket of her jeans. "Yes."

"What happened?"

Hannah couldn't think of a single way to make the truth sound any less dire. "Someone killed him."

"What?" A lost look crept into her roommate's eyes, as if she had no idea how to deal with an event her tea leaves hadn't foretold. "How will we get home? I told Dick I could work miracles just as well on a secluded beach, but he insisted on the mountains. I knew we shouldn't have come up here. I get a bad vibe at high altitudes." She rubbed at the frown lines between her eyes. "I can't think straight. I warned Dick. I warned him."

Dick was Dr. Copperfield, Hannah's boss and the man who'd hired Irene. Taking the group out of their element so that they'd learn to rely on each other had been Irene's idea. Doing it at twelve thousand feet had been Dr. Copperfield's.

"How will we get home?" Irene repeated in a distant murmur.

"Don't worry." Hannah squeezed the older woman's arm, offering a confidence she didn't quite feel. "Everything will be okay."

Irene retreated into the tent with a jerky nod and a vow to find her crystals and meditate on Frank's passing. While the other woman grieved and worked through her shock and fear, Hannah descended the short slope to the nearest tent.

The Defoes—the alumni couple funding this re-treat—weren't even awake yet, judging by the snoring rattling through the thin nylon walls. Over in the next ravine, she could hear Professors Butler and Robinson arguing over the best way to arrange the rocks and grate around the fire pit. Why hadn't they responded to her shout for assistance? Or had they truly not heard her?

Shaking off the twinge of resentment at going unno-ticed yet again, Hannah scrambled down the gravelly in-cline that led to President Copperfield's tent. She knocked on the metal pole that held up the tent's front canopy. "Dr. Copperfield?"

She heard scrambling sounds, a thump and a curse from inside. Great. She'd wakened him. He'd already labeled her an annoying know-it-all. At their introduc-tory meeting, he'd informed her that if it weren't for the Greene name, he'd have let her go from the college. He needed professors with more flash and credits on their résumés, not just ones who could teach and do research.

Under the circumstances, though, he could damn well be annoyed with her. The stubborn Greene genes she'd also inherited were acting up. She knocked again. "It's Hannah, sir. We have a problem."

An instant later, the president popped his head through the opening flap, clutching it close beneath his chin so that all Hannah could see was his overly tanned, handsome face and receding brown hairline. "What is it, Greene?"

"Sorry to catch you so early, sir. But I think you should be made aware of the situation." She thumbed over her shoulder. "I found Frank dead in his tent this morning."

"Dead? Are you sure?"

"I'm sure. I think the stake through his heart was a pretty good clue."

"A stake?" Copperfield frowned as if she'd spoken a foreign language. "You mean he was murdered."

"Yes, sir."

The whole tent shook as if he was moving inside. Pulling on his pants, perhaps? "When did you find him?"

"Just a few minutes ago. But I think he's been gone for several hours." She patted the phone at her hip. "I tried to call for help, but we're out of cell-phone range up here."

"Probably the altitude or distance from the nearest tower. Or both."

Duh. Being dumb had never been her problem. "I'm sure you're right."

"We need to do something."

She *was* doing something. "That's why I woke you."

"You didn't wake me."

Hannah heard a giggle from inside the tent. Dr. Copperfield suddenly disappeared and lectured someone in hushed tones. Sometimes, she needed to be hit in the head with a rock to understand the whole male-female relationship thing. Of course. She hadn't awakened him. She'd interrupted him.

Interrupted *them.*

Natalie Flanders, President Copperfield's executive assistant wasn't anywhere to be seen this morning. But Hannah could hear her. And, judging by the shushing sounds and months' worth of rumors, Hannah could bet the statuesque blonde wasn't in the tent taking dictation.

Dick Copperfield poked his head through the tent

opening again. "Give me five minutes to get dressed. I'll be right there."

Though she hadn't actually seen any impropriety, Hannah politely turned her head away from the happy campers. "Yes, sir. I'll meet you at Frank's tent."

Scuffing aside a rock with the toe of her hiking boot, Hannah headed back up the slope. She heard footsteps shuffling behind her before she felt the anxious touch on her arm. "Is Frank really gone?"

Hannah turned to face William Hawthorne with a wry smile. "I'm afraid so."

The white-haired gentleman, whose stooped figure put him at eye level with Hannah's five-foot, five-inch frame, reached for her hand and patted it between his arthritic fingers. "Rowdy told me about all the blood. I was out for my morning constitutional when he stopped me. He's quite beside himself. Threw up outside our tent. I'm so sorry you had to find the body. Is there anything I can do to help?"

"Got a map on you?" Sarcasm leaked out on a humorless laugh.

His rheumy blue eyes blinked. But he saw the problem, too. "We're somewhere on Mount Moran in the Tetons of Wyoming."

Somewhere. "Exactly."

She hadn't paid close attention to the names of the canyons and passes and rock formations Frank had pointed out. Like the others, Hannah had been too engrossed in the scenery, too afraid of falling behind, too reliant on their guide's expertise. "I'm going to look through Frank's gear to see if I can find a radio and some way to contact Extreme, Inc., headquarters."

He nodded at the name of the extreme vacation adventure company that had organized this excursion for them.

"Good idea." Professor Hawthorne released her and pointed a gnarled finger in the air. "I'll see if I can get the fire going, maybe make a signal out of it. I'll check the food supplies, too. There are too many trees and the terrain's too rugged to land a helicopter at this altitude."

Hannah agreed. "Whatever happens, we'll have to hike out."

"It took us two and a half days to get here," he reasoned. "It'll be at least that long before we're rescued."

Two and a half days. On their own. With a dead body in one tent and a killer on the loose.

A flare of panic hastened her steps. "I'd better find that radio."

Piercing eyes watched them running from tent to tent. Cursing. Crying. One of them actually threw up.

Idiots.

"Like chickens with their heads cut off."

Only one of them seemed to fully grasp the danger they were in. She thought she was so smart. But she wouldn't be a problem for long. None of them would be a problem anymore.

This plan was so ingenious, and his ally so easily duped that it was almost too easy. If this group could destroy the reputation of a proud private college that had been around for generations, then they could easily destroy themselves.

And there wasn't a one of them there who didn't deserve punishment of some kind. Fear was good. Terror, even better. And for one, in particular? Death was the only acceptable retribution.

Revenge was a grand thing. So entertaining. So satisfying.

Time to sit back and let the drama unfold.

Chapter 2

"Hello? SOS? 911?" Hannah pressed the button on the side of the hand-held radio she'd uncovered in Frank's backpack, searching for something besides static to answer her. "Can anyone hear me? Hello?"

Dick Copperfield had been appropriately shocked and concerned when he'd checked the dead body. He'd gathered everyone around the empty fire pit, informing them of the situation. Lydia Defoe had fainted into her husband's arms, scattering them all back to their tents in a desperate search for smelling salts and cool water. Five minutes later, they'd returned empty-handed, but Lydia was awake. While her husband, Charles, cooled her with a battery-powered rotary fan, Professors Butler and Robinson resumed their never-ending debate, this time arguing over the proper way to dispose of a body when there was no mortuary at hand. Rowdy asked if anyone had brought a weapon to defend themselves against the killer and Dr. Hawthorne limped away to gather wood.

Before Copperfield could regain control of the chaos, Hannah excused herself. Her ideas never seemed to get heard when everyone talked at once, anyway.

She was tired of being the quiet one, surrounded by all the strong personalities she'd grown up with, and now worked with. Something inside her, a voice held in check for far too long, demanded to be heard. She sensed that she needed to stand up and really fight for herself this time—or else this crude excuse for a vacation might be her first, last and only adventure.

Hannah fiddled with the dials some more. "Mayday. Mayday. Calling Moose, Wyoming. Can anyone hear me? Mayday."

Static cleared the line, leaving a moment of deafening silence. Hannah held her breath. "Mayday?"

"Enough, lady. You're coming through loud and clear." Hannah gasped, her whole body smiling with relief as a deep, growly voice boomed from the radio. The low-pitched timbre of the terse words resonated along each nerve ending like a rough caress.

"Who is this?" She rose to her feet and paced the small confines of the tent.

"Rafe Kincaid at Extreme, Inc., headquarters in Moose. Who the hell is this?"

"I'm Hannah Greene. From Kansas." She didn't know whether to be reassured or intimidated by the strength of that voice.

"Well, look, Hannah Greene from Kansas—" He paused, as if catching himself from saying something he'd regret. "You do realize you're on an airway that's reserved for emergencies only."

"That's what this is. An emergency."

"What kind of emergency?" His clipped tone softened.

She held the radio in both hands, talking to it as if it was the man's face. "I'm with the Randolph College wilderness camping adventure."

"Frank Brooks's expedition?"

"Yes. You know who we are?"

She heard a crunch of noise in the background, the sounds of movement and typing. "I've got your group up on the screen now," he reported. He continued reading from his computer. "Ten novice climbers from Kansas taking the historic CMC route up the mountains. Why isn't Frank calling in?"

His sharp demand startled her for an instant. But she'd answered to that same tone and more from her father, so she quickly responded with the plain facts. "He's dead."

If there'd been any hint of static, she might have thought she'd lost the connection.

"Frank?"

"Yes. If he was a friend of yours, I'm sorry." Hannah knelt beside the cot, lifting the blanket and gently searching through Frank's pockets for a billfold or something that would indicate whether or not he had any family. She hadn't even thought to check that; she'd been too consumed with her own fears. "We don't know our way off the mountain. And it doesn't look as if you could land a chopper up here."

"You can't."

She endured another painful pause. "Like I said, I'm sorry to be the one to give you the bad news."

She'd avoided the front of Frank's bloody shirt and the gruesome piton, but finally Hannah noticed the stiff rectangular shape inside his right chest pocket. Had that folded piece of paper been there before? She'd probably been too shocked to notice it. Intellectual curiosity and a real desire to help the situation had her sliding the paper free and reading the message inside.

By the pricking of my thumbs,
Something wicked this way comes.

Hannah frowned. Frank Brooks hadn't struck her as the literary type. "That's *Macbeth*."

"What?" Rafe Kincaid's response turned her attention back to the radio.

"The Scottish play."

"I have no idea what you're talking about."

"The three Weird Sisters—witches—in the play, they foretell of death." Confusion became a deep, sinking feeling of foreboding. "And more deaths to come."

"I'll tell you who the weird sister is, lady—"

"Listen." Hannah shot to her feet, crammed the note into her pocket and turned her back to the dead man. "I'm scared up here, Mr. Kincaid." Her tone wasn't quite a reprimand, wasn't quite a desperate plea. But it was edged with the foreboding that colored her thoughts. "I don't believe Frank's death was an accident."

"What happened?" The sarcasm that had tinted his voice a moment ago was replaced by something harder, more intense. It was definitely a voice accustomed to taking charge.

"I found him on his cot. One of his climbing pitons,

you know, the stakes that he drove into the rocks to help us climb—"

"I know what a piton is."

"It's stuck in the middle of his chest."

An unimaginative string of curses filled the airwaves. But Hannah thought she detected sorrow as much as anger in those words.

"Mr. Kincaid?" she whispered softly, tuning into his pain and apologizing for the shock her news must have given him. "Are you all right?"

She held her breath in the silence that followed.

He released a deep-pitched sigh that danced against her eardrums and suffused her with a prickly sense of awareness that had nothing to do with fear or compassion.

"Don't worry about me, Kansas." His words denied what his silence had told her. "I need you to do exactly what I say." She heard nothing pained or angry now. Only a confidence that inspired her first bit of hope. "Is anyone up there injured?"

"No. We're all fine. Just lost."

"Stay close to the campsite. Get a fire going if you can. Don't eat anything but the rations you brought with you. I'll be up there by nightfall."

Nightfall? "But it took us over two days to get here. Do you even know where we are?"

"Trust me." He was moving again. "I'll find you."

Rafael Kincaid ran his canoe aground on the western shore of Leigh Lake, stowed his paddle and climbed out onto the grassy bank. With his eyes tilted toward the flat-topped peak of Mount Moran rising above him, he breathed in deeply, assessing the temperature of the air and the scents on the wind.

The sun was high in the sky, the breeze light, the ground marshy beneath his boots as the spring thaw gave way to summer heat. He tossed his pack onto a patch of gravelly mud and hoisted the canoe onto his shoulders, carrying it to the framed-up rack of logs where six other canoes had been dry-docked. He slid the canoe onto the top rack and paused a moment to inspect the knots before readjusting the protective tarp to cover his boat as well.

"Frank's been here, all right," he muttered out loud, recognizing the distinct handiwork of a left-handed man with army Special Forces training.

Skewered by a piton. Not an easy thing to accomplish against a man with Frank's unique background. In order to get close enough to drive a stake into his heart, Frank would have to have been unconscious, overpowered— or duped by someone he trusted.

None of those possibilities endeared the staff of Randolph College and their spiritual guide to him. He mentally flipped through the list of names and backgrounds he'd quickly researched before departing. Everything from a retired widower to a Forbes 500 millionaire had popped up in his search. A college president with the slick charm and influential connections of a politician. A former showgirl who'd worked her way through an accounting degree. Two professors—one with a series of sexual harassment complaints filed against him, the other with ties to a graduate student who'd been missing for almost three years.

And the young woman who belonged to that sweet voice on the radio. *Are you all right?* The dulcet tones of her concern for him had him thinking of starlit nights and intimate conversations between a man and a woman.

"Sounds more like a twisted version of *Gilligan's Island.*" He chided himself before his neglected hormones and angry heart could take that image any further.

He had a job to do—for his friend, for his company. He'd damn well better get to it.

Rafe pulled the tarp tight and retied the knots, thinking of the last time he'd seen Frank Brooks. They'd tossed back a couple of beers at a bar down in Jackson, Wyoming, celebrating the success of their last mission together. That had been what, two weeks ago? Rafe had been called out of the state after that, to assist with a search and rescue in Utah. By the time he'd gotten back home, Frank had departed with Hannah Greene and her cohorts from Kansas on one of the challenging climbing and camping excursions that Extreme, Inc., was known for.

And now Frank was gone?

Gripping the top log in his long, nicked-up fingers, Rafe inhaled a deep breath, urging the resentment from his bones and clearing his head. There'd been too many people in his life he'd never gotten to say goodbye to before losing them. Starting with his own mother all those years ago.

Rafe adjusted the long hunting knife he wore on the side of his belt beneath his cotton sweater, and scooped up his gear. Equal weights of regret and determination settled on his shoulders as easily as the backpack.

He would have liked to have said goodbye to Frank—if Hannah Greene's claim was true and his friend was truly dead. He would have liked to have gotten closure on at least one relationship in his life before fate or his job or his own charming personality forced him to watch the people he was close to leave.

And if Hannah Greene was lying—if the woman who belonged to the soft, husky voice was manipulating him in any way…

Rafe tipped his nose into the air as the wind shifted, a symbolic portent of his own dark mood should this hike turn out to be some kind of a game or trap. The suspicions brewing inside him receded a notch. The mountain was trying to tell him something.

Hurry.

Unlike a woman, the mountain didn't lie. Rafe heeded that warning.

He slipped on the dark sunglasses that hung from a lanyard around his neck, and in long, sure strides, headed toward the rocky path at the base of the tree line.

Thank God the sun was still shining.

The gathering clouds and shifting winds warned Rafe that his good fortune wouldn't last long past sunset. Still, he gritted his teeth, counted his blessings—however temporary they might be—and forged ahead.

Dropping his pack by a tow line so that it hung low beneath his hips, Rafe turned and squeezed his shoulders through the narrow crevasse, keeping his eyes focused on the shards of sunlight filtering in above him. He secured his boot on a blind toehold and pushed himself upward. The passageway was little more than a yard in height, but the granite closed in around him like the hug of an angry grizzly bear. Trapping him. Pinning him down.

The shadowed walls were cold to the touch, and the dampness that clung to the rock face soaked through the cotton of his T-shirt and chilled his skin. He closed his eyes and flashed back to a memory of cold, utter blackness. His nose crinkled, remembering the suffocating stench of stale air and dirt and decay. His heart pounded with the recollection of all he had lost that day.

Swearing as the stupid childhood fear tried to sink its claws into him and snatch him from the reality at hand, Rafe thrust his arm through the opening. He scraped a strip of skin off his elbow before finding a knob of rock for his fingers to latch onto.

The sting of pain was brief, but it was enough to clear his head. He clung to the warmth of the sunbathed rock above him until he could bury the dark memories. His size and strength became his ally once more as he pulled himself up and out of the crevasse. He braced his feet on the crowning ledge and leaned back against the pillow of the sweater he'd removed and tied around his waist. Drawing his pack up through the crevasse and setting it at his feet, he unhooked the tube from his water pack and swallowed a few sips to rehydrate himself while the sun re-warmed his body.

Ignoring the tight passageway below his feet, Rafe scanned the horizon and breathed deeply. Though travels with his archaeologist father had taken him all over the world, he'd always come back to the mountains of Wyoming. Something about the vast expanses, the unspoiled air, the lack of man-made walls and the confinements of civilization had always appealed to him. Maybe, as his younger brother liked to tease, the size and space of the Tetons was the only place in the world big enough to accommodate all six-foot-four, two-hundred-and-fifty pounds of him.

Or maybe, as his mother might have told him in a bedtime story decades ago, there was simply a wildness to the land that spoke to the untamed spirit inside him.

He liked that explanation best because that meant he still shared a bit of a link to the mother he'd lost down in that black hole twenty-five years ago.

Rafaela Sanchez Kincaid, a native Indian of Central America, had possessed some sort of mystical powers, according to Rafe's father. She'd been more in tune with the earth and its treasures and the history of its peoples than any map or textbook or university could put together. Rafaela and Lucas, Sr., had been a happy couple. Adding two boys, they'd become a happy family. They'd shared adventures and love, created good memories and weathered bad times together. They'd lived a charmed, if not quite typical, life, until that fateful summer day in the middle of the jungle when Rafe had learned what hell truly was.

As a boy, he'd loved exploring the tombs and secret passageways of the archaeological expeditions on which his parents had taken him and Luke. But an earthquake and cave-in at the Mayan ruins on Isla Tenebrosa had forever changed that love into fear and bitter memories. As the ancient stones and weakened support beams collapsed on top of him, his mother had pushed him into a sarcophagus and sealed the lid. He lay trapped inside that black stone box for hours, running out of air and hope. He'd nearly suffocated that day. But when his father's workmen finally unearthed him, Rafe knew he'd been saved.

And he knew his mother hadn't been so lucky.

"Hello? Mr. Kincaid? Are you there? Hello?"

The muffled female voice was sharp enough to cut through his thoughts, stalling out the darkness growing inside him.

Miss Kansas was on the line again. Rafe grinned at the

bossy insistence in her tone. Hoisting his pack onto his hip, he carefully replaced his water and dug out his radio.

"Please, Mr. Kincaid. If you can hear me, you must answer."

Hannah Greene's succinct articulation reminded him of his sixth-grade English teacher, Miss Chapman. An ageless wonder of the world, Miss Chapman had been a petite stick of a woman who hadn't backed down from lecturing him and sending him to the office for drawing pictures on his tests instead of answering the questions, even though, at age twelve, he'd already towered over her by a good foot and a half. He'd had a lot of respect for Miss Chapman, but she'd forever forged his image of a spinster schoolmarm.

Rafe hooked his pack over his shoulder, lifted the radio to his mouth and hit the call button. "If you're going to use the radio, Kansas, why don't you learn to use it right? Over."

"Thank God, you're there. It's such a relief to hear your voice." The weight of her sigh hovered across the airwaves and settled like a shared smile into his bones. Rafe tried to recall the last time anyone had sounded so happy to hear from him. It was even harder to remember the last time a woman had spoken to him in such sweet, welcoming tones. But sweet and welcoming was followed just as quickly by a huffy sound of protest. "Excuse me, Mr. Kincaid, but I got hold of you, didn't I? More than once. I have to be doing something right."

He shook his head at the foolish notion that some kind of connection had just occurred between them. She was nothing more than a voice on the radio, he warned himself—a sharp voice that baited him to respond in equally concise tones. "There's a procedure to follow when you're making a call. Identify yourself and who you're trying to reach. Hannah Greene from Kansas calling base camp, for example. When you're done speaking, you signal the other end by saying 'over.' Over."

"Oh, no," she gasped, almost as an aside. "Please don't tell me you're still at the headquarters building."

Rafe straightened his stance, and the sprawling vista of the Teton Mountains shrank to the sound of her voice. The timbre of it had changed again. It had grown more feminine, softer—hinting at desperation, but with a backbone that kept her fear under control. For the moment, at any rate.

Rafe heard his own voice soften in a rumbly, low-pitched effort to reassure her. "Easy, Kansas. I'm over halfway to your position already. Assuming Frank followed the climbing plan he filed, that is."

"I wish I knew," she answered, without waiting for his *over* signal. "I hate feeling so lost."

The circuitous route Frank would have taken to Targhee Meadow would have provided the opportunity to teach and practice various outdoorsman and climbing skills. Rafe's unmarked path was neither for novices to mountaineering, nor for strangers to the mountain.

"I've got a pretty good map inside my head," he assured her. He clipped the radio to his lanyard and wedged it between his ear and shoulder, freeing up both hands so he could re-position his gear and resume the climb. "I'll be there for dinner. Over."

"If there's anything to eat. I thought we had provisions for another couple of days, but we went to fix lunch and all we've got is a nearly empty bag of marshmallows." She hesitated. "Um. Over?"

Barely noticing her concession to his rules, Rafe

cinched the last strap and paused. The tension in him had knotted just as tightly. Hannah Greene and her friends might be in bigger trouble than he'd first suspected. He stared hard into the rock wall in front of him, as if its craggy surface might reveal her expression and let him know whether or not she was serious. "Your food's gone?"

Frank wouldn't make such a mistake in prepping for an expedition, especially with a group of first-timers. In fact, he'd pack extra rations instead of risking that they'd run short. First Frank's death—his murder, according to Hannah—and now a missing stockpile of food? What the hell was going on?

"You forgot to say 'over,'" she stated, with a prickly matter-of-factness that amused as much as annoyed him. "Maybe an animal got into our supplies. Over?"

Rafe plugged in his hands-free radio transmitter, tucked the receiver into his ear and adjusted the tiny microphone beside his jaw. "You'd know if an animal got into your food. There'd be chewed up plastic, scattered evidence. Pawprints and scratch marks." Eyeing the steep granite slope above him, Rafe sought out a secure handhold and resumed his ascent. "You're sure one of your cohorts didn't panic and decide to horde the food for himself? Over."

"Shoot." Hannah's ladylike curse made him think she hadn't considered the possibility that someone in her group might be trying to sabotage the excursion, whether intentionally or just to save his own hide. But the suggestion didn't seem to surprise her. "I'll see what I can find out. A couple of our members are trying to build a trap so they can catch something to grill. Thank God they don't have a gun, or they'd be arguing about hunting. Ov—"

"They can't do that. You're in a National Park."

"I told them that. Maybe if they heard it from an authority figure…" Rafe froze, his long limbs spread-eagled against the rock face. What the hell kind of mess was he climbing into? Apparently, Hannah Greene from Kansas was waiting for some kind of response, some kind of guidance beyond his mountain-climbing expertise. "Rafe?" Not the formal clip of "Mr. Kincaid," but a breathy plea. "Over?"

Her voice had faded to that husky whisper again. Its soft, rhythmic cadence took him back to starry nights and cool breezes, with nothing but hot words against his ear and hotter skin against his own to keep him warm.

Man, he had to let that idea go!

Shaking aside the pleasurable image forming in his mind, Rafe concentrated on the facts at hand. His friend was dead. His company was responsible for a group of inexperienced climbers stranded high on Mount Moran—apparently without any food.

Women were not his best thing—judging by his track record of failed relationships spread few and far between the work and adventure that consumed him—but he was better at his job than just about anybody on the planet. He might fantasize about a woman who could keep up with him and accept the risks he took. But at the end of the day, Rafe knew that his satisfaction would come from pushing his body to its limits, conquering a mountain or a mission—not snuggling up against a woman who…

"Rafe? Are you still there? Over."

…sounded like sex and vulnerability and a hint of attitude, all rolled into one mysterious package.

So much for clearing his thoughts and focusing on facts.

"I'm here." He let a grunt of exertion explain his silence as he purposely reached for a handhold a few inches beyond his fingertips. Savoring the pull of muscles through his arms and torso, he stretched to anchor his grip and pull himself up. He spied an outcropping of granite about ten feet above his head. Once he hoisted himself up and over that, he'd be on an easier, vegetated slope, and would simply have to keep his bearing amongst the trees to complete his journey.

"Who's in charge of that chicken outfit up there?" His frustration came out gruffer than he intended, but that little dose of guilt went a long way toward getting his priorities straight again. "Over."

"That would be Dr. Copperfield. President Copperfield. He's president of the college, not—"

"I could figure that out." A frustrated sense of urgency overrode communication etiquette. "Put Copperfield on."

"He's not here right now."

Did these eggheads have a death wish?

"I told you to keep everyone close to camp. Where is he?"

"His assistant was a little spooked about having a dead body around, so he took her for a walk."

"Get them back to camp." Before they fell off the side of the mountain or got attacked by a bear or puma. The predators wouldn't be out hunting in the heat of mid-afternoon, but they wouldn't hesitate to defend their territory from neophyte hikers who wandered too far off the path. Rafe paused as he reached the outcropping. Then he leaned back, defied gravity and scrambled over the top. He rolled over onto his backside to catch his breath and speak some sense. "Do whatever you have to do to get control of the situation. If no one else is stepping up, then you have to take charge."

"Me? How?"

Hell. Though she'd given him snippets of a seductive voice, he'd just assumed there was more bossy schoolmarm than damsel in distress to her. "What's your job back in the real world?"

"I'm an English professor, with a specialty in grammar and the history of the English language."

"A grammar teacher?" Rafe groaned at how perfectly Hannah Greene from Kansas was falling into his stereotyped image of her. He'd lay odds she was plain as a post, pinched her hair back into a bun and didn't know how to smile. Of course, that image was more in keeping with his memories of Miss Chapman than with the pictures this woman's sexy voice had conjured in his mind.

"I also have an extensive background in literature, but that's not what they pay me to teach. Is any of that helpful?"

Priceless. Yeah, the ability to diagram a sentence or quote Shakespeare would come in real handy when it came to trekking down the mountain. Rafe wanted to laugh. But with the campers' situation growing more dire by the moment, instead of indulging any sense of humor, he stood and altered his gear for hiking.

"Yeah, Kansas. That helps. Pretend they're your students." *Or me,* he added silently, wondering if she realized how little trouble she'd had snagging *his* attention. "They'll listen."

Chapter 3

With the sun balling into an orange glow behind the snow-capped peak of Mount Moran, Rafe emerged from the forest that formed the jagged southern border of Targhee Meadow. Peering through the cloud of his warm breath in the cooler air, he paused to wipe the sweat from his forehead and take stock of the chaos. "Hell."

Tackling the mountain in one day was a piece of cake compared to corralling these tourists bent on self-destruction.

Rafe stalked into the campsite—silently cursing the pile of trash that broke park rules and invited wildlife to pay a visit. He overlooked a collapsed tent, strode past the woman curled up like a pretzel and chanting about *Calm* in a patch of itch-weed that would come back to haunt her by morning, and approached the circle of campers gathering around an argument that was quickly becoming a brawl.

"I saw you come out of that tent!" A blond man, decked out in L.L. Bean from head to toe, ignored the woman with her hand braced against his chest and shoved her forward in his effort to get at the man he accused.

"Ed," she protested. "Stop this."

Ed Butler. The first name from the list kicked in.

A black man, sporting shoulder-length twists of hair, shouted over the top of the woman's bronzed curls. "I was paying my respects. What, are you spying on me now? Haven't you done enough to screw up my life?"

"Keith—" She tried her luck with him. Keith Robinson. Rafe memorized the face to go with the dossier.

"You're the one who mucked up that grant, not me."

"You son of a—"

Ed shoved.

Keith shoved back.

Someone in their audience shouted, "Gentlemen!" No one listened.

"If I die up here in this godforsaken—"

"I'm happy to oblige—"

The woman jostled between the men's chests, her shapeless figure the only thing keeping their fists from landing their targets. A khaki-clad shoulder knocked her narrow-framed glasses off her nose as she twisted around to beg for help. "Dr. Copperfield, do something!"

Rafe dropped his pack beside the cold firepit and plunged into the circle of shocked faces. He knocked Ed Butler aside, wrapped his arm around the woman's waist and lifted her out of the fray. Her startled gasp was drowned out as the feud between the two men heated up with a string of obscenities and a throat-grabbing lunge.

A shaggy-haired hulk backed off a step as Rafe carried the woman out of harm's way. "Whoa!"

He tuned out the blond kid's awestruck response and ignored the curious stares and sputtering protests of the gallery of onlookers who'd been too frightened or indifferent to intervene.

"You can put me down now," the woman ordered, squirming against his chest.

Hints of a familiar voice drew his entire attention to her for an awkward moment. With his hand palming the swell of her hip and his forearm wedged beneath the generous weight of her breasts, Rafe realized *shapeless* hadn't been an accurate first impression of her. She had more curves to her than most, in fact, camouflaged beneath her baggy clothes. But before he allowed his body to respond to the impression of such lush femininity, he set her safely down behind him.

Returning to the business at hand, Rafe pried the black man's fingers from his opponent's collar and twisted his arm up behind his back. "Ow! Who the hell are you?"

Butler wavered, debating whether to help his *buddy* escape or take advantage of him being restrained.

Rafe made the decision for him. Holding on to one man, he glared the other into submission.

Ed, the tussler dressed like an outdoorsman catalog ad, wisely retreated. Keith Robinson went still, finally understanding he had no advantage over Rafe's brawnier build and expertise in dealing with human nature as well as Mother Nature.

"Let me go, dammit," Keith pleaded, breathing hard and wincing at the inflexible grip on his wrist. "This isn't any of your business."

"The hell it isn't." Ed snapped to when Rafe addressed him, "Get the lady's glasses."

While Ed scrambled to do his bidding, Rafe kept his eyes on the campers closing in around them, making sure no one else tried to jump in and reignite the battle.

"Why the hell didn't any of you break up this fight?" he demanded.

"I was going to," a mid-life crisis of a man insisted. Rafe quickly identified him as Dick Copperfield. The devilish points of his receding hairline deepened as he arched a condescending eyebrow. "You just beat me to it."

In a pig's eye. Copperfield couldn't let go of that blond showgirl turned office manager, Natalie Flanders, long enough to take any useful action. But maybe it wasn't fading testosterone so much as wanting a shield to protect himself that made the college president hold on to his assistant so tightly.

"We function as one unit, one team, up here on the mountain," Rafe explained in succinct terms even the two hotheads could understand. "Or else we die on this mountain. Do I make myself clear?"

While his words were absorbed by silence and the cooling summer air, Rafe made a few quick impressions of the people he'd come to rescue and wondered which—if any—of them had the brass and motive to murder Frank.

They matched his research to a T. Irene Sharp, New-Age airhead and suspected con artist. Rowdy Trent, overgrown surfer boy stuck in the flatlands of Kansas. His petty juvenile crimes and poor grades had raised questions about how he'd ever landed a teaching assignment. William Hawthorne, apparently more frail than his age might indicate. Charles and Lydia Defoe, real estate magnates who looked as out of place in a rustic campsite as he'd look at a black-tie party. And, of course, Butler and Robinson, who'd carried an old grudge up the mountain with them.

The fact he didn't see one spinsterly, pinched-face, Miss Chapman type in the bunch brought Rafe's gaze back to the woman he'd pulled from the fight. *She* belonged to that sex-under-the-stars voice that had served as both inspiration and distraction on his grueling climb.

He watched as she accepted her glasses and wiped them clean on the hem of her flannel shirt. The only lines on her fresh, flushed expression were the dimples beside her mouth, putting her closer to thirty than to retirement. She'd never tame that riot of sun-kissed amber curls back into a bun. And he didn't want to read too much into how perfectly her pretty gray eyes matched the snow-capped granite of the peak above them.

"You made your point crystal clear," she replied when no one else would. "I'm afraid we've been working on the *team* idea now for several days without much success." Her gray eyes fluttered self-consciously when she slipped on her glasses and finally saw how intently he'd been studying her. But, dismissing his interest, she tilted her chin. "Mr. Kincaid, I presume?"

He nodded. "Kansas?"

"Hannah Greene," she confirmed and corrected in one sentence. Rafe grinned. Miss Chapman's spirit was alive and well, despite the new and decidedly improved packaging. "I appreciate your help, but I think you can let Dr. Robinson go now."

Rafe cautioned Keith Robinson to mind his temper before freeing him. The black man rubbed his arm from shoulder to wrist and sulked his way back into the circle.

"So you're the roustabout superhero who's come to rescue us?" The man who'd ignored Hannah's plea for help extended his hand and flashed a smile. "I'm Dick Copperfield, president of Randolph College. This expedition was my idea." Like that was some claim to fame? "As you can see, we still have a few issues to work through. I must admit, I hadn't planned on staying alive being one of them, however."

"Rafe Kincaid." Rafe shook his hand just to get the niceties over with and move on. "Let me assure you that even though you signed liability clauses, Extreme, Inc., will see your party safely down the mountain." He propped his hands on his hips and scanned from side to side, including everyone in his instructions. "But in order to do that, I need you to do exactly as I tell you, the moment I tell you to do it."

Copperfield smirked. "Frank Brooks used a much more patient, scholarly approach as our guide. He made this a fun, educational experience for us."

Rafe's gaze swung back and nailed the president. "And look where that got him."

Copperfield's beady black eyes narrowed, giving Rafe a glimpse beneath the good ol' boy facade. The guy wasn't all charm and PR. "Are you insinuating something, Mr. Kincaid?"

My friend's dead, and the ten of you are the only people I've seen on this mountain all day. Making accusations now wouldn't endear him to anyone, and would put the killer on his or her guard if, indeed, one of these so-called academics had taken Frank out. Despite the suspicions that beat a strong pulse inside him, Rafe bit his tongue. Far better to focus on survival at this point, and keep his eyes and ears open for leads of any kind.

Besides, there was still a possibility that someone from Frank's past had gotten to him, that the killer was someone adept at tracking, hiding and making an undetected strike. Stranding these people could simply be collateral damage—an unfortunate consequence to pulling off a murder.

Heeding his own advice, Rafe turned his speculation down a notch. "I'm just saying that time is critical. I understand there's a food shortage. Plus, the National Weather Service predicts stormy weather by tomorrow noon. That means our climbing time will be cut short. In the interest of safety, at that time we'll take shelter until the storm front passes." That earned a few worried murmurs. "I want to get you down to headquarters, then come back for Frank's body as quickly as possible. But I don't want anyone getting hurt in the process."

"You're damn straight he'll get us out of this mess ASAP." Charles Defoe, a man of about sixty, made his presence known with a thump against Copperfield's chest. "I paid good money to finance this fiasco. You promised me that Randolph would return to its glory days if you could get your faculty to resolve their differences and work together. So far I haven't seen anything resembling cooperation—or competence." He pointed that same polished finger up at Rafe. "If anything happens to me or my wife, the college won't be the only one hearing from my lawyers."

A chorus of hear-hear's and stony silences told Rafe just how fractured this supposed *team* truly was.

Dr. Copperfield introduced the man who'd just threatened to sue. "Mr. Defoe is an alum of the college, and one of our most reliable investors." The two men exchanged contemptuous looks hidden behind fake smiles. It seemed that Copperfield liked Defoe's money more than the man himself. "This is his wife, Lydia."

"Ma'am."

The refined redhead acknowledged Rafe with a nod and a threat of her own. "I was against this stupid idea from the start. I want to be home in my hot tub by tomorrow night."

Rafe shook his head. "Not possible, ma'am. I figure we have at least two more nights on the mountain, and that's providing we leave here first thing in the morning."

"Two nights?" Lydia scoffed. "That's entirely unacceptable."

"Two nights to get to a clearing where we can safely land and load a chopper. Three if we go all the way back to the canoes."

"Why, I… You—" Temper dotted her cheeks to match the color of her hair. "I have appointments. I have a life." She turned to her husband. "Charles?"

"My wife is trying to put on a brave front here. But we're all thinking the same thing. We're not safe." Charles wagged an accusatory finger. "And I'm not talking about mountain-climbing. After the tragedy that befell Mr. Brooks—"

"Mr. Defoe, Lydia," Hannah argued, stepping into the conversation with a rebuke that was too gentle to do much damage. "Rafe can't help what happened to his friend. Or to us. We should be grateful that he's finally here. That we're going to get home, period."

There was something a bit Miss Chapman-like and unexpectedly intriguing about a woman who barely reached his shoulder jumping in to defend him. Still, Rafe had faced tougher crowds than this on his own. "I don't intend to let anyone else get hurt, Mr. Defoe. But you'll make my job a lot easier, and this trip a lot safer, if we all cooperate. Keep in mind that I'm willing to leave a friend behind in order to see you and your wife and the others home just as soon as I can."

Dick Copperfield finally made an effort to sound like the voice of authority. "Well, I, for one, am relieved to see you. What do you need us to do first?"

Rafe didn't like the feel of this place. These people. The mountain was telling him something was amiss— there were too many secrets, too much tension that he couldn't attribute to fear alone. Something very wrong was brewing beneath the surface of all this bravado. But they had only one problem he was compelled to deal with at the moment. Survival.

"We'll be losing daylight in about ten minutes," he warned. "You, you and you—" He pointed to the most able-bodied men. "Gather wood and get a fire going."

"We lost our matches, dude." The beach boy, Rowdy Trent, shrugged. "They were with the food when it disappeared."

"Fine. I'll get the fire started if you bring me the wood. I need dry stuff, deadwood you find on the ground. And stay in sight of the tents. I don't want to search for anybody after dark." Once Rowdy and the dueling professors had scurried away into the trees, he turned and snapped orders to the others. "Assemble any and all food from your tents and packs on the table— everything from an energy bar to a breath mint. Make sure you're dressed in layers to conserve body heat. Professor Hawthorne?" He addressed the white-haired gentleman with the stooped shoulders. "Do you know how to pitch a tent?"

"I sure do." The old man smiled. "And it's William."

The sparkle in his eyes made Rafe think the old man was sharp and willing, even if the body couldn't quite keep up.

Rafe grinned, respecting the energy he conveyed. He nodded toward the collapsed tent. He figured it was the least strenuous job at hand since it required no climbing or heavy lifting. "Can you fix that?"

"I sure can. But that's Ed and Keith's tent."

The two combatants bunked together?

"They're a little busy right now. Do you mind?"

Seeming pleased to do Rafe's bidding, Hawthorne laid a hand on Dr. Copperfield's shoulder. "C'mon, Dick. I'll need your help."

With a reluctant nod from the alleged man in charge, the remaining campers scattered to do Rafe's bidding.

As the group cleared, Rafe sought out the closest thing to an ally he had on the mountain. "Kansas."

Hannah paused on the slope above him, giving him a glimpse of denim clinging to some interesting curves before she shifted direction to climb back down. "Yes?"

A shower of dirt and gravel swept beneath her boots as she turned, carrying her feet along in a current that moved faster than the rest of her body. She wobbled, and her arms wind-milled to keep her balance. But before she landed on her backside, Rafe reached up, spanning his hands at either side of her waist to set her squarely on the flat ground in front of him.

"Try to keep your center of gravity closer to the mountain," he advised, automatically shifting his hands to her stomach and the curve of her hip and buttock to demonstrate the technique. "Lean in to the slope when you're facing it. Bend your knees a little and sit back when you're going the other way."

"Oh." Her fingers pinched into the muscle beneath

his skin, almost like an urgent caress, and suddenly Rafe was as curiously aware of the soft swells of woman filling his hands as he was of her clinging to the sweater and skin around his biceps. She nodded along with a breathy reassurance that buzzed across nerve endings and awakened dormant parts of his body. "I'll try to remember that."

Though she tried to hide it with a man-size flannel shirt, *shapeless* was definitely the wrong adjective for the ample figure beneath his big hands. And those gray eyes were pinpoint in focus—even above the rims of her glasses—turned up to his superior height in a completely innocent, completely captivating...

Rafe plucked his hands away almost as quickly as she reached up to center her glasses back into place. "What did you need, Mr. Kincaid?"

You? Sex? A swift kick in the pants?

Silently damning the untimely arousal of hormones, he tuned in to her actual words. *Mr. Kincaid.* What happened to *Rafe?* Like a splash of icy water, the subtle distancing cleared his head of those scattered impressions of her and put him firmly back in the moment and his need to assess the situation. "What was that fight between Butler and Robinson about?"

"The radio." She seemed to breathe easier now that the charged moment between them had passed. Feeling more like himself as well, Rafe followed as she crossed to the camp table and pointed out what was left of shattered plastic, shredded wires and crushed computer circuits. "I left it in Frank's tent after the last time we talked. I figured no one would bother it since no one wanted to go in there. About a half hour ago I went to get it to let you know the natives were getting restless, and…" She gestured at the mess on the table. "That's how I found it."

"And Robinson was the last one in the tent?"

"That's Ed's claim. Though I didn't see him there." She tucked a springy curl behind one ear. But it popped right back out of place, masking the red welt that was deepening in color across her cheekbone. "But then I didn't realize I needed to be watching everyone. Now I don't know who to trust."

"Trust yourself," he advised. Rafe reached out with one finger to brush the curl aside and frowned at the evidence of the earlier fight. "It doesn't look like there's anyone else up here to take care of you."

Rafe savored the heat creeping into his fingertip as a blush stained Hannah's cheeks. Was she feeling this connection, too? Or was she embarrassed that the big, tough mountain man she barely knew couldn't seem to keep his hands to himself?

With almost a shy duck of her head she broke the contact and turned away. Rafe curled his finger into his palm, respecting, if not liking, the don't-touch-me message she sent. "But I'm supposed to trust *you*, though. Right?"

"Yes," he answered honestly, though a smart woman would take the time to get to know a man before investing that kind of faith in him.

She quirked an eyebrow in doubt, giving her expression a sassy sort of class that reminded him of a favorite sixth-grade teacher. "Uh-huh."

One thing that marked all the Kincaid men was that their word was good. Dissing the family honor was not allowed. Even if the criticism was couched in the halfway teasing banter she challenged him with. Rafe splayed his fingers at his hips, and reminded her of all he'd done for her today. "I promised I'd be here tonight. I'm here."

"So you are." Maybe she *was* being smart, sensing the spark between them and purposely trying to distance herself so they could concentrate on more important matters. "All right. I trust you. Just don't make me regret it. Please."

"I won't," Rafe vowed, granting her that space, and silently thanking her for keeping him on track as well. He turned his attention to the radio. "This has been destroyed on purpose."

"That's what I thought. The second I mentioned it, the accusations started flying. I think we all panicked when we realized we were completely out of touch with the outside world."

She hadn't panicked, Rafe noted. She'd been trying to keep the peace and had gotten banged up for her effort. He admired Hannah Greene's toughness. He hated that she'd had to be.

"Can you fix it?" she asked.

He picked up the remnants of Frank's radio and let the pieces trickle through his fingers onto the table. "No."

He hated this whole mess. Sabotage. The kind where the perpetrator drops the equipment down a canyon wall, or goes after it with a sledge hammer.

A murdered guide. Missing food. A broken radio.

This wasn't about Frank Brooks or his work with the Watchers, the uniquely trained, covert group of men and women that Rafe himself still answered to on occasion. This was about Randolph College. This was personal. He looked up and saw that Hannah suspected it, too. "Someone's going to a lot of trouble to make sure you never get home."

She shivered, though he'd guess the temperature still hovered somewhere in the forties. "I've been thinking about that. If someone out here wants one of us—or all of us—dead, and they're willing to kill Frank to strand us so that it looks like some kind of accident, or so there are no witnesses…" She trained her gaze deliberately up to his. "Then that person isn't going to be too thrilled that you showed up to replace him."

Rafe ignored the urge to squeeze her shoulder or take her hand to offer his warmth and comfort. No touching was the key to concentration. "The same thought occurred to me."

"There was a note in Frank's pocket, that *Macbeth* quote I read you."

"Do you still have it?"

She nodded and pulled the crumpled paper from her pocket. While Rafe unfolded it, she voiced her fear. "To me—to anyone who understands literature—that note's a threat. A promise that more bad things are going to happen to us. Did you notice it was typed?"

He'd noted the same detail. The plain paper told him nothing, but the letters sent an unmistakable message. "That means Frank's death was planned out ahead of time, when this note was prepared—or that someone up here is hiding a battery-powered keyboard and printer."

She shivered again and rubbed her hands up and down her arms. "I've only read murder mysteries. I've never lived one."

This time he did give in to the urge to touch her. Reaching out, he smoothed aside that silky curl that refused to stay in place. "I'll get you home, Kansas. I promise."

"I want us all to get home, Rafe."

He might have resisted those soft gray eyes and tipped-up chin if she hadn't couched her concern in the seductive balm of that voice. But it was too late. Something inside him shifted in a dangerously personal direction. Suddenly, he was leaning in to taste the lips that framed that voice. His fingers were swallowed up by a riot of silky curls. He was bending closer, inhaling the earthy scents of the mountain that clung to Hannah's skin and hair.

He was going to kiss her. He hadn't kissed a woman in months. But this one needed kissing. He needed…

A gentle hand, pressed firmly to the middle of his chest stopped him. "What are you doing?"

Making a mistake.

Rafe retreated a step and scraped his hand across the prickly crop of his own short hair. He should apologize. He should explain.

He did neither. He turned away from the question in her eyes and called himself every name in the book. They had a murder on their hands, for cripes sake. One of his best friends was gone and these people were in danger.

Not just Hannah. Everyone—and it was his responsibility to protect them. He needed to concentrate on their three-day descent. He needed to focus on keeping them safe from the killer on their trail, or uncovering the killer amongst them.

He couldn't afford to be distracted by anything Hannah made him feel.

"I told you before, don't worry about me." Rafe retrieved the radio hooked onto his pack and tucked it into his pocket. It wouldn't be the first time in his life he'd had an imaginary target painted on his back. It wouldn't be the first time he'd screwed up a relationship with a woman, either. He was either gone too much, or wasn't cultured or civilized enough, or he didn't know how tell a woman how he... Hell!

Sparring on the radio and thirty minutes of face time scarcely constituted a relationship. *Focus.* "Is there anyone in this group with something to hide? Any secrets someone would go to these lengths to in order to cover them up?"

Though her eyes remained clouded behind her glasses, Hannah shrugged. "We all have secrets of one kind or another."

Touché. "Are you speaking metaphorically? Or does Professor Hannah Greene from Kansas have something to hide?"

"It's just Hannah, Mr. Kincaid," she answered with a weary huff and a Miss Chapman-like tilt of her chin. "We're a troubled bunch of brainiacs. That's why we're here. To find a way to get over ourselves and work together. But believe me, I'm not interesting enough to have anything to hide."

Rafe wanted to argue that last point. Instead, he let the subject drop. "Before the others get back, I'd like to say goodbye to my friend." He was too late to do it right, but he intended to make amends as best he could after the fact by completing Frank's assigned task, finding out who murdered him and why he'd had to die. "Do you mind showing me the body?"

"Of course not." Seeming willing, even eager, to move away from the scene of that almost kiss, she pointed to a tent separated from the others on a small outcropping. "This way."

Rafe fell into step behind her, taking note of the others' locations around the camp when he really just wanted to enjoy the view.

We all have secrets. So what kind of secret did Hannah Greene have to hide?

And whose secret was worth killing for?

Chapter 4

*D*amn. *Damn. Damn.*

Where had the Incredible Hulk come from?

One slight miscalculation in timing his return to Frank Brooks's tent, and a whole new, *big* problem had arisen.

It was that Greene woman's fault. He'd sorely underestimated her. To think a quiet mouse like that would pick this particular occasion to grow a backbone and get to the radio before anyone else could.

No, that wasn't quite true. She'd had backbone enough when she'd stood up at that dissertation review and announced that although the culmination of several years of hard work were interesting, the results were flawed.

Rejected. Denied.

And to think, he'd wanted to do her a favor by asking her out. Linking himself to the Greene name would have been quite the coup. She'd have been grateful for his attentions.

But no more.

She'd be dealt with like all the others. The new guide from Extreme, Inc., was a problem he could handle, too.

He'd already spotted the little flickers of attraction between the mountain man and the bookworm. No accounting for taste. But it provided a weakness. A weakness he'd have no trouble using to his advantage.

Rafe Kincaid's arrival might have thrown a wrench into a perfect plan, but the outcome was still inevitable.

Revenge was inevitable.

Time to take care of business.

Rafe Kincaid was more man than she'd ever seen live and in person. He was tall. Broadly built. Packed with muscle from his rugged jaw to his booted feet. A true outdoorsman, big enough to conquer the mountain and the threat of murder.

And he'd wanted to kiss her.

Hannah frowned against the morning sun that was already being masked by the gathering drift of rainclouds. She was still working on that one. Why? She wasn't a hottie. Murder and sabotage weren't exactly conducive to romance.

And yet there was something there. Some inexplicable bond that had been forged by the two of them over the radio, intensified by fear and compassion and a gallant rescue from a fight. There was something mysteriously deep in the shadows of his cinnamon-brown eyes, something extraordinarily unnerving about his penchant for touching her. There was a bold confidence about him. A deceptive nonchalance about him that indicated he didn't do a damn thing he didn't want to.

And he'd wanted to kiss her!

It was heady, arousing—and confusing as hell.

She'd been so dumbfounded by the possibilities, so distrustful of the why's and wherefore's—so afraid he'd be disappointed when the real deal didn't live up to his curious expectations—that she'd pushed him away.

A phone call to her sister might give her some clues as to whether Rafe Kincaid was truly into her, or whether she was just projecting her own gratitude-fed attraction onto him. But there was no phone. No sister. No innate trusting her gut when it came to men.

There was only this…connection.

While she buttoned her flannel shirt and stretched the kinks from her body, Hannah sneaked glances at the nearly au natural view of Rafe stripping off his shirts beside the table near the firepit. He splashed his face, neck and shoulders in lieu of a shave, then patted everything dry with his white T-shirt before slipping the garment on over his thick biceps and tapered back. Though several feet of rock and a sharp incline separated them, they were the only two up and out of their tents to see the sunrise, and the solitude made the stretch of craggy peaks and endless sky feel like a private room.

Running a comb through her shoulder-length curls, she watched him tuck in his shirt and sweater. Then he went to work, restoking the fire and putting together the makings of coffee from his pack. He was as at home in these natural surroundings as she was in her classroom. His taut features and once-broken nose kept him from being truly handsome, but there was an ultra-masculine appeal to his short crop of earth-brown hair and economy of movement that tripped through her pulse the same way the cavernous depth of his voice had done over the radio yesterday.

They certainly didn't build many like him back in the halls of academe. Maybe in the tomes of mythic literature—he could be a Hercules or a Beowulf. Jane Eyre's Mr. Rochester.

And like that plain, bookish heroine, Hannah found herself irresistibly drawn to the big, mysterious man who had barged into her sedate, predictable world like a force of nature.

"Yeesh." Hannah buried the fanciful notions back in her imagination and quickly tucked her hair into a ponytail, pulling it through the back of the ball cap she used to keep the stray tendrils out of her eyes when they climbed. "He's just a guy."

A guy whose presence made her feel safe in an unfamiliar situation. A guy whose halting goodbye and whispered vow for justice over his friend's dead body had touched her heart. A guy whose pupils had dilated and whose breath had stilled in anticipation of kissing her.

"Get over it, girl," she chided herself.

Maybe if she had a little more experience with men, live and in person, instead of the ones she met in her books, she could make sense of what was going on between her and Rafe. She wouldn't question his motives or second-guess his attraction to her.

But she didn't have that experience. Piper was the femme fatale of the family. Hannah had always attracted study-buddies and intellectual types whose idea of meeting behind the stacks meant to locate books and do research. She could be counted on as a teammate in Trivial Pursuit and a back-up escort when a real date fell through. She'd been on a couple of curious forays into the process of having sex—but passion? love? Unless her obsession with the English language and all the wonderful ways an author could put words to paper counted, she was out of luck when it came to understanding and dealing with her feelings for Rafe.

So she'd stop peeking, stop pondering, stop wishing—and go about the business of her day.

After stashing her comb inside the tent, Hannah closed the flap behind her so as not to disturb Irene's slumber. It was at this time yesterday that she'd planned to meet Frank—before the others had roused from their sleeping bags. A subconscious memory blipped into her mind, diverting her attention into an equally disturbing train of thought.

She wasn't the only one who'd been awake at dawn yesterday. Rowdy had startled her at Frank's tent. Irene had been up doing her yoga. Professor Hawthorne had been out. Where? Exploring? Dr. Copperfield and Natalie had been…well, they hadn't been sleeping. And she hadn't actually *seen* Lydia and Charles inside their tent.

For a bunch of night owls, there'd been an awful lot of activity going on before sunrise.

Could one of them have seen or heard an argument in Frank's tent? Did they hear his final cry or last gasp of breath? If so, why hadn't they shared that information with the group? Why pretend to know nothing about the murder? Unless one of them needed an alibi. And needing an alibi would indicate…

An uneasy feeling crawled up Hannah's spine. She didn't want to believe a group of her so-called colleagues could be hiding a murderer in their midst. But how else could she explain the unusual activity in camp yesterday morning?

That uneasy feeling spread through her bones, leaving a trail of suspicion in its wake. Since she and Irene had the highest vantage point, it was easy for her to look from one tent to the next on the terrain below. Were they all occupied this morning? She glanced back over her shoulder and even wondered if Irene was only feigning sleep.

"That's a frowny face." The deep voice from below her feet startled her from her paranoid imaginings. Rafe stood with his hands splayed at his hips in a stance that emphasized the bulk of his shoulders and arms. A probing curiosity glinted in his warm brown eyes. "Should I say good morning? Or is this not your best time of day?"

"No, I love to start my day early. Good morning." Hannah mustered a civilized greeting and a smile. She used her diaphragm to give her voice more *oomph* to carry against the breeze.

But Rafe heard her. He smiled, and that rugged, beard-dusted face sent something much more pleasant than suspicion shimmering along her spine. "Morning, Kansas."

Their positions on the gravelly, grass-studded slope gave their conversation an intimate *Romeo and Juliet* feel. But since doomed, star-crossed lovers wasn't exactly the way she'd envisioned a romance for herself— or even this pointless crush she had on Rafe—Hannah decided to join him at the firepit. Her pulse simmered as she remembered his coaching from the night before. But, concentrating on the skill, not the teacher, she sat back a little over her knees and climbed down the six-foot slope to the main campsite.

Rafe watched her descent with an approving nod. "I see you're learning how to handle the mountain."

Her temperature rose as if he'd just called her beautiful. Hannah adjusted her glasses to hide the irrational blush. "I had to think about it, though. Your balance seems second nature to you."

"I've been climbing since I was a kid. You'll get the right moves if you practice enough." And, oh, how she wanted to practice with him. But he was talking about mountain-climbing, not kissing or her desire to learn *everything* he could teach her. Her flustered thoughts put her off guard, leaving her unprepared for his next question. "So what's wrong?"

Standing close enough to smell the outdoorsy scents of pine and smoke and chilly air on him, Hannah got a quick reminder of the easy sensuality that had made her stop and stare in the first place. She turned to answer and got an eyeful of taut, ragg wool sweater blocking her view. Big. Broad. Masculine. And he smelled good. *Yeesh.* She wisely stepped away before she embarrassed herself.

"I was thinking about Frank." She busied her hands righting his enameled metal coffee cup and retrieving one for herself from the supply bag he'd set on the table. "The more I go back through what happened yesterday, the more convinced I am that someone here in camp must have seen or heard something."

"Are grammar teachers known for their detective skills?"

This one was going to be since their lives might depend on uncovering the truth.

"I'm the only one who admits to being up early yesterday. But I know I wasn't. And leaving a quote in

Frank's pocket tells me it's a message for us." She glanced around at the noiseless tents before seeking Rafe's intent gaze. "We're a bunch of literary nuts. I think the killer's trying to say something that only people like us would get. He's speaking our language. There has to be a reason for that. It's a taunt. A warning."

"You think it was written by one of your fellow nuts?"

"Either written by, or intended for. I sure don't think it's a random clue." She tightened her grip around the cup in her hands. "That could explain why everyone was so edgy yesterday. One of us knows what really happened to Frank. He or she's either a witness or the killer. We might have both in our midst."

Rafe's jaw dipped in the slightest of nods. "I'm suspicious of your buddies, too."

"You are?" He believed her?

"I walked the perimeter of the camp at first light. There are no tracks leading into or out of the area except my own." He picked up the nylon sleeping bag that had been spread out beside the firepit and shook it, scattering bits of dirt and grass. "Frank didn't shoot himself. And if the killer isn't out there, then he's one of us."

"You don't suspect me, do you?"

"A sassy little thing like you kill someone? Did anyone else try to contact Extreme, Inc., for a rescue?"

"No."

"Why call for help when you could get rid of all your witnesses by leaving them stuck up here, or use the tragedy of a lost expedition to mask your real target? You're smarter than that." He grinned in a way that aroused her curiosity and quickened her pulse. "Besides, you remind me of somebody I once knew. She couldn't commit murder, either."

Though Rafe's easy trust empowered her in a way praise from her family never had, Hannah adjusted her glasses to study the bemused expression that accompanied his odd statement. "Of whom do I remind you?"

"Of *whom?* Exactly." His smile broadened into a sexy, mysterious curve at the private joke which eluded her. And while his unexpected humor tempted her to smile along with him, he'd triggered a nagging need to know about that unnamed person from his past she resembled. Instead of answering, he shook his head and knelt down to roll up his sleeping bag. "You don't want to know."

Who could it be? An old girlfriend? A current girlfriend? A wife? Her gaze dropped down to assess the ring-free finger on his left hand. Embarrassed by the relief coursing through her at the verification of his single status, Hannah turned her attention to other details. Rafe was packing up his bedroll and supplies. Here. By the firepit. He hadn't pitched a tent of his own. She realized now he hadn't even brought one. Hannah frowned. "You slept outside last night?"

She thought she detected the first glitch in his amazing control when a shiver rippled across his back from shoulder to shoulder. Hannah shivered, too, thinking about how cold it must have gotten in the middle of the night with nothing but a few embers from the dying fire to warm him.

An altogether different kind of shiver raised goose bumps along her arms as Rafe turned on the balls of his feet and stood up. Craning her neck to keep his face in view, Hannah fought the urge to retreat. The tension in his body was as rigid as the line of his mouth where his smile used to be.

"Rafe?" she questioned in a small voice.

The stiffness in him vanished like a popped balloon. "Considering yesterday's events, I didn't want any surprises sneaking up on me. Besides, it was a clear night and I enjoy watching the stars." He tossed his sleeping bag up onto the table and began lashing it to his pack. "Tonight we won't be so lucky."

He seemed awfully busy all of a sudden—as if the sexy smiles and teasing banter and unspoken trust between them had never happened. Why get so defensive? Why was it a big deal for her to know he'd slept outside? But if he needed to change the subject, Hannah would let him. For now.

Looking up into the silver-blue sky, she took note of the line of clouds gathering just beyond the mountain's peak. "You think today's storms will last through the night?"

"I called in to headquarters a few minutes ago. That's what the forecast—"

"Dude!"

Hannah whipped her head around toward the shout from the trees. Rafe's hands stilled their work for a split second. And then he was moving. He bounded to the top of a granite outcropping and dropped out of site into the ravine on the opposite side, heading toward Rowdy Trent's anguished cry.

"Oh, my God. Dude!"

"Rowdy?"

"Somebody help me!"

Hannah dropped her mug and scrambled after Rafe. Landing on her bottom on the other side, she slid down the rockface until her feet hit relatively level ground. Swatting the dirt from her jeans, she followed the uneven excuse for a path—more of a gulley worn by wind, water and gravity—into the trees. Breathing hard in the thin air, she slowed when the canopy of evergreen branches marbled the sunlight and cooled the air by several obvious degrees.

"What is it?" she rasped, spotting Rafe and Rowdy kneeling beside something golden brown among the gray shadows and rocks. "Is it a mountain lion?" she asked as the mass began to take shape.

She could hear the others in the camp, stirring behind her. Muffled questions and panic in the distance. Footsteps hurrying their way.

Rafe pushed to his feet as she approached. "Stay back, Kansas. It's Hawthorne."

At first she mistook the dirty white she saw on the ground as a lingering patch of snow. But before Rafe's shoulders could block the view, she blinked the tan jacket and white hair into focus. "Is he…?"

Rafe's hands were on her shoulders, trying to push her away from the gruesome scene. But she wrapped her fingers around his forearms, planted her feet and lifted her gaze to let him know she could handle this challenge.

"I'm sorry," he whispered, in that deep, protective pitch that had comforted her over the radio. "The tracks weren't here earlier. This shouldn't have happened on my watch."

"It's not your fault." Hannah reached up and laid her palm against the prickly contours of his cheek and jaw. She kept it there, despite the startled question in his eyes, reassuring the man she'd thought needed no kind of reassurance from anyone.

A controlled burst of energy replaced the tension in him. With a quick nod, he pulled her hand from his face and reached for his radio. "I'm calling this in to headquarters."

Though she couldn't help but feel dismissed, Hannah knew this wasn't the time or place to stew in her feelings. As Rafe stepped away, she turned her attention to the real tragedy and squatted down beside the dead body crumpled amongst the rocks.

"Poor William." With gentle fingers, she brushed the snowy white strands of hair from his cold, ashen cheek. She felt almost as cold herself. Did a person ever get used to this? "He seemed to be the only one who was truly enjoying himself up here."

On the other side of the body, Rowdy sniffed back a noisy sob. "He left the tent a couple of hours ago to take a leak. When I woke up and realized he hadn't come back, I went lookin'… Do you think he had a heart attack?"

"I don't know. Maybe the stress…" Hannah looked into Rowdy's teary eyes, not liking how readily her compassion was tainted by suspicion. "When did you leave your tent?"

"A few minutes ago."

Had she been so absorbed in watching Rafe that she hadn't seen Rowdy sneak out of camp? She let her gaze slide over to the man on the radio. Even though he'd crossed several feet away and was absorbed in his proper "roger that" and "over" conversation with someone named Luke, Rafe's gaze instantly locked on to hers. No, he was too sharp, too aware of people and his surroundings. Even if she'd been too distracted to notice Rowdy sneaking out of camp, Rafe would have seen him.

Without answering the query in his eyes, Hannah turned back to Rowdy. He shivered as soon as she looked his way, though the impression of bristling in self-defense could be explained by his shorts and short sleeved shirt, and by the cool, rain-laden air.

"Do you think it was his heart?" Rowdy asked, punctuating his question with a sniffle. "I found his medicine in the tent. They were the same pills he used to give his wife. He didn't have them with him. Ironic, huh? That they should both die the same way?"

Before she could ponder the irony of Rowdy using a term like *ironic,* Hannah's fingers caught in something as sticky as cold molasses. She slowly pulled her fingers from Hawthorne's hair and splayed them in the air. "I don't think he had a heart attack."

Blood. Dark red. And plenty of it soaking into the ground beneath his head.

"Oh, dude." Rowdy scrambled from his knees onto his haunches and landed on his bottom in his haste to retreat. "He must have tripped and hit his head on that rock."

A deep voice resonated above them. "I think the rock hit him."

Hannah suddenly felt herself cocooned in a circle of warmth as Rafe knelt down, wrapped an arm around her shoulders and pulled her to his side. She needed the solid contact and comfort, and couldn't help leaning in to his indomitable strength and abundant heat.

"Look." He pointed to the lichen-encrusted edge of the fist-sized rock, then flipped it over to reveal its smooth, weather-worn side. "This has been moved."

Murder number two. Not a heart attack. Not an accident.

"But why?" Hannah blinked back the tears that stung her eyes. "Who would want to hurt a sweet man like that?"

Rafe's arm tightened around her and she wanted to turn and bury her face in the security and strength of his chest. But just as her nose began to nuzzle, Rafe shot to his feet, startling her an instant before she heard footsteps skidding to a halt behind them. "Hold up," he warned.

A woman shrieked. "Oh, my God."

"Not again."

"What the hell is going on around here?"

Hannah got the sense that Rafe was protecting her, though maybe that was wishful thinking. He might just be blocking the view of the body the way he'd tried to shield her from seeing it. Either way, she didn't feel quite so alone in dealing with yet another senseless murder.

"More death." Irene Sharp circled around the body and laid a comforting hand on Rowdy's shoulder as he shakily stood. "Just like Frank's note foretold. This is bad karma. I knew this altitude was bad for us. I just knew it."

Ed Butler helped Charles Defoe sit his wife, Lydia, on the ground before she could faint. "Hawthorne was one of the founding fathers of our college. Along with Cyrus Randolph. Poor man. What a loss."

Keith Robinson walked a wide berth around Rafe and stood beside Rowdy. "At least he can be with his wife, Bernice, now. They were married what—fifty years? Spent most of that last year in the hospital with her."

Hannah nodded. "He seemed so relieved when her suffering ended."

Charles Defoe pulled off his hat to fan his wife. "Hawthorne was the first advisor I had at Randolph. I always remember he and Bernice and Cyrus hanging out in the administrative offices together. Like the Three Musketeers."

"Cyrus introduced William to Bernice," Lydia added between noisy sighs, joining the reminiscences. "It will crush Cyrus to hear that the last of his old friends is gone."

"Where's Copperfield?" Rafe's succinct question halted the sentimental journey for a long, silent moment.

Then everyone started talking at once.

"Boinking his mistress. Where do you think?"

"They're probably planning ways to skim more money from the college funds."

"Those allegations were never proved."

"Did you get a raise this year? Were your programs and research cut?"

"Don't get me started."

"He's losing his hair over this. Literally. Just because the money's missing, doesn't mean he's..."

The familiar arguments buzzed into white noise that swirled around her as Hannah's focus zeroed in on the white paper triangle peeking from William Hawthorne's slacks pocket.

"Rafe." She reached out and tugged on his pant leg. "Rafe?" Any lingering hope that Hawthorne's death might have been a tragic accident vanished. "There's another note."

He knelt beside her, and the group held its collective breath. "What does it say?" he asked.

With a quick apology to the dead, Hannah pulled the folded paper from his pocket. Like the note in Frank's shirt, this one had been neatly typed and properly punctuated.

Trouthe is the hyeste thyng that men may kepe.

Rafe was reading over her shoulder. "Translation?"

"It's Middle English. From Chaucer's *Canterbury Tales*. Truth is the highest thing that men may keep."

"And what does *that* mean?"

"Either someone believed Professor Hawthorne lied, and punished him for it," She peeked over the top of her glasses to meet Rafe's probing gaze. "Or somebody silenced him so he couldn't tell the truth."

Rafe nodded, as if he had suspected as much, even without the cryptic note. He stood, wrapping his hand around Hannah's arm and pulling her to her feet. "Let's move his body into Frank's tent. I'll secure the area. The rest of you, pack your things."

"Oh, my God. Not William." Dick Copperfield chose that exact moment to join them. As Hannah spun to face him, she couldn't help but notice all the unspoken accusations flung his way by her colleagues. No wonder he fidgeted and blanched an uncharacteristic shade of pale beneath his artificial tan. "Our problems are worse than you think. Natalie's disappeared. I can't find her anywhere."

Tension radiated through Rafe's fingertips into Hannah's arm. "What the hell kind of game are you playing here, Copperfield? I can't mount a search for her and take care of you people at the same time. Not with everything I've seen up here."

"I don't want you to conduct a search. Think of me what you will, Mr. Kincaid—all of you." A sheen of perspiration dotted his forehead. He shifted back and forth on his feet, looking as nervous as a sheep cornered by a pack of hungry wolves. "But you have to get us off this mountain. Now. Before somebody else dies."

Chapter 5

"This has been cut." Rafe had long since inured himself to the rain that plastered his hair to his scalp and trickled down the back of his neck. He ran his thumb along the smooth edge of the severed rope. "The core's still dry," he muttered to himself.

The sabotage was recent.

If he had eyes in the back of his head, he couldn't pinpoint any more accurately where each member of the Randolph group had positioned themselves. Eight drenched hikers waited on the path behind him through the trees, resting their bodies, catching their breaths and anxiously hoping that he'd found a shortcut to warmth and safety.

But the fifty-foot expanse of the Osprey River gorge and the dubious means to cross it stood in their way.

Rafe dropped the rope where it hung from a detached

pulley and rose to his feet to check the rest of the rigging attached to the wooden platform. A rough-hewn beam anchored one end of a series of ropes that carried a bosun's chair back and forth above the storm-fed river like a midair ferry.

The remaining equipment seemed solid enough, but without that third line to anchor it, the hanging basket might not be able to sustain the weight of a full-grown man with a back-pack. Hell, unless he could get a look at the rigging on the opposite side to see whether or not it had been tampered with as well, he wouldn't trust that basket to carry anything.

"Trent, Robinson," he called to the group. "Drop your packs and give me a hand. The rest of you stay put."

Shedding the weight of his own gear, Rafe grabbed the lead rope and pulled. Odd that the basket was at the far side of the river. Though Rafe had by-passed the gorge completely on his ascent yesterday, Frank would have brought the group up this way and left the basket on the Targhee Meadow side, closest to their camp.

The loss of the line made the bosun's chair heavy to pull across—even with the muscle power of three men. The rain spattered on the wood at their feet and in the branches of the surrounding trees, melding with the roar of the river crashing over rocks below them and dampening the sounds of wet rigging straining through creaking pulleys.

"Can we still use it to cross the river?" Lydia Defoe shouted from her perch on top of her husband's pack. "I don't know how much farther my feet will take me."

Rafe bristled at her petulant tone and put his back into dragging the basket across. They'd only been hiking half a day, their pace slowed to a crawl since the sky had opened up an hour ago. Lightning still rippled through the clouds above them, filling the gray air with enough static electricity to stand the hair on his arms on end. Lydia's feet had better take her a good five miles more today, or it'd be a week before they got back to headquarters.

But Rafe bit back his retort. These people weren't used to the altitude or terrain. They weren't used to murder. "I'm not sure, ma'am," he answered. "But I intend to find out."

"Should the basket be swinging that much?" Hannah asked. Her voice at his shoulder told him she hadn't obeyed his instructions.

"Didn't I tell you to stay put?" A crack of thunder splintered the air, ringing in his ears and giving his concern a lot more bite than he'd intended.

"I'm only trying to help."

He glanced down to see her picking up his backpack. Despite the bill of her cap, raindrops dotted her glasses. Rafe battled the strangest urge to take his finger and wipe them clean so she could see clearly. He was even more tempted to remove them entirely so he could look deep into the steady depths of her eyes and apologize for jumping down her throat.

But he kept his hands at their task and softened his voice instead. "Sorry. I appreciate you lookin' out for me." Her answering smile was more reward than he deserved. He nodded toward the clearing in the trees above them. "Now get back with the others so I don't worry about you falling off the edge here."

"Yes, sir." The arch of her brow gave her compliance a sassy twist. Rafe grinned. The spirit of Miss Chapman was alive and well. But coupled with that seductive voice and those amazing eyes, Hannah Greene was doing crazy things to his professional detachment and emotional equilibrium that his sixth-grade grammar teacher certainly never had.

"It's here, Kincaid," Keith Robinson reminded him of their task.

"Go." Rafe pointed up the incline, telling Hannah to get her pretty little butt in gear. When he looked back, the bosun's chair *was* weaving back and forth like a pendulum. That much movement on too few lines could certainly spell disaster. But if there was a possibility of shortening the journey…

"Grab the basket," he commanded, holding on to Robinson's belt as the black man slithered close enough to the end of the platform to grasp a rope handle. Together the three of them tugged the high-sided basket onto solid ground. Already, Rafe could feel the unusual weight of the thing. What else had been tampered with? "Tie it off."

While Rowdy Trent secured the basket to the log fence surrounding the platform, Rafe untied the basket's door and looked inside. He jumped back just as quickly, startled, sickened, angry. "Damn."

"Rafe?" That was Hannah, concerned for him. Curious.

Her voice was enough of an anchor for him to move past the image of frozen blue eyes and a swollen tongue.

"It's Natalie," he announced. Amidst the cries and curses, Rafe went back inside the basket to untangle the rope from around Natalie's pale neck and feel for a pulse. He straightened with a silent curse of his own. "She's dead."

"Natalie?" Dick Copperfield lurched to his feet, looking ashen beneath his tan. Hannah tried to grab him before he stumbled down the incline. Instead of staying put, she slid after him. "That can't be."

He knelt in front of the slumped figure and picked up Natalie's cold, stiff hand. "Oh, Nat. Sweetie." He was crying now. "This can't be right. We've been through so much together."

Hannah slipped in beside him and wrapped her arms around his shoulders. "Dr. Copperfield."

"This wasn't supposed to happen." He looked right at Hannah. "It wasn't supposed to happen like this."

Hannah frowned and lifted her gaze. Rafe shrugged, wondering the same question she did. *What wasn't supposed to happen?*

"I can tell you right now, Mr. Kincaid, my wife and I are not riding on that thing." Charles Defoe seemed to have little sympathy for the president's distress.

"Make yourself useful, Defoe." Whether it was arrogance or fear that fueled the wealthy man's lack of compassion, Rafe wasn't going to let him dictate who did what on this rescue mission. "Come get your buddy here and calm him down."

Though Lydia was the one who actually huffed at her husband being given an order, Defoe reluctantly picked his way down the slope, stuck his handkerchief in Copperfield's hand and led him back to the relatively level path.

"Oh, man, I can't take this. We're all gonna die. All this Shakespeare and Chaucer and Latin crap. We're gonna die." Rowdy grabbed his gut and doubled over. For all his physical strength, the shaggy grad assistant had a weak stomach.

Rafe nodded toward Keith Robinson. "Get him out of here, too."

Irene Sharp came down to help get Rowdy up to the

trail. Ed Butler opened his canteen and gave the young man a drink. "Do you think we're all targets?" Butler asked, starting an inevitable debate with his professorial rival.

Robinson snatched the canteen to take a drink for himself. "That witch probably deserved what she got." Cold. But no one argued with him. "Do you honestly think Copperfield is smart enough to doctor the books on his own? As soon as he made president, she became his right hand."

"And his bed partner."

"Exactly. There's something hinky about having departmental funding cut while Copperfield and his mistress shack up in a new mansion together."

"Sounds like motive to me."

"Are you accusing me of something?"

"Keith. Ed." Irene tried to shush them. "You're filling the air with negative energy."

"Oh, come on, you looney…"

Thunder rumbled overhead, rolling across the sky like the fusillade of battle in the distance. As Mother Nature's sounds faded, the bombardment of words behind them increased. But it all disappeared into another world when Rafe heard Hannah mumbling softly at his feet. "…accused of taking money from the school, but never proven. Rumors suggest Professor Hawthorne let his wife die by withholding her medicine. Couldn't prove a mercy killing."

Rafe went down on his haunches beside her and touched her shoulder. "Kansas?"

He quickly realized she was thinking out loud. "Look at the note pinned to her blouse."

Like the other two bodies, Natalie had been left with

a message. *Mors ultima ratio.* "Is that Latin? Mine's even rustier than my English lit."

"*Mors* is death. *Ultima* means last or final."

"Does *ratio* have to do with numbers?"

She nodded. "You could translate it as accounting. Natalie was the chief accountant for the school. 'Death is the final accounting.' It's an old Latin proverb."

"She was killed because she was an accountant?"

"Natalie was killed because someone thinks she got away with taking money from the school."

Hannah turned, bracing her hand on his knee. Despite the instant frisson of awareness that seeped through soaked denim and skin, the fear in those deep-gray eyes cut right through him. "I think I've figured this out. We all have secrets. What if that's the connection? There have been rumors and accusations surrounding each of us on this retreat. None of which have ever been proven."

Someone meting out retribution on the faculty and staff of Randolph College? Rafe took her by both shoulders and tried to nudge her out of that dangerous train of thought. "What kind of crime could someone like you have committed?"

"Beyond being a huge disappointment to my family?" She swiped at a wet curl that had fallen loose from her cap and was dripping into her eye. "I don't know. Dr. Copperfield's always resented that I've never used my family connections to bring money into the college. I could have offended someone somewhere along the line. Failed a student. Stuck my nose in where it wasn't welcome."

"I doubt that."

She pushed at the annoying curl again, tucking it behind her ear and holding it there—exposing the purplish bruise that marred her smooth cheek and giving her an air of such vulnerability that Rafe had to fight the urge to sweep her into his arms. She still needed to talk, and he had a feeling he needed to listen. "What if someone thinks they know the truth? That we're being punished for getting away with murder or embezzlement or some other crime?"

"You're joking, right?"

Her voice dropped to a low, urgent whisper. "Ed Butler has been accused of sexual harassment more than once, supposedly even trading sex with students for grades. But the charges never stuck. Keith was accused of stealing the research for a series of national articles he published. Though he claims it was a joint project, the graduate assistant he allegedly stole from dropped out of school and hasn't been heard from since."

That curl sprang free and bobbed against the earpiece of her glasses. With shaky fingers, she tried to bat it away. Rafe could see there was more nervousness than discomfort in the repetitive gesture. He reached up and brushed it aside himself, cupping her wounded cheek to warm the chill on her skin that might not be due entirely to the rain, either.

"I read that in the report. Nothing has been substantiated. There is no proof."

"What report?"

"I ran a background check on all of you before heading up here."

Hannah pushed her glasses squarely in front of her eyes and squinted. "You spied on us? Isn't that illegal?"

Hell. He was trying to reassure her, not raise more worries. Yeah, he had a real tender touch with women.

"I've got the clearance to do it legally. With Frank's murder, I wanted to know what I was getting into before I came up here."

"What kind of clearance are you talking about? Are you a detective?"

How did he talk his way out of this one? The Watchers weren't public knowledge. In fact, they'd been disbanded and disavowed until Homeland Security came into being, and the need for a covert group to handle security, rescue and retrieval situations without the government being officially involved had arisen. "It's a complicated story."

"Tell me."

"We have other priorities right now."

Raindrops splashed her upturned face and ran down her cheek in rivulets that caught where his fingers still cupped her jaw. The smell of ozone had long since been washed from the air, leaving the earthy scents of mud and pinewood and Hannah herself rising between them.

Rafe waited and watched and inhaled as she debated their hushed conversation inside her head.

"Am I stupid to trust you?" The soft husk of her voice reached deep inside him, crumbling the last vestiges of personal detachment into dust.

He framed her face in his big hands. "Would I tell you if you were?"

She arched her brow and tapped a finger against his chest. "Don't be logical with me, Rafe. My gut says you're a good guy. But then my gut doesn't have much experience."

Oh, hell. He closed the distance between them and kissed her. Long enough to feel her soft lips move against his, to feel them part and shyly invite him inside—not long enough to stake a claim the way he ached to. Long enough to feel her palm brace against his chest and her fingers dig into sweater and skin and muscle beneath—not long enough to pull her into his arms and feel her whole body pressing just as urgently against him. He kissed her long enough to drop his guard and let her into the secret places inside him—not long enough to admit how close she'd gotten to his heart.

It was a tender taste of heaven. A welcome. A promise. When Rafe pulled away, he couldn't seem to move his hands from her face. And it took every ounce of his will to catch a normal breath and lift his gaze from those sweet, pliant lips to her clear, questioning eyes.

"Trust your gut, Kansas. I won't hurt you." He swept his thumbs across her lenses, making sure she could see the true depth of his vow. "And I'll be damned if I let anyone else hurt you."

Her shaky nod humbled him. "Okay. I'll try to keep the faith." She smoothed her palm across his chest, and though he imagined she was straightening his sweater, it felt like a caress. "It might seem pretty lame, but I'll do my best not to let anyone hurt you, either."

He might have laughed if he hadn't seen how serious she was. Imagine—a buxom brainiac like her protecting a man like him. He'd never imagined himself needing protection from anyone. He was too strong, too well-trained, too well-educated in the game of survival. But he liked the idea of Hannah watching his back. He liked the idea of Hannah taking an interest in him, period.

But there were others to consider. And they still had miles to go. Rafe pressed a quick kiss to the arch of Hannah's brow and pulled her to her feet as he stood. "Now go on up with the others. Let me wrap Natalie's body like I did Frank and William's. Then we can move out."

"I can help."

Was there any challenge this woman wouldn't face? Rafe relented. He'd feel safer with her close by his side, anyway. "Can we use your sleeping bag?"

With a quick nod, she hurried to retrieve it. By the time they had Natalie's body securely wrapped and hung back out in the basket to protect it from scavengers and the elements, the others had cooled their jets to a simmering suspicion of the world and each other. But they were ready to take orders if it meant getting back to civilization.

"We have to go back up and down along that ridge." Rafe pointed to the tree-crowned slope above them. "There's a rope bridge we can cross about a mile downstream."

"A bridge made out of rope?" Keith Robinson sounded skeptical enough for all of them. "What if it's been tampered with, too?"

"The drop-off's less steep down there," Rafe explained. "If we can't use the bridge, it'll be easier to climb down and ford the river." He shouldered his pack and instructed the others to do the same. "I don't know if Miss Flanders wandered away from camp, making herself an easy target for the killer, or if she was specifically singled out and then brought to this place so we'd be sure to find her and the sabotaged crossing. But from now on, we stick together. No one goes off by themselves. Not even to take a whiz. Understood?"

Robinson nodded. The others chimed in with agreements of their own.

"All right, then. Let's move out."

He took Hannah by the hand and pulled her up to walk beside him. The others fell into step behind them, single file.

This time, even Butler and Robinson didn't argue.

"Oh, God, I don't think I can do this."

Hannah eyed the white-knuckled grasp of the woman in front of her on the rope bridge. "Lydia, you can't stop now."

Twenty feet above the winding Osprey River, Hannah could feel the spray of water, chilled even in summer by snow melting at higher altitudes. As Rafe had said, this crossing was a lot easier in the acrophobic department, but there was also nothing to prevent her from looking down to see the current sweeping beneath her feet, swirling into eddies where it caught against rocks before roaring on downstream.

Lydia was looking down, too. "Should I tell you now that I don't know how to swim?"

All the more reason to hurry across. Hannah swallowed the panicked retort and took a deep breath. If Lydia couldn't get her nerve back, then Hannah was stranded with her. The single rope they walked on, with V-shaped supports on either side didn't allow any room to walk around a person.

Not that she could abandon Lydia, anyway. She tried a little encouragement first. "Lydia, look at Charles on the shore already." She glanced ahead to the graveled clearing amongst the trees where everyone except Rafe waited. He'd crossed over first to check the bridge's reliability, then come back to be the last one over to ensure they all made it safely. "You're halfway there already. Don't give up now."

"But the water just hit me in the face. What if I fall in?"

Hannah unclipped the security line that hooked her belt to the bridge's guide rope.

"Kansas, what are you doing?" That was Rafe behind her. The sharp clip of his voice, though gruff, betrayed his concern.

"I'm helping Lydia." Trusting her shaky balance and the security of the bridge, she walked the rustic tight-rope until she stood right behind the frozen older woman, and reclipped her line to the same section with Lydia. "I'm right behind you," she cautioned.

"Lydia, darling, what's wrong?" Charles called to his wife now. "Keep walking."

"I can't!" Her bright red fingernail polish seemed to be the only color on her trembling body.

"You need to breathe," Hannah coached her as calmly as she could. Lydia was shaking so badly that Hannah could feel the tremors through the ropes at her hands and feet. "In through your nose. Out through your mouth. You don't want to pass out up here."

"No, I don't. I'll fall!"

"You won't fall."

Over the rain and the water, she heard the methodic rustle and clicks of Rafe attaching his gear. "I'm coming to get you."

"No!" Hannah shouted over her shoulder, not risking turning completely around. "You said two people on the bridge at a time. You'll be too heavy."

"Dammit, Kansas—"

"Stay back!"

After sparing a moment to wipe her glasses clean and take a steadying breath, Hannah spoke gently but succinctly to Lydia. "I'm going to take your hand. We're going to move it forward a few inches on the rope, and then we're going to take the next step together."

"I don't want to."

"Lydia, we're both soaked to the bone. It might be sixty degrees out here, but I'm cold. I want to get to the other side so we can make camp and start a fire. Don't you?"

Lydia nodded. Creature comforts had always appealed to her. "I want to be warm."

"Okay, then." Hannah slowly reached out and wrapped her hand around Lydia's chilled fingers. "Let go of the rope and hold on to me."

"Lydia?" Charles was frantic with his wife's predicament.

"Just listen to my voice," Hannah reminded her. "Take my hand."

With a cold, stiff grip, Lydia twisted her fingers and latched on to Hannah with a tight fist. Her nails dug into Hannah's skin, but Hannah ignored the pinch of pain and moved their hands forward, wrapping them around the guide rope.

"Let's do your right hand now." They repeated the process on the other side. Lydia had drawn blood across Hannah's knuckles, but the woman was moving. "Now your right foot." She nudged the back of Lydia's boot. "Now your left." Hannah moved up behind her. Six inches. A snail would have zipped across faster than this, but Lydia was moving.

"C'mon, Kansas." She thought she heard the words through the cacophony of Mother Nature's noise. The gruff encouragement schooled her patience and kept her calm.

They repeated the process. Two steps. Three.

"This is taking too long!" Hannah glanced across to

see Charles pacing the opposite shore. The others had gathered around, waiting anxiously.

"You're doing great, Lydia." They'd covered five feet now. She unclipped their anchor lines. "I'm going to reconnect us to the next section. Here we go. Next step."

"Darling, I'm coming to get you." The bridge lurched beneath Hannah's feet and she nearly lost her footing.

"Charles?" Lydia reeled backward.

Hannah grabbed her flailing arm and lunged to reclaim a grip on the ropes. "Hold on!"

"Defoe, no!" Rafe shouted from behind her. But Charles was striding out onto the bridge. It swayed. It bounced. "Defoe, secure your line!"

It was too late. Charles's eagerness to help his wife had doomed them all. Lydia tumbled, taking Hannah with her. They swung out, freefalling until her belt jerked at her waist, cutting off her air. Their security lines had caught and held, but they dangled over the river like twisting, swirling bait.

Lydia's screams drowned out Rafe's commands. "Charles! Charles!"

The rebound of lost tension on the lines quivered down the length of the bridge. Charles Defoe toppled from his perch and plunged into the icy river below.

Chapter 6

Hannah blinked her dizzy eyes into focus. Like Hector, storming through the Greek battle lines of the Trojan War, Rafe snapped his anchor line to the bridge and charged toward her.

In an extraordinary feat of strength and balance, he looped his anchor line around hers and pulled her in. He pulled her right up against his body, his hand on her butt, her hips wedged against his. Then his arm and chest wound around her somehow and she was crushed against him, her nose buried in the damp warmth of his collar, his mouth brushing against her temple.

"Don't you ever scare me like that again," he whispered savagely against her ear.

Hannah latched onto his shoulders and held on for a split second, absorbing his hard strength, sharing her own. "I'm okay, Rafe. I hooked up everything the way you taught me. I'm okay."

"I know. I know." He repeated the words as if he didn't quite believe her, but he was already setting her down. Her feet touched the rope and took her weight. "Can you make it across on your own?"

There was an almost desperate quality to his bone-deep voice. He was pushing her away, though he didn't want to let her go. But she understood his urgency. There were other lives to save. Hannah nodded, reassuring him by taking the ropes into her own hands and moving toward the shore. "Help Lydia."

Though she couldn't watch Rafe behind her, she could tell by each gasp between Lydia's screams that he'd grabbed the hysterical woman and was carrying her across the bridge. Hannah's legs wobbled like jelly by the time she set foot on solid ground. Irene was there to help her to a flat, broad rock where she could collapse, catch her breath and watch Rafe step off behind her.

Carrying Lydia tucked to his side like a football, he set her down and barked an order to the closest person, Rowdy Trent. "Get a blanket and cover her so she doesn't go into shock."

Then he was off and running, shedding his pack as he dropped down between the rocks and out of sight below the bridge. Hannah found the strength to stand and started stripping off her own gear. *No one should be alone.* That was the rule, wasn't it?

"Honey, you should rest, too." Irene tried to push her back to her seat. "Let the men handle this."

"No." There was concrete in her legs now. An untapped strength of will and purpose coursed through her, firing her up from the inside out. "I'm helping Rafe."

Keith and Ed had already climbed down to the river and were running alongside to keep Charles Defoe's bobbing head and flailing arms in their sight. "He's down here, man!" Keith yelled.

Hannah hit the flat, gravelly bank in time to see them pull up beside a nest of gray-green boulders, worn round and smooth by eons of the river hitting them at full force before veering to the south. The bend in the river at the wall of rocks formed a swirling eddy that sucked Charles' bald head beneath the water, then flung him back to the surface where he smacked into the rocks.

"Help!" He swallowed a mouthful of water and spat it back out. "Help me—aagh!"

He grimaced with pain and was pulled under again.

"Charles!" Hannah yelled.

When he resurfaced, the water came up to his chin and swirled around him. He sputtered again. He wasn't bobbing up and down anymore. He was trapped, his head tipped back, his nose barely above the rushing waterline.

Ed climbed out onto a rock, but the moss covering it was slippery and he slid off, landing knee-deep in the water well beyond Charles's reach.

"Stay on the bank!" Rafe hollered. He unhooked his long nylon rappelling line from his belt and dropped it to unwind behind him as he knotted the other end around his waist and waded into the river. "Tie it off!" he ordered, pointing directly at Keith who was helping Ed climb to shore. Rafe waded in, his powerful thighs parting the water until the current caught him and he was swimming toward the rocks.

Hannah ran up beside Keith and Ed who stood by in dumb shock, ignoring the rope snapping past their feet.

"Grab that line!" she yelled, stomping on the end with her foot while all three of them scrambled to pick it up and hold on until they could get it knotted and hooked around an angular rock. When she was confident it was secure, she left Ed and Keith behind and scrambled around the boulders to keep Rafe in sight. "Don't let that go!" she shouted over her shoulder as though the other two professors always listened to what she had to say.

"C'mon, Charles." Rafe had reached the drowning man. "Give me your hand."

"I can't," Charles sputtered as water flooded into his mouth. "My foot's caught."

"Ah, hell." With Ed and Keith holding the line so he didn't crash against the rocks himself, Rafe dove beneath the surface.

Fear fisted around Hannah's heart. He was down way too long. Too many seconds had passed. "Rafe? Come back, Rafe."

He'd just kissed her for the first time, awakening every needy, hopeful thing inside her. She didn't want that kiss to be their last.

He shot back up to the surface and sucked in a huge gulp of air. "Too tight. Too small."

Gripping a rock for balance, Hannah inched out over the whirlpool. Rafe was pale as a ghost, and muttering to himself. "What's wrong?"

Treading water, he spun around and stared at her with wide eyes that frightened her. "His foot's wedged in a tiny little space beneath the rocks. I'll have to swim underneath."

"Are you too big? Do you need me—?"

"No!" he barked. "I will do this!"

Something in his tone told her this wasn't entirely about keeping her out of harm's way. He wasn't balking at the physical challenge of saving Charles. This uncharacteristic hesitation was about facing something else. Something inside him.

"Rafe?"

With a roar of determination and a deep, deep breath, Rafe dove beneath the surface again. Hannah held her own breath. After too many endless seconds, Charles popped free. But she felt no relief until Rafe surfaced behind him. She jumped to her feet and splashed through the water toward their position. "Pull them in! Pull them in!"

A minute later, Ed and Keith were hauling Charles up onto the bank. "My ankle," Charles moaned. "Oh, my ankle."

Rowdy had come down with another blanket the three men wrapped around Charles. But Hannah reached for Rafe as he stumbled across the rocks, gasping hard. His arms wound around her and he sank to his knees, dragging her down to the ground with him.

"Rafe? Oh my, God. Rafe." She ran her fingers along everything she could reach, checking for head injuries, cuts, scrapes, broken bones.

His knuckles were battered, his skin cold, his eyes dazed. "I hate that. I hate it."

"Hate what?" She tried to reverse their positions, to wrap her comparatively warm body around his colder one. "I need a blanket!" she shouted to the others.

"It was so dark and small. I couldn't breathe." Rafe's ragged voice trailed away as his eyes regained focus. They were spicy brown as they bored into hers, and she didn't guess his intent until his arms tightened around her and he fell back, pulling her into his lap and covering her mouth with his.

His rough hands swept the cap off her head and freed

her soggy ponytail so he could tunnel his fingers into her hair and clasp the back of her head. His tongue plunged into her mouth, deeper than before, seeking, demanding, taking.

Hannah wrapped her arms around him and held on, letting him anchor her even as his kiss led her on a wild thrill ride. The moans in his throat hummed in her ears like erotic music. Every move he made—every touch, every taste—she tried to learn and give back to her teacher. Rafe leaned back even farther and Hannah sprawled across his chest, sinking into him in a way that reminded her of all the stunning, wonderful differences between a man and a woman. His hands slid down her back, creating a delicious friction as he squeezed here, rubbed there. He palmed the hips that had always given her self-conscious fits and dragged her up against a part of him that was very warm, very solid.

He groaned against her mouth. "You're killing me. This is crazy to need you this—"

"Well, at least this trip hasn't been a complete waste of time for some of us."

A shadow fell across them and Hannah froze as if she'd just been tossed into the river herself. Rafe's hands stilled and his expression hardened like granite. "Go away, Butler."

Hannah tried to roll off Rafe, but he trapped her in his arms and sat up with her, spilling her into his lap again.

All the heat that had blossomed inside her at Rafe's fiery kiss rose to the surface and dotted her cheeks with embarrassment. But Rafe held on, giving her no opportunity to run and hide or regroup.

Ed Butler pushed his hat back on his head and held up his hands in mock surrender. "Don't get me wrong,

Kincaid. I'm all for gettin' some whenever a woman throws herself at me, too."

"You jerk." Rafe's grip on her arm was the only thing that kept Hannah from falling when he abruptly jumped to his feet. All his fear was gone, all his passion spent.

He made a move toward Ed, but Hannah shoved against his chest. "Rafe, please. Don't."

Unlike Ed himself the evening before, Rafe listened to her request and held himself in check.

But his steely glare over the top of her head was enough to send Ed into retreat. Rafe Kincaid was clearly not a man to be messed with. Not now. Not ever. "Sorry, pal," Ed apologized, leaving off the insinuations. "I just wanted to know what the next move is."

Though the tension in him never eased, Rafe looked over to where Charles sat on the ground, moaning about his ankle. "Can Defoe walk?"

Ed shrugged. "I'm no medical expert, but I think his ankle is twisted pretty good."

"There's a first-aid kit in my pack. We'll need to get his ankle wrapped," Rafe instructed. "You two help him back up to the others. We'll make camp at the bridge clearing. Find an extra shirt and soak it in the river. We'll use that for an ice pack."

"Roger that, big guy. You want us to get wood for a fire?"

Rafe shook his head. The rain had let up to a steady drizzle, but the sky wasn't clearing. "Everything will be wet. I'll take care of that."

Ed doffed a salute, then went over to help Keith carry Charles between their shoulders. Hannah pried herself free and picked up her ball cap. The rubber band she'd secured her hair with was nowhere to be found, so she finger-combed her curly mop as best she could and plopped the hat on top. The three men were gone by the time she bent down to retrieve the blanket Charles had used. "Where's Rowdy?"

It was a rhetorical question, whispered out loud as she realized the graduate assistant had disappeared. But Rafe answered. "Hopefully, he went back with the others."

A now-familiar unease crept in to mingle with the lingering sexual tension she felt. "We'd better go check. He shouldn't be by himself."

"Hannah."

He'd said her name. Not *Kansas*. That alone was enough to make her stop and turn. And worry. "What?"

Water glistened in the stubble of his day-old beard. But she didn't think that was why he swiped his hand across his jaw. "I'm sorry. Kissing you like that was crass. Going from 'pleased to meet you' to making love on the rocks… I'm sure that's not your style, you being a teacher and all. But the adrenaline was still kickin' through me. I shouldn't have—"

"Kissing me was a mistake?"

"I shouldn't have done it here. Not like that. Not with an audience." He spoke the words over her worried speculation, emphasizing his point. He reached out and tucked a stray curl beneath the brim of her cap. "A classy lady like you? I should have waited for someplace more private. Read you some poetry or something." He pulled away and busied himself with the rope still tied at his waist. Now *he* seemed to be the embarrassed one. "Not that I'm any kind of a poet. I should've minded my manners, been a little more civilized about it."

He thought kissing teachers was uncivilized? She pressed her lips together, suppressing a self-conscious giggle that threatened to turn into tears. He thought she was dignified. *Yeesh.* Apparently, her klutzy maneuvers hadn't impressed him. She wasn't sexy or irresistible like her sister. She wasn't the kind of woman a man lost control with. Hannah Greene was classy. Scholarly. A man should be a little more restrained with her.

Sort of like an old book.

"I'm glad you weren't so civilized."

"Yeah?" He almost smiled. Almost. Maybe he sensed that some of the heady pleasure she'd gotten from that life-affirming embrace had already been tainted by his apology.

"You weren't the only one who was scared. I needed that assurance that we were alive and safe right at that very moment myself." But those long-ingrained feelings that she was a little too plain, a little too plump, a little too smart had her making a joke out of what had passed between them. "I'm just glad I was here to help out."

"Help out?" He definitely wasn't smiling now. He reached for her. "Look. Maybe I didn't say that right. I didn't want just any warm body to get me through the moment. I know that's how it might have seemed—"

Hannah pulled away, but summoned a smile to try to alleviate any guilt or concern he might feel. *She* was the one who didn't measure up. "We'd better get back to the others and help set up camp. I have a feeling it's going to be a long night."

"The superhero has to go."

The man with the piercing eyes looked down from his vantage point among the trees and watched his colleagues move around the flickering fire like weary moths drawn to a flame. The clouds had moved past to the east, leaving the horizon painted with the strokes of a lavender and gold sunset.

But he had no interest in the beauty of the sky; he was only here because the setting was so convenient. They all should have fallen into a deep hole or broken their necks by now. But Rafe Kincaid had gotten in the way.

And now his accomplice was having a damned panic attack, forgetting the roles they were each supposed to play. He hated that his companion had risked this conversation before darkness could cloak their meeting. The fool was getting nervous. More mistakes could happen. "Did you get his radio?" he asked.

His companion held out the portable transmitter and headset. "I took it out of his pack while he was playing hero and rescuing Charles."

The man with the piercing eyes took the radio. He was tempted to grind it beneath his boot, to take symbolic satisfaction in imagining it was Kincaid's head. But his plot for righting the wrongs these people had committed wasn't about impulsiveness; it was about careful preparation, striking in ways that would hurt the most. Eliminating anyone who might be lucky enough to decipher the truth. The terror and distrust and rampant suspicions brewing among Randolph's finest were almost as satisfying as the end result would be.

He tucked the radio into his bag, wondering when Kincaid would first miss it. Certainly there'd be no chance to call in back-up or an early helicopter to rescue them once they reached the high, flat meadows of Bridger Pass tomorrow evening. He'd have one more night to complete his task. He'd need it. Thanks to the mountain man and this one's spineless incompetence, he had already fallen behind schedule.

He picked up his binoculars to get a closer look at the camp. "I could have gotten rid of Defoe today. Maybe even that Greene woman if it weren't for him."

His companion lacked his patience. The fidgeting was getting annoying. "*I* could have been on that bridge. It could have been *me* drowning in that river. Is that what you want?"

"Calm yourself. You know what I want." He lowered the binoculars. Even if the risks changed, his goal remained the same. "All we have to do is get rid of Mr. Kincaid, and everything will fall back into place."

"Impossible."

"Relax. Take a deep breath. There's still a full day's hike and another night ahead of us. If they last that long." He let his gaze slide to the sheer drop-off behind him. There were easier routes to get to the meadows, but he'd made friends with a little C-4 explosive, and had kept abreast of the rock-slide and avalanche warnings. The erosion caves and wash-out gulleys that pockmarked this side of the mountain would make a much more interesting route for the group. "I've spotted his weaknesses."

"He doesn't have any." His companion halted as the light of comprehension dawned. "You mean *her?*"

"Do exactly as I tell you and I promise you'll be home counting your money and gloating over our triumph in a matter of days. I'll take care of my end of things. You take care of yours." He pulled a neatly folded paper from his bag. "Here's the note. And here's this." He handed over a small plastic box. "Be very careful. I trust you know what to do with it?"

"You sure you don't have something like this planned for me?"

"You know I need your help to do this." He smiled in a way that had never failed to put others at ease. He'd fooled all the others, he'd fool this simpleton, too. "We'll be just fine. We're a team, remember? No one suspects we're in this together."

Rafe lay on top of his sleeping bag, looking up at the stars and listening to the mountain. He'd left his jeans on, but had draped the rest of his clothes over some rocks to dry beside the fire. He dozed on and off frequently enough that he'd pass for rested come morning. But even though his body ached with the physical strains of the day, he couldn't find deep sleep.

Sure, a part of him would always be on guard against whatever was out there—or closer to home—that wanted these people dead. But there was more to his restlessness than his years of training with the Watchers. There was more than Charles Defoe's snoring or the music of the mountain after midnight that kept him awake.

There was Hannah.

Hannah Greene from Kansas with the mystical eyes that spoke more than words. The woman with the sweet, sweet lips and luscious body that didn't know when to quit. The woman with more brains and guts than a dozen good men he could name.

A woman had never kept him awake before. And yet, after little more than a couple of days, all he could think about was the sound of her voice, whispering to him with the same earthy magic as the mountain itself. All he could think about was her dangling over a rushing river by a single rope. All he could think about was that narrow black shelf beneath the water he'd had to swim into to free Charles Defoe, and how he'd crawled out to see Hannah on the shore, running to him, calling his name, caring about his hurts and fears. She'd unleashed a powerful need in him to claim her. To absorb her strength. To renew himself in her eager passion.

"Hell." Rafe rolled onto his side and propped his elbow beneath his head to watch the last glowing flames of the fire before it burned down to embers. Hannah set him on fire inside like that—his body, his head. She'd even ignited something inside him he wasn't sure he knew how to use anymore—his heart.

He picked up a small stick and chucked it into the firepit, listening to the wood crackle and watching the sparks fly. "Damn straight Miss Chapman never got under my skin like this." Miss Chapman never made him hard as a rock just thinking about her.

But a woman from the flat plains of Kansas and a man from the mountains? A woman who could quote Shakespeare when he wasn't even sure he could spell the name right? He couldn't even get the right words out to talk to her sometimes. He was too gruff. Too blunt. He'd tried to apologize for being such a lusty idiot at the river instead of the gentleman she deserved, and he'd wound up hurting her somehow.

Hell. He wasn't apologizing for kissing her. He was apologizing for not doing it right. For maybe not being the right man to do it. He'd spent too much time on the job, too much time in the company of other men or on his own. His brother, Luke, would have handled this afternoon better. He'd know the right words to say to a woman like Hannah. The right way to treat a lady.

The final kicker was that when this was all over and it came time to tell her goodbye, he'd probably screw that up, too.

A concussion of sound in the distance, like a muffled sonic boom, echoed through the night. Rafe rolled over onto his back and studied the stars again as a rumble of thunder shook through the mountain. Clear sky.

Rafe sat up. Though he knew that sound well enough, he couldn't pinpoint its exact location. Rock slide.

A natural enough occurrence in the mountains. Fault lines cracked rock. Moisture settled in. Ages passed and the weight of the rock would become too great. It would break off and gravity would carry it down the mountain, gathering debris in its path and altering the terrain.

But tonight, the whispers of the mountain weren't natural. With three murders and the threat of more surrounding them, Rafe unsnapped his knife from his belt and pulled on his socks and boots. Something was out there. Something beyond the sleeping tents and shadows. He could feel it.

By the time he heard Hannah scream, he was already on his feet, rushing to her tent.

"Rafe! Rafe!"

She burst through the exit flap, dragging Irene behind her. He barely raised his knife out of harm's way before she slammed into the middle of his chest.

"Easy, Kansas. What is it?" He latched onto her arm to steady her and quickly realized two things. She wasn't wearing anything beneath her thermal shirt, and she wasn't letting go.

Hannah released a dazed and sleep-rumpled Irene and crawled beneath his arm, sliding around behind him where she hooked her fingers into his belt and pressed her nose into the middle of his back. "In there. On my blanket." She gasped for a breath. "Oh, my God.

I left my glasses in there. That's how I could see it. It was right there. Huge. In front of my face."

Rafe stuck his knife blade between the tent flaps and lifted one aside to check for intruders. "What did you see?"

Irene shoved her hair out of her face, slowly waking up as the others filed from their tents to see what the commotion was about. "She just started screaming. Woke me plumb out of the best sleep I've had since we walked up this mountain. I didn't see anybody."

"No. Not a person," Hannah insisted. He could feel her trembling. He tried to turn around to read her expression and offer comfort, but she jerked on his belt, keeping him squarely between her and whatever had spooked her inside the tent.

"What the hell's going on now?" Dick Copperfield had stumbled out of his tent, along with Rowdy Trent. Keith Robinson was buttoning his shirt as he jogged up behind Ed Butler. Lydia poked her head out of the tent she shared with her husband.

Rafe waved her back inside. "Go back to sleep, ma'am. It's nothing."

"The hell it isn't!" Hannah argued from the middle of his back. "It's a monster. The size of my fist. A huge, killer spider-monster."

Robinson swore. "A spider? Lord, woman, I thought you were being attacked."

"I was. He was on my hand, right by my face. If I hadn't heard that thunder—"

"You woke us up over a bug?" Rowdy scratched his head, still too groggy to grasp the situation.

"Come on, Rowdy." Copperfield had been understandably subdued ever since finding Natalie. His somber mood seemed to have finally made him a better leader. "We're all a little jumpy. I, for one, am relieved it's not another dead body." He started ushering the others back to their tents. "There's nothing to see here, folks. Go back to bed. If that's all right with you, Mr. Kincaid?"

"Sure." Though Hannah had loosed her grip on him, he wasn't quite ready to say the danger had passed. Better to keep everyone calm and accounted for until he was clear on what had happened. "Irene, I suggest you go ahead and bunk with the Defoes. It'll be a while before I can get your tent thoroughly checked for other critters."

"What about Hannah?"

"She's bunking with me."

"Oh?" Irene wasn't the only one gaping at his decision. But she was the first one to smile and accept it. She even winked. "Oh. Well then, goodnight, you two."

"Goodnight."

Once they were alone, Hannah turned to face him. She had her arms crossed beneath her breasts and he had to concentrate to keep his focus on her prim, nervous expression instead of the generous bounty farther down. "What do you mean I'm bunking with you? You don't even have a tent."

He nodded toward the isolated bedroll near the fire pit. He intended to be firm about this. He couldn't think of any way to quit worrying about her except to keep her where he could touch her or see her. "Go get in my sleeping bag and stay warm while I check this out."

"But, Rafe—"

"Go, woman. If you're not in that bag when I get back, I will track you down and carry you there myself."

She opened her mouth to protest. "Unless you'd rather check out the tent with me and the spider?"

Her lips snapped shut just as quickly and Rafe itched with the desire to kiss them. To comfort her, to reward her for her cooperation—hell, he just wanted to kiss her again.

But Hannah thumbed over her shoulder toward the firepit before he could force his coarse charms on her. "I'll be in your bed."

With those suggestive words sounding way too right in that unconsciously seductive voice of hers, Rafe finally admitted he had it bad for this woman. He watched her walk away and knew that finally saying goodbye was going to be more than awkward.

Chapter 7

By the time Rafe returned several minutes later, Hannah was up, grinding a circle into the ground as she paced around his sleeping bag.

He allowed himself a moment to simply watch her move. He couldn't exactly call her graceful, but there was a force about her—a combination of mental energy, hope and selfless natural beauty—that spoke to him in a way no other woman ever had.

He'd nearly lost her today. Twice. If the mountain hadn't talked, hadn't woken her, she might be dead.

When she spotted him, she squinted him into focus and hurried to meet him. "I'm so not a nature girl, am I? Did I totally embarrass myself with my little phobia?"

Rafe walked right up to her, palmed the back of her head and kissed her soundly before she could make another joke about herself or any other thing that had happened between them. The kiss grounded him and bamboozled her enough to keep her quiet for the moment. "You're a smart girl, Kansas." He held up the spider skewered at the end of his knife. "Not quite as big as your fist. But this guy's poisonous."

She jerked back from the point of the blade and the nickel-sized menace at the end. But she wasn't so squeamish that she didn't tiptoe back for a closer inspection once she realized the eight legs weren't wiggling anymore. Like a curious scientist, she moved in really close. That was when he realized she wasn't wearing her glasses. It was also when he realized that he was damn well going to find the proper way to tell her how he felt about her.

"Could his bite kill me?" she asked.

Rafe nodded and flicked the tiny carcass into the fire. "Not instantly. But left untreated, you'd have a slow and painful end. Paralysis around the wound would be almost immediate. It'd make it damn near impossible to hike out of here."

"Yeesh." After the initial shock of his explanation, the color crept back into her cheeks. "How did he get into my bed?"

Tender admissions would have to wait. "I'm guessing someone put him there. He's not indigenous at this altitude. Besides," He pulled a crumpled note from his pocket. "I found this inside your, um…bra."

"Oh, God." Though he'd already memorized the weight and shape of her beneath her shirt, he found it endearing when she crossed her arms in front of her. "I forgot."

He sheathed his knife, handed her the note and pulled her to him in one smooth motion. "I think you and I are past the point of modesty with each other. Go on. Read what it says. I'll be right here."

She held herself stiffly, tapping her fingers against his chest as if she was afraid to let her hand rest against bare skin. She cleared her throat. "Did you find my glasses?"

"Yeah." He didn't immediately pull them from his pocket, though. "I'm not done lookin' yet."

"Looking at what?"

"You're a beautiful woman, Hannah."

Her hand stilled. She blushed, then laughed, then waved aside the compliment. "Get real. I'm the brains. My sister's the pretty one."

Rafe cupped her chin and bent down close enough so that she could read his sincerity. "She doesn't have prettier eyes than you."

"You haven't even met…" Her voice trailed away as she considered his words. When she finally relaxed against him, Rafe thought that maybe, finally, he'd done right with her. "I never expected poetry from you. Thanks."

Poetry? From a man who'd spent a good portion of sixth-grade English in the prinicpal's office? He could imagine his brother laughing at his pitiful effort. But if his words made Hannah smile, then they were good enough for him.

"Read the damn note."

She reached up and touched his face with that gentle caress he was learning to like a little too much. "My glasses?"

He was still holding her when she read the note.

"Will you walk into my parlor?" said the spider
to the fly;

"'Tis the prettiest little parlor that ever you did spy."

"Don't I know that from when I was a kid?" Rafe frowned. Now the killer was into nursery rhymes?

Hannah fiddled with that wayward curl at her temple. "'The Spider and the Fly' by…Howitt. Mary Howitt."

"So you know who wrote it. What does it mean?"

He tucked the curl behind her ear and watched the various possibilities change her expression. "Just the spider killing me is too obvious. He's talking about a web, a trap. He wants us in his parlor, to go somewhere in particular. He's daring us to. He's set a trap for us."

"The only place we're going is down to Extreme, Inc., and to the cops and hospital in Moose."

She leaned back against his arms to meet his gaze. "But there's more than one way to get there, right?"

"Yeah. With Defoe's ankle, I thought we'd circle southeast by Lewis Springs. It's a longer route, but it's an easier grade to carry a man."

"Is there a way to get him to help sooner?"

He didn't like where this was going. "Sure. We could cut straight through to Bridger Pass and call for a chopper. But it's a more dangerous route. We'd have to deal with sheer rock walls, maybe some rappeling, and a drop-off or two that I don't want you anywhere near."

"One way's a trap. Maybe both are. Which way does he want us to go?"

Rafe pried the note from her fingers before she got too agitated with speculation to sleep. "Either route is dangerous enough that we'll need to be rested and sharp."

He led her to his sleeping bag, unzipped it and urged her to slip inside. He tossed another log onto the fire to build up the heat and pulled on his T-shirt before he sat on the ground beside her. "Go to sleep, Kansas. I'll decide which route we take in the morning."

"You can't sleep out there on the ground," she protested. She flipped the bag open and sat up, scooting as close to the far edge as possible. "Wyoming's idea of a summer night is about forty degrees. Now get in here."

Rafe grinned at her bossy invitation. "Do you know how close we'd have to be to fit inside a sleeping bag together?"

"I don't mind."

He waited a moment to make sure she completely understood what might happen if he crawled into those close quarters with her. She didn't budge.

Minutes later, he'd kicked off his boots and spooned himself against Hannah's back. His arm slid naturally around her waist, his hand beneath her shirt. He palmed the smooth skin of her belly and brushed aside her hair to kiss her nape. Helplessly, his hand slid higher until he caught the weight of her breast in his palm.

"Is this too much?" he asked.

Hannah moaned at a husky pitch that sent a rush of pure liquid heat straight to his groin. She shook her head, stirring her silky hair against his cheek. His chest expanded in an uneven breath at her acceptance. He buried his nose in the fragrance of her skin and kissed the warm pulse beat beneath her ear.

"This?"

"Are you sure?" Her whisper drizzled against his ears like a sultry breeze.

He kissed her again. "I'm sure."

He squeezed his fingers together and found a taut,

pearlized nipple begging for his attention. "How about this?"

Hannah pressed forward into his hand. Her breathing grew as ragged as his own. "More, Rafe. More."

It was the most seductive plea he'd ever heard from a woman.

He unhooked the snap of his own jeans, then wrapped himself around her, nudging her bottom with the proof of just how much he wanted her. "Too much?"

His brainy lady surprised him by lacing her fingers through his and dragging him down to unzip her jeans and guide his hand inside to her warmth. He kissed her. Held her. Touched her. He savored every kiss and touch and verbal caress she bestowed upon him in return.

"You tell me when, Kansas," he whispered against her ear, sliding into the very heart of her.

They didn't speak again until morning.

Had things changed irrevocably between her and Rafe? Hannah wondered. Was she a one-night stand? A foray into the world of large and lovely women? Was there any chance he'd still say and do such beautiful things back in the real world off the mountain?

She was the last person in line this morning as Rafe led them toward Lewis Springs. He was all business today, urging them to quickly break camp, police the area, then switch off carrying Charles on a lashed-up stretcher or hauling his gear for him. Rafe led them on a steady, winding descent through the thickening spruce forest.

But Hannah was having trouble concentrating on the hike. Up ahead, Rafe's short brown hair glistened whenever he crossed through a patch of sunlight, reminding her of its soft texture against her palms. His massive shoulders and terse orders reminded her of his strength, but they also reminded her of his gruff charm and fierce protection that had comforted her, warmed her and seduced her last night.

Making love with Rafe under the stars had been thrilling. Naughty. Uniquely their own intimate experience. He'd shown the perfect mix of tenderness and urgency, of need and consideration. She'd thought he'd be too big, too rough, that she'd be too amateurish, too little of what a man of his appetite for life and danger needed.

But he'd been perfect. He'd made her feel…perfect.

"Take that, Piper."

Not that she wished her sister any ill will. But last night, she'd felt a lot less envious, a lot more as though Hannah was the Greene sister who was all that. Last night she'd finally understood that she didn't have to win a Pulitzer Prize or earn a million dollars a year or outshine anyone else in her family to be proud of who she was. She liked the woman she was becoming. In fact, she had a hard time imagining Piper scaling down a mountain, snuggling inside a sleeping bag, making love in the great outdoors, and falling in love with a man like Rafe.

"Damn."

Startled as she was by the discovery of her true feelings, the curse wasn't her own. Rafe had stopped at a clearing where the ground seemed to fall away at his feet. Even from her vantage point, she could see the ripped-up trunks, like oversize match sticks that had been pushed over by a giant's hand. A fine layer of dust coated the surviving branches, transforming their rich blue-green color into a dull shade of gray.

"What happened?" Hannah asked, joining the others as they gathered around the edge of the fifty-yard-wide gap in their path. "Was there an earthquake?"

"Rock slide."

"That thunder we heard last night." But this time the earth, not the sky, had trembled.

Rafe nodded as he dropped the extra pack he carried and pointed to the U-shaped valley of rocks, gravel and debris where the trees used to stand. He tipped his head and scanned the higher elevations where the rocks had once been part of the mountain itself. But he was frowning. This couldn't be good. "Someone's not playing nice."

"What do you mean?"

He glanced down past his shoulder at her. "Mother Nature didn't do this."

"How do you know?" Irene asked.

"Blast marks." He turned and faced the group. "Probably rigged by the same person who stole my radio to keep me from reporting in at headquarters this morning."

A pall of deadly silence filled the air a moment before the inevitable protests began.

"Are you accusing one of us?"

"We're all gonna die."

"We have no means of contacting anyone?"

"Who would do such a thing?"

"Who took it?"

"Who hates us that much?"

Hannah fisted her hands to combat the contagious wave of panic. "Shut up! All of you!" She centered her glasses at the bridge of her nose and stared them all down. "If we could think rationally for one minute—if we could work together as a team instead of wasting our energy making excuses and accusations—if we could set aside our egos and fears—" she swung her arm toward Rafe "—and actually listen to someone who knows how to lead us...then maybe we could finally get the hell off this mountain!"

That burst of temper left her feeling light-headed. It also left her feeling as if she'd finally broken free of the Randolph College curse. Copperfield stared at her as if he didn't recognize her. Irene covered her gaping mouth in shock.

Rafe grinned as though something about her tirade amused him.

And then the clapping started. One solitary set of hands. Charles Defoe sat up on his stretcher—his clothes torn and dirty, his bald head bruised—wearing the biggest smile she'd ever seen on the man. He finished his round of applause and winked at her. "Now that's what I'm paying my money for. It's about time somebody stepped up and kicked this outfit into shape."

It wasn't exactly the breakthrough moment of the bonding retreat that Irene had been training them for, but it was enough to unite them. For the time being, at any rate.

"All right. So what now, Kincaid?" Keith Robinson groaned as he and Rowdy set down Charles' stretcher. He nodded toward the pool of boulders and trees. "Can we cross it?"

"Not with all this loose rock. There could be cave-ins, or more slides if we take a wrong step. We can't risk it without the right equipment. And not with an injured man."

"We'll have to go the other way then, won't we?" Dick Copperfield suggested. "Through the high caves and crevasses you pointed out earlier?"

Hannah read the tension that wiped out the last vestige of humor in Rafe's expression. She knew a thing or two about phobias; she'd figured out that he had a secret, too. Rafe Kincaid would rather don a suit and tie than take them through the narrow passageways and dark confines of the erosion tunnels.

"Turn around, folks. We're going through the caves." As everyone shrugged into their packs, Rafe reached out and squeezed her hand. Was he offering reassurance? Or seeking it?

His grim apprehension was a tangible thing that radiated through his fingers into hers. "Your spider's forcing us into his trap."

"Hell." Rafe wedged his body through the narrow passageway that had been used by Native Americans and outlaws more than a century ago. He'd bet damn good money that none of those cowboys and Indians topped out at his size and weight. With his neck bent at an awkward angle to dodge the low ceiling and his body twisted sideways, he found it hard to breathe, much less make much headway.

Of course, his stopped-up lungs and the cold sweat beading across his forehead had as much to do with the haunting scents of dirt and damp that filled his nose as they did the crick in his neck. Though the tomb that had claimed his mother's life and forever cursed him with this irrational fear had been man-made, these corridors that had been carved by Mother Nature felt just as close, just as confining. And as he scraped his cheek across the cold, wet slime of niter clinging to the granite, he felt as if these walls were trying to bury him, too.

But eight people were counting on him to lead them to safety. Hannah was counting on him. He'd promised he'd get her home. It was a promise he intended to keep.

They were nearly through the length of the corridors formed by shifting tectonic plates and erosion. Maybe an eighth of a mile more, and the mountain would open up into a cavern and out onto a cliff where the only dangers he'd have to worry about were steep drop-offs and snakes and slippery footing. But he'd be able to breathe. He'd be able to see illumination beyond the beam of his flashlight. He wouldn't be so damn afraid of a cave-in that he could barely remember someone wanted them dead.

In his eagerness to find freedom and fresh air, Rafe turned to squeeze through a narrow archway. But he knocked his elbow against the wall, hitting his funny bone. His fingers popped open and the flashlight crashed at his feet, went out and rolled away into the darkness.

Rafe closed his eyes and swore, damning the darkness, damning the walls that rushed in at him, damning his own useless hide. This was panic, pure and simple. It was a weakness. A curse. A horrible reminder that—

"Rafe." He heard Hannah's voice and snapped his eyes open. He felt her hand on his shoulder and inhaled a welcome breath. "I'm here with you. Let me squeeze past you. I can see the light from outside. We'll be okay."

"I should be able to handle this." He squeezed the unconvincing protest through his teeth.

"*We* can handle this. We're a team. Over?"

He wanted to smile at that reference to their conversations over the radio—how she'd intrigued him even then. "Got it, boss."

"You forgot to say *over.*"

Her voice was as hushed and seductive as it had been
that first day on the radio. And with every fiber of his
being, he homed in on that sound. Even when he removed his pack and she squeezed past him, rubbing
nearly every delicious inch of her body against his, Rafe
was listening for her voice. Then she had his hand in hers.
She kept talking, asking about things he could barely remember. His brother's name. How old his father was.
Why he loved the mountains so much. That voice eased
his fear, strengthened him, lured him like a siren.

"You can open your eyes now. We're here. It's…"
She fell silent for a moment and he reached for her,
wanting to hug her, thank her. But she pulled her hand
from his, disappearing into the darkness.

Her soft gasp cut through his hazy gratitude and lingering fear, leaving deadly suspicion in its wake. "Kansas?"

Rafe blinked his eyes open to four feet of head room,
the dim light shining in from outside, and the sight of a
silver-haired stranger holding a gun to Hannah's head.

"If you prick us, do we not bleed? if you tickle us,
do we not laugh? if you poison us, do we not die? and
if you wrong us, shall we not revenge?"

Hannah cringed at the lyrical recitation, fully grasp-
ing its deadly meaning.

"Nice sentiment, old man. Now get the hell away
from her." Rafe's low-pitched threat rattled along her
nerves, but the distinguished gentleman with the gun
wasn't fazed.

"I don't think so, Mr. Kincaid. Allow me to introduce
myself."

But Hannah whispered the announcement first.
"Cyrus Randolph." She cleared her throat, shivered

against the gun at her temple and spoke more loudly. "*The Merchant of Venice.* So you know your Shakespeare. Is that what this has all been about—revenge?"

"I knew you were the smartest one of the bunch, Miss Greene. I could leave clues and you'd worry, become frightened. And when I needed you to follow them, you did."

Dick Copperfield stepped forward, shaking in his boots, though whether from fear or anger, it was impossible to tell. "You killed Natalie."

"You destroyed my school. So we're even. And technically, I didn't kill her. I only moved the body." Cyrus Randolph, retired president of Randolph College, the last surviving member of the school's loyal old guard now that William Hawthorne was dead, swept his gaze around the stunned faces inside the cavern. "Clean-up will be so much easier having you all die in one place like this."

Rafe, ever alert, was looking up. Hannah nudged her chin up to follow his gaze. She saw them, too, the wires running across the mouth of the cavern from one brick of putty to the next. She'd only seen them in movies and television, but she recognized explosives. "You've rigged this place to blow."

"Yes, and if my accomplice hasn't completely muffed his instructions the way he did with you, Miss Greene, then the entrance where you came in will also collapse."

Lydia squealed. "You're burying us alive."

"All but Miss Greene here. I believe I'll use her as insurance to keep Mr. Kincaid from trying anything heroic."

"What about the rest of us?" Keith Robinson challenged the real enemy this time. "What if we get a heroic urge to stop you?"

Cyrus laughed. "Not likely. I've been watching you people for the past three years, tearing apart everything my family built over generations. Dick and Natalie stealing money from the college accounts." He turned his attention to Copperfield. "Do you know that even after you took that bimbo to bed, she continued siphoning funds into her own private account?"

"What? No, we did that together. We agreed. A million dollars and then we'd…" He stopped when he realized how his words damned him.

Nodding with contempt at the president who'd replaced him, Cyrus moved his accusations to his next victim. "Ed and Keith. I hired you both for your ideas to revitalize the college. But I didn't know how lazy and decadent you could be. I found that young man whose research you stole, Keith. He's bussing tables at a fast-food establishment, trying to raise money to sue you and the college. I paid him ten thousand dollars and promised to save him the trouble. And Ed…" Cyrus clicked his tongue with disgust. "What you have done to the reputation of my college. How many girls filed protests against you? Six? Seven? Did you pay them off to drop their suits and leave Randolph?"

Ed seemed stunned to be the current focus of Cyrus's vengeance. "I talked them out of it. They got the grades they wanted. They were of legal age. It was their choice."

"Getting rid of you now is *my* choice."

"And us?" Charles Defoe had taken his wife's hand to protect her as well as a crippled man could.

While Cyrus explained his disappointment in his

wealthiest alumni for not safeguarding the college following his departure, Hannah tried to piece together everything she'd seen and read and heard thus far. An accomplice. Cyrus hadn't killed three people on his own, hadn't tried to murder her without help. He had an inside man.

Who?

Who had been unaccounted for the morning someone cracked open Professor Hawthorne's skull and Natalie had disappeared? Who would be strong enough to overpower Frank Brooks? Who would Cyrus trust? Who could he blackmail or pay into helping him?

"...I loved Bernice, but she chose him. And then William let her die. I could have loved her better than that."

Like the killer, Irene had provided them each with a daily quote. Was that too easy? Too much coincidence?

All that Shakespeare and Chaucer and Latin crap.

Rowdy had said that. At the suspension ferry before he'd run off to get sick. The kid who couldn't tell e.e. cummings from a Yeats ode had named the classic quotations and Latin language—*even though he'd never seen the note on Natalie's blouse!*

Hannah defied the gun at her temple, interrupting Cyrus's neatly rehearsed list of accusations. "Who's Rowdy Trent to you?"

The older man stuttered in the middle of his speech. Then he laughed. It was a cold, heartless sound that echoed through the cavern. "Bravo, Miss Greene. Rowdy's my grandson. Who, by the way, had a very good dissertation presentation until you stood up and ruined it for him."

Oh, God. *That* was the crime she was being punished

for? "He didn't know what he was talking about. His facts were wrong, his conclusions made no sense—"

"He was a Randolph heir!"

"You wanted us to make Randolph College a better place. I stood up for the truth and the reputation of the department and school."

"You… You four-eyed twit!" She'd just dug the first chink into his choreographed plot for revenge. Cyrus's cheeks burned bright red and he looked as if he wanted to curse. But such a basic expression of honest emotion was beneath his skewed sense of values and honor. "Rowdy! Did you set the charges the way I showed you?"

"Yeah, Grandpa." Rowdy sidled around the group and their mute threats at the surfer dude who'd fooled and betrayed them. "But I didn't think we were supposed to act like we knew each other. Do I need my gun now?"

"It's over now, you idiot. Yes, point your gun at the mountain man and get outside."

Rowdy reached into his backpack and pulled out a black steel gun that looked as big and deadly as the one grinding into her skull.

"Do you have the detonator for the rear entrance?"

"In my pocket." When Rowdy pulled the device from his pocket, it caught on a wire and dragged out Rafe's radio with it. The radio dropped to the ground and skidded across the floor toward Hannah's feet. "Oops."

"You were supposed to destroy that one, too."

"I didn't have time. The big guy was watching. I'll get it."

Cyrus shoved him back upright when Rowdy bent to retrieve it. "Leave it." He dug his fingers into Hannah's arm and dragged her with him out onto the ledge beyond the cave's mouth.

The heat from the sun beat down on the top of her head, raising goose bumps on her skin after the cold, damp night of the cave. Hannah's stomach lurched with concern. Rafe couldn't stay in there. His claustrophobia would make entombment a particularly cruel way for him to die.

"Rafe?" She looked straight at him. Gray eyes met brown across the gulf of a few feet that spanned an eternity of unspoken feelings and hopes and regrets between them. "This isn't the end. I won't let him do this to you. I'll find a way to help you."

Rafe's eyes never left hers as he stripped off his pack and dropped it to the cavern floor. His expression was still as a stone mask. His knife. Did Rowdy remember that Rafe had a knife?

"Touching final words, Miss Greene. Maybe someone will write them down for posterity." For a brief moment, he removed the gun from her temple and flashed it at the others to keep them cowering inside the cavern as he backed several feet closer to the lip of the cliff. "The rest of you stay where you are. If it's any comfort, I'm sure archaeologists will find you in a few millennia or so."

"I will find *you*, Randolph," Rafe promised. Hannah had heard that promise before. She found as much strength and inspiration in that vow now as she had the first time she'd heard his voice. "I'll find you."

Cyrus jabbed the gun into Hannah's temple, knocking off her glasses, plunging her into a blurry world of color and motion. "Make one move against me and I'll dump her over the side of this cliff."

"Fine with me."

Rafe wasn't abandoning her, he was choosing his target.

A big blur of brown fury charged Rowdy. The two men crashed to the ground. She felt a jerk on her arm, slinging her toward oblivion. Hannah fought back.

"No!" Cyrus screamed and stumbled into her as the two goliaths rolled into his legs. Hannah hit the ground hard. Rocks bruised her bones and cut into her skin. Cyrus landed on top of her, knocking the wind from her lungs.

"Get out! Everyone! Now!" She was vaguely aware of Dick Copperfield shouting orders.

The scramble of feet and panicked cries was soon eclipsed by an awful rumbling noise, echoing through the cave, flying at them like retribution from the bowels of the earth. The ground shook. Hannah and Cyrus slid toward the edge of the cliff. She sucked in a deep, painful breath and dug her nails into the rock, trying to shake loose the man on top of her while she found purchase on a rock, a clump of grass—anything.

A gunshot rang out and Hannah screamed. "Rafe!" A ghoulish scream drowned out her panicked cry. A shower of tiny rocks and debris pelted her. "Rafe?"

"I'm coming!"

He was safe. He wasn't hurt. Her relief was so immense, she didn't immediately feel her toe popping out over the edge of the cliff, sliding toward certain death on the rocks below. "Rafe!"

"No! Rowdy!" A rough hand grabbed her by the back of the collar and yanked her to her feet. Her heel skidded off the edge and Cyrus jerked her back up beside him. "You killed my boy! You'll pay for what you've done to me and my name! Now she dies!"

Cyrus pushed.

Hannah staggered backward, her arms swinging out, latching on to nothing but air. She screamed.

A flash of something, silver and bright, sailed through her line of sight. She heard Cyrus gasp, felt him buckling beside her. Her fingers sank into a handful of his jacket and she squeezed tight, holding on for her very life. But Cyrus was falling, too. Falling faster with the momentum of Rafe's knife planted squarely in his chest knocking him off the edge of the cliff.

"Hannah!"

She heard Rafe's shout as she tumbled over. Without her glasses, she couldn't see the jagged rocks and un-bending trees below. All she saw was the wall of gray granite.

And the roots.

Hannah reached.

Her fingers scraped past wood and rock. Splinters rammed beneath her skin. Falling. Flying. Fighting for her life. Her right arm wrenched in its socket as she found her grip at last. She jerked to a halt and swung violently back and forth as her body absorbed the shock of stopping so abruptly.

"Help me," she breathed, wanting to cry, she hurt so bad. "Help me." She spoke a little louder, refusing to die. "Help!"

Her left hand found a rock to steady her swing. But there was no place for her feet. Her arm was so sore. Her fist was shaking. Slipping.

"Hel—!"

Five warm bands of steel latched on to her wrist. Five strong fingers. The biggest hand she'd ever seen on a man. A warm, strong, loving hand.

"I've got you, Kansas."

Hannah looked up into Rafe's battered, bloodied face, and at last the tears fell.

He dangled halfway over the edge of the cliff himself as he latched on to her other arm and pulled her up. Keith Robinson was there, too, anchoring one of Rafe's legs. Ed Butler braced the other leg. Dick Copperfield crouched near the edge to grab a handful of Hannah's shirt to help haul her over the edge. Lydia took the blanket that Charles pushed into their hands and brought it over to cover her as Rafe pulled her up into his arms.

Rafe rolled over, away from the edge of the cliff. He crushed her to his chest, wrapped his arms and legs around her, buried his nose in her hair and whispered raggedly against her ear. "I didn't lose you. Thank God, I didn't lose you. I wasn't ready to say goodbye."

Hannah huddled against his warmth and strength, too spent to offer more than a nod when Irene handed her her glasses.

The threat was over.

They could all go home.

But Hannah never wanted to say goodbye.

Chapter 8

Rafe slipped his key into the back door of the Extreme, Inc., offices and wearily pushed it open. He didn't bother looking at his watch. Judging by the stars, it was close to three in the morning.

He was too late.

After his brother, Luke, had picked them up off the high grassland of Bridger Pass and helicoptered them all down to the town of Moose, Wyoming, Rafe had filed a report with his father for Extreme, Inc.'s attorney and the rescue team who were heading up the mountain to retrieve the bodies of Frank, William, Natalie, Rowdy and Cyrus. He'd taken a few stitches and been declared free of any major injury at the hospital in Moose. He'd given his statement to the sheriff's department and park security, and notified his commander at the Watchers of Frank Brooks's death.

He'd done his job. He'd conquered the mountain one more time and saved eight people from certain death.

He shoved the door closed behind him and leaned against it. The darkness of the empty hallway walls surrounding him didn't even raise his pulse.

He was too damn late. Again.

Hannah was gone. He'd left her at the hospital with the others while he'd handled his responsibilities. But when he'd gone back to see her a few minutes ago—just to watch her sleep and know that she was safe again—the night desk clerk informed him that all of the Randolph College parties had checked out.

"I didn't get to say goodbye."

He'd had her in his arms. She was alive, she was safe. And now she was gone.

"Son?" A deep-pitched voice, so like his own, echoed from the shadows. Lucas Kincaid, Sr., rose from the chair in his office and came out to lay a hand on his older son's shoulder. "Did you get everything taken care of?"

Except telling Hannah how he felt. But he nodded. "Yes, sir."

The squeeze on his shoulder became a quick hug. "I'm glad you're home safe and sound. You had us worried when you failed to report in this morning."

"I figured somebody would come looking for us."

"We Kincaid men take care of those we love." It was a statement of fact, and a true declaration of the bond the family shared.

It gave him the strength to muster a smile. "I need to shave and get cleaned up. Then hit the sack for about twenty-four hours."

"Sounds good. But you might want to check your office first. You have a visitor. Goodnight, son."

"'Night, Dad."

A visitor at three in the morning? Rafe couldn't be civil right now. If it was work, he didn't want to deal with it. If it was the sheriff again, he could wait. He stalked past his office door, heading toward the apartment upstairs where he lived.

"Rafe?" That warm, seductive siren's voice called to him out of the darkness.

Hannah.

He spun around, hit the light switch and walked straight across his office to scoop up the woman bundled up in a blanket in the chair behind his desk. He turned with her and sat, nestling her in his lap, crushing her in his arms and kissing her until he felt the blood of possibilities pounding through his veins once more.

"I thought I'd never see you again." He kissed the arch of her brow above her glasses. "Thank God you're still here. I was afraid I'd missed the chance to say goodbye."

Hannah wrapped her bandaged hands around his wrists and pulled his fingers from her hair. The confused frown on her face was as precious as any smile she'd shared. "Why do you want to say goodbye?"

"For closure." Ah, hell. He wasn't sure how to explain this. But words were so important to this woman, he had to try. "I never got to say goodbye to Frank or my mom or…" He brushed aside the kinky amber curl that shaded her cheek. "There have been too many relationships in my life that I didn't get to finish right."

"And we're finished?"

"You're headin' back to Kansas, aren't you?"

Hannah pushed herself out of the chair, out of his lap, beyond his reach. He would have followed to snatch her back, but she turned on him and pointed a finger that kept him rooted to the spot.

"You know, nothing against wheat and sunshine and friendly people, but why in the hell would I want to go back to Randolph College?" He loved it when she went all Miss Chapman on him like this, caring enough to set him straight, standing up to him before he did something foolish that could ruin his life. "I mean, sure, we made some headway as a team. But the authorities have already arrested Dick for embezzlement. Randolph's Board of Trustees will launch an investigation into Ed and Keith's activities. Irene says she's giving up her consultation business and moving to southern Florida. The Defoes are on their private jet trying to decide whether they want to sue the college or just withdraw their funding, so there's not an awful lot at Randolph I'm anxious to see."

A spark of hope made him smile. He thought maybe it was safe to stand now. "I wouldn't want to go there."

Hannah adjusted her glasses on the bridge of her nose. She inhaled a deep breath and took one step toward him. "I hear they have colleges here in Wyoming."

He moved a step himself. "Some of the country's best."

She reached up and laid her palm against his craggy, unshaven cheek, gently touching him as if *he* was precious to her. "You know, I'm even certified to teach middle and high school English."

"No kidding?" The spirit of Miss Chapman was gonna save his butt yet. He rested his hands at her waist, pulled her closer. "Did I ever tell you that you remind me of an English teacher I once had?"

She wrapped her arms around his neck. "Is that a good thing?"

"Very."

"What if I stayed?"

"What if you stayed?"

They blurted the question in unison. They answered together, too.

"Yes."

And when Rafe Kincaid kissed Hannah Greene, he knew there was no need to say goodbye. I

Everything you love about romance...
and more!

Please turn the page for Signature Select™
Bonus Features.

Bonus Features:

BONUS FEATURES

CORNERED

EXCLUSIVE BONUS FEATURES INSIDE

Author Interview:

A conversation with
LINDA TURNER

*USA TODAY bestselling author Linda Turner began
reading romances in high school and began writing
them one night when she had nothing else to read.
She's been writing ever since. Recently, she took some
time out from her busy schedule to chat with us.*

**Tell us a bit about how you began your writing
career.**

It seems like I've been preparing to be a writer my
entire life. I've always loved to read—anything and
everything. I read every biography in elementary
school I could get my hands on, especially those
about American women throughout history—
Martha Washington, Betsy Ross, Sacagawea. I
eventually graduated to Nancy Drew, then romances
when I was in high school, but not just category
romance. I loved *Pride and Prejudice, Gone with the
Wind* and *Romeo and Juliet.* My high-school English
teacher wanted me to be on the school newspaper,

but I was such an introvert and journalism really didn't appeal to me. Then, after I graduated from college and was working for the FBI in D.C., I didn't have anything to read one night. I started writing what I liked to read, and I've been doing it ever since.

Was there a particular person, place or thing that inspired this story?
I wanted to do something fun, something a little different from a regular detective story. I've always loved Spencer Tracy and Katharine Hepburn movies, and I wanted that kind of chemistry between the hero and heroine. I also didn't want it to be a heavy, who-done-it kind of story. Once I added the parrot, the story just seemed to flow. I can't remember the last time I had so much fun writing a book.

What's your writing routine?
My writing routine isn't nearly as disciplined as I need it to be. I like to start writing by eight, but I'm lucky if I get going by nine. At the moment I have six dogs, three cats, five chickens, two ducks and seven guinea fowl to feed every morning, plus I need to make sure the cows have water. I was a city girl all of my life—until I moved to the country two years ago. It's wild, especially when the coyotes are howling and my dogs join in, but I love it. Once everyone's fed, I settle into my bed with my laptop and write until about four. When I'm on a tight deadline, I sometimes work until midnight.

How do you research your stories?

When I first started writing, I tried to travel to the location of my stories to research the settings and get the feel of the place, but that was before I had six dogs, three cats, etc. So I try to write about places I've been. As for researching jobs for my hero and heroine, I talk to people in the same field when I can or have my twin sister research it on the Internet. I hate to confess it, but I was born in the wrong time period. I'm completely computer illiterate!

How do you develop your characters?

As for developing my characters, I start out with a certain character type for every character in the book, but they don't always turn out the way I expect. They take on a life of their own and usually develop into characters I wish I'd thought of. I don't know quite where they come from. I know it sounds weird, but there's a voice in my head that I go with—that's the only way I can explain it.

When you're not writing, what are your favorite activities?

When I'm not writing, I'm antiquing, doing something crazy with my sister or working on my house. In 2000 I bought a house that was built in 1920 and had it moved thirty-five miles to the eleven acres I own in the country. The house had absolutely no architectural details except for ten-foot ceilings and a built-in ironing board, so I'm gradually restoring it and adding character as I go. I love it!

What are your favorite kinds of vacations? Where do you like to travel?
Growing up with a mother who loves to take country roads she's never been on before, I started traveling at an early age. I've been all over the United States. I attended the 1984 summer Olympics in L.A., the 1988 winter Olympics in Calgary and spent a year working for the FBI in Washington, D.C. I would love to go to Tuscany, or take a train trip through New England in the fall. I don't care for cruises—the ship moves too slowly in the water—but I love driving anywhere and everywhere.

Any last words to your readers?
I would love to thank the readers who have been so loyal all these years. I don't usually do book signings—I think that goes back to being a twin and getting a lot of attention from the day I was born. My sister jokingly told me when I first started writing that she didn't care how famous my name became, but my face—and hers!—was another matter. Not that I'm in this for fame—I just love a good romance. And I'm very grateful that my readers do, too. Because if they didn't, I'd have to go out and find a real job!

Author Interview:

A conversation with

INGRID WEAVER

USA TODAY bestselling author Ingrid Weaver has won the Romance Writers of America RITA® Award for Romantic Suspense, as well as the Romantic Times Career Achievement Award for Series Romantic Suspense. She enjoys creating stories that reflect the adventure of falling in love. Recently, she chatted with us as she took a break from writing her latest book.

8

Tell us a bit about how you began your writing career.

It seems too easy to say that I started writing by reading, but that's how it began. I consumed books voraciously, anything from mystery to romance to science fiction, so I thought actually writing a book of my own couldn't be that hard. It took three worn-out manual typewriters, eight rejected manuscripts and five years of stealing writing time from my job as a stay-at-home mom before I sold my first book. But it was all worth it to be able to earn a living doing something I love.

Was there a particular person, place or thing that inspired this story?
Aside from chocolate? Because as a writer I spend much of my time in a make-believe world, I find the blurring of the line between fantasy and reality fascinating. Perhaps this is why I could relate so closely to Erika when she struggles to figure out what is real.

What's your writing routine?
I'm an unrepentant morning person. As a child, I loved the day each year when daylight savings time kicked in, since it meant I could get up an hour earlier. I'm usually at my computer well before dawn and I work until noon. Afternoons are more flexible, especially in the case of emergencies such as nice weather or gardening.

How do you research your stories?
If I can't find the background information I need in my reference shelves or in my husband's collection of scientific and technical books, I use the local library or the Internet. But my favorite method is simply to ask someone. Most people, writers included, love to talk about their professions.

How do you develop your characters?

I believe our personalities are shaped by heredity and by the crises we endure in life. At the same time, the way we behave in a crisis reveals our true character. When I create fictional characters, I like to delve back into their formative years and figure out what shaped them. Then I toss them into one crisis after another and show who they are by how they react.

If you don't mind, could you tell us a bit about your family?

My children, whom I stayed at home to raise, are all grown up now. Luckily, none of them are writers, so I'm hoping there won't be a tell-all book someday about how I raised them.

If you don't mind, how did you meet your husband?

We were both attending university—he was studying chemistry, I was pursuing an English degree—and we met when his roommate invited me to dinner. That was it. We *knew*. We've been together ever since.

When you're not writing, what are your favorite activities?

Every now and then I go on knitting or jigsaw puzzle binges, but generally my non-writing time gets swallowed by our farm and our chronically expanding gardens. And of course, my dog happens to be the world's most adorable and energetic springer spaniel, so I'm often out walking the back forty with him.

Do you have a favorite book or film?
That's hard to choose. I have always loved Anne McCaffrey's Dragonrider series, particularly the initial trilogy, *Dragonflight, Dragonquest* and *The White Dragon*. Ms. McCaffrey's such a wonderful storyteller. I reread her books every few years as a restorative.

Any last words to your readers?
Absolutely. If you enjoy a book, if you're moved by a story, then please, tell the author. I treasure every letter and e-mail I've received—it means I've done my job.

Author Interview:

A conversation with
JULIE MILLER

Julie Miller is an award-winning author and teacher who attributes her passion for writing romance to the fairy tales she read growing up. Inspired by the likes of Agatha Christie and Encyclopedia Brown, she believes that the only thing better than a good mystery is a good romance. Recently, we spoke to her about writing, life and romance.

Tell us a bit about how you began your writing career.

My earliest stories were adventures that I created for my Barbie and G.I. Joe dolls when I was about 8. Even back then, before I had a concept of romance, I knew what made a great hero.

My novel-writing career began when my son was one. We'd just moved to a new town in a new state, and I had the opportunity to be a stay-at-home mom for a year. As much as I loved that time with my son, creatively, I needed something more. So when he napped, I wrote—challenging myself to see if I could write an entire novel like the mysteries, romances and romantic suspense books I loved to read. I'm proud to say that I could both write a complete book and raise a terrific son. I entered that first novel into a few contests, joined Romance Writers of America (and helped charter our local group, Prairieland Romance Writers) to learn about the business end of things and gained a wonderful critique partner and support group—I even had that novel considered by the Silhouette Shadows line. The line folded, but that editor's encouragement to send something else stayed with me. Eventually, I sold three paranormal romances to Dorchester books, but my dream of writing romantic suspense for Harlequin stayed with me. I eventually got another manuscript done, targeted specifically for Harlequin Intrigue, which I sold. That book was *One Good Man,* the beginning of my successful, seven-book TAYLOR CLAN series for Intrigue. I've been happy writing a variety of projects for Harlequin ever since.

Was there a particular person, place or thing that inspired this story?
I've been a big Agatha Christie fan since high school, some-odd years ago. It's been a fun challenge over the years to try to read every book and play she's written. One of my all-time favorite mysteries by Agatha Christie is *And Then There Were*

None. As a reader, I love the intellectual challenge of trying to solve that perfect murder. There's such suspense in knowing that there's a murderer among the group of people upon whom your very life depends.

And I've long been a fan of action-adventure movies—*Raiders of the Lost Ark, The Mummy, Speed,* etc. So it was a delight creating a real man of action like Rafe Kincaid. I had lot of fun merging my intellectual and adventurous halves into this story.

What's your writing routine?
I try to keep the same hours I did when I was teaching (fifteen years of junior high English!), so basically 8:00 a.m.–5:00 p.m. Though when I'm close to a deadline or the creative juices are really flowing, I'll write late at night—that seems to be my natural creative time, probably because that's when I wrote while I was still teaching. I was forced to be creative and produce pages after the family went to bed.

I generally start by reading/editing/revising the scene or chapter I wrote the day before—that accomplishes the revision task, plus gets me into the story and characters to start me on a productive day. I write ten to twenty pages a day on average, unless I'm really stuck. Then I try to distract my brain by doing some of the less creative aspects of writing: answering fan mail, doing research, organizing PR, planning workshops, etc.

I try to give myself regular breaks about once an hour—walk the dog, throw in a load of laundry, etc.—so my back doesn't give me fits later on. I find those breaks are also good for some mental planning on the work in progress or upcoming stories.

How do you research your stories?

My favorite mode of research is to either experience the thing myself (and I try to get involved with a variety of workshops and community projects to give me a range of life experiences and contacts), or to interview someone who has that experience. I made a great friend at the Kansas City Fire Department that way when I wanted to know more about firefighters and the KCFD. I've also participated in community emergency preparedness drills. I have a background in theater, so it's a lot of fun to role-play the victim of a plane crash with a sucking chest wound. The paramedics, hospital staff, police officers, etc., who are being tested by the drill have always been great about answering my questions about such things as procedure and their daily lives. I've also been a part of the state of Nebraska's IMPROV program—this is a program that teaches teenagers theater skills to use in presenting scenes that help to educate others and generate discussions about a variety of topics. Many professionals from a variety of backgrounds work with the youth as well, counseling them and educating them (and me) on everything from drug use to safe sex to traffic safety to peer pressure. Through IMPROV, I've gotten to know a variety of different people: cops, DEA agents, rape trauma survivors and therapists, sheriffs, highway patrol officers, K-9 officers and nurses. I've been fortunate that they've all been happy to answer my questions—even eager to see if they recognize some part of their story or advice in my books.

Beyond that, I love to read, and I have several nonfiction books that I use as reference guides. Plus, the Internet is my friend.

How do you develop your characters?

I suppose I always look at either the hero or the villain first. (Seems my heroines always have some element of my personality or background in them, so they're easier to put together.) In my heroes, I tend to put together a man who's larger than life in some way—physically, intellectually, emotionally. He definitely has to be someone I, as a reader, can fantasize about and fall in love with. I try to develop what it is that makes him unique—a certain skill or talent he possesses, experiences that he's survived and learned from, a fear, a quest. My hero needs to have a deep internal conflict of some kind, so that he has room to grow throughout the story— becoming a better man, or accepting that he's a better man than he gave himself credit for, thanks to the love of the heroine. And I always want my heroes to have a code of honor of some kind, and since I write a lot of law-enforcement heroes, that often comes out of the job. But I like to imbue them with some tenet that is more deeply ingrained than what their training has given them, for example to always treat a lady with respect, protect the innocent or strive for justice and truth, even if it means sacrificing his own life or happiness.

I do something similar with the villains/antagonists. They need to be larger than life so that the villain is a worthy, tough adversary for my hero and heroine. To me, the best villains have great skills and talents themselves, and they believe their crime is a necessary means to an end or is unavoidable according to the code of honor that they live by. If my villains are unique, smart, strong and resourceful, then my hero and heroine are that much smarter, stronger and more resourceful for conquering them in the end.

If you don't mind, could you tell us a bit about your family?
I have a husband who is a teacher (and former juvenile probation officer), a teenage son (big into music, sports and Scouts) and an all-American dog who has become my constant writing companion. I'm very close to my folks, who live in another state, but whom I call, e-mail and visit as often as possible.

If you don't mind, how did you meet your husband?
Our first real date was to visit the university
observatory and look at Halley's Comet. At the time,
he worked with a friend who had been my college
roommate. Being new to the state and community,
when his birthday came around, he threw his own
party and invited his coworkers and their friends. I
was a tagalong at the party. I knew he was
somebody special because, even though I'd always
been tremendously shy, I had no problem talking to
him. The intense blue eyes and cute backside didn't
hurt, either. By the end of the party, we'd made
plans to go see the comet.

**When you're not writing, what are your favorite
activities?**
Spending time with my family. Reading. Watching
movies or favorite TV shows. Traveling.

**What are your favorite kinds of vacations? Where do
you like to travel?**
I love to go places where I can see the sights—
either historical or geographical. I've been most
fortunate to have grown up in a family that likes to
travel so I've seen a lot of the United States, as well
as Canada and parts of Europe. Some favorite
places have been Yellowstone, Teton and Glacier
National Parks, Stratford-on-Avon, England's Lake
District, Scotland, the Ozarks, Washington, D.C.,
and Williamsburg, Virginia.

Do you have a favorite book or film?
Ha! Too many to possibly list them all. But a few classics that I've always loved are *And Then There Were None, Jane Eyre, To Kill a Mockingbird, Rose In Bloom, Gone with the Wind*. Some contemporary authors I read voraciously are Suzanne Brockmann, Debra Webb, Kylie Brant, Nancy Warren and Rachel Lee.

Movies are a hobby of mine so I love a lot of them—ones I own and can watch over and over include *The Lord of the Rings* trilogy, *The Mummy,* Disney's *Beauty & the Beast, Shrek, White Christmas, Silverado, The Sound of Music, Pirates of the Caribbean, Speed, Star Trek IV* and *Star Trek VI* and on and on...

Any last words to your readers?
Share your love for reading with others.

Author's Journal: An Interview with Rafe Kincaid of EX-TREME, INC.

Vital Stats

Name—Rafe Kincaid

Age—35

Height—6'4"

Weight—250 lbs.

Job Title—Vice-president and Expedition Coordinator, EXTREME, INC. SURVIVAL ADVENTURES

Job Description—Mountain climbing expedition leader and outdoor survival expert—physical guide to coordinate with private vacationers, corporate retreat participants and thematic bonding groups

Hobbies—Anything outdoors

Tell us a little about your company and how you made the career choice to become an extreme adventure guide.

EXTREME, INC. is a company that plans adventure vacations for its clients, and has several guides with specialized skills to see them safely through a variety of experiences and locations. My dad, Lucas Kincaid Sr., runs the company with my younger brother, Luke, and myself. Forming the company was my dad's way of getting us to settle down—as much as the Kincaid men seem to be able to.

My mom passed away shortly after Luke was born, so Dad raised us. He's a retired archaeologist now, but when I was growing up, I always thought he was the real Indiana Jones. When he was working, he always made a point of keeping the family together, so he took Luke and me with him all over the U.S. and the world on his expeditions. He put us to work, taught us about each environment, as well as the history and culture of a place. We got to taste a little bit of everything—from mountain climbing in the Andes to kayaking in Iceland to wilderness camping in Australia's Outback. It made for one heck of an education—better than any classroom. I guess Dad's adventures inspired me. I'm happiest outdoors, working with my hands, pushing my body to its limits on occasion. Since EXTREME, INC.'s incorporation, we've hired associates to assist with the management end of the company so that we can get back out into the field more often, where I, personally, prefer to be.

According to your résumé, you've lived or worked on all seven continents at some time in your life. What is it about Wyoming and the Teton Mountains that made you want to call it home?

The easy answer is, that's where EXTREME, INC. is headquartered. I suppose the more complicated answer you're looking for is that I know who I am. I couldn't live in the city or be cooped up in a regular office. Hell, I hate to be cooped up anywhere. In the Tetons, there's plenty of space to move around, and not a lot of people to mess with. The air's clean, the sky's blue, and the mountains talk to me—the way a lover would. You know, in a way that's special and intimate, but not many people on the outside can understand.

Describe your training to lead expeditions into the mountains, and assist on other—how shall I say it?—"dangerous" vacations. What has prepared you to guide novices and experts alike on an adventure they'll never forget?

Life.

You said the mountains talk to you the way a lover would. Speaking of love, what do you look for in a woman?

I don't. I haven't met one yet who can keep up with me, or who wants to put up with me. Luke's the lady's man in the family. I'm not big on sweet talk or candlelight or poetry, and women seem to need that stuff. They like being warm at night, too, and that's not necessarily a requirement for me.

What's your best-kept secret?
Well, if I told you, it wouldn't be much of a secret, now would it?

Is there any truth to the rumor that you and other employees of EXTREME, INC. have conducted covert missions for the government and private individuals to search for and recover artifacts, retrieve citizens kidnapped on foreign soil, etc.?
That'd be quite a story, wouldn't it? I'd have to say, no comment. I'm just the mountain guy.

TEN QUOTES
Smart Readers Should Know
by Julie Miller

Like my heroine, Hannah, I believe it pays to know a thing or two about classic literature. Through my years as an English teacher and avid reader, I've collected, memorized and analyzed quotes from many works of literature, including the writings from many genres and authors. Knowing your quotes can be essential to help understand references in other stories, or on television or in a movie. Citing a quote or two can add real pizzazz to an ordinary conversation. And in extreme cases—like Hannah's—knowing the words just might help save your life.

How's your general knowledge base? How many quotations from the story did you recognize? Did you know the literary work? The author?

Here is a sampling of some of my favorite quotations. (by no means complete, and in no particular order)

1 "It was the best of times, it was the worst of times..."
　　　—*A Tale of Two Cities* by Charles Dickens

2 "Double, double, toil and trouble; Fire burn and cauldron bubble."
　　　—*Macbeth* by William Shakespeare

3 "Do not go gentle into that good night.
Old age should burn and rave at close of day;
Rage, rage against the dying of the light."
—"Do Not Go Gentle into That Good Night"
by Dylan Thomas

4 "What happens to a dream deferred?
Does it dry up like a raisin in the sun?"
　　　—"Dream Deferred" by Langston Hughes

5 "How do I love thee?
Let me count the ways."
　　　—"Sonnets from the Portuguese" by
Elizabeth Barrett Browning

6 "Two roads diverged in a wood, and I—
I took the one less traveled by,
And that has made all the difference."
—"The Road Not Taken" by Robert Frost

7 "All the world's a stage,
And all the men and women merely
players."
—*As You Like It* by William Shakespeare

8 "All for one, and one for all..."
—*The Three Musketeers* by Alexandre Dumas
(The Elder)

9 "Quoth the Raven, 'Nevermore.'"
—"The Raven" by Edgar Allan Poe

10 "My dear, I don't give a damn."
—*Gone with the Wind* by Margaret Mitchell

TOP TEN

Reasons Women Make
Good Sleuths

10 Being a sleuth is a great way to meet guys.

9 Being a sleuth is also a great way to discover which guys you don't want to meet.

8 Women have plenty of patience for stakeouts—if men had to wait for anything, the human race would have died out after nine months.

7 Women have a high tolerance for discomfort, for the same reason as number 8.

6 Superior intelligence: this goes without saying.

5 Women are naturally curious. Just ask Eve or Pandora.

4 Keeping secrets is second nature to any female. Just ask a woman her age.

3 Phenomenal memory: women can relate conversations word for word several years later.

2 Any wardrobe changes needed for disguises are tax deductible.

1 Women are always right.

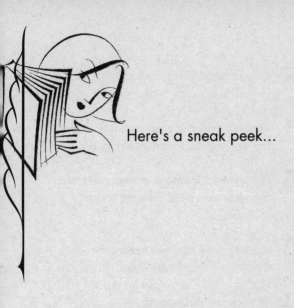

Here's a sneak peek...

ROMANCING THE RENEGADE

by
Ingrid Weaver

*Don't miss Ingrid Weaver's Romancing the Renegade,
available in October 2005 from Silhouette Intimate Moments.*

SNEAK PEEK BONUS FEATURE

$ $ $

"I know you said you wanted me to drop you off," he said, "but it doesn't seem right for me to just leave you on your own with only thirty dollars and ninety-five cents. Especially with a bunch of guys cruising around who like to mug lone women. Sure you don't want to call the cops?"

"I can't."

"Why not?"

She hesitated, fiddling with the arm of her glasses. "I don't want the police to know where I am."

He pretended to digest that for a while. And in fact, it did take him off guard. This was the kind of confidence he'd been hoping for, but he hadn't expected her to open up so soon. "Are you on the run?"

Her hesitation was longer this time. "Yes."

"From the cops or those guys with the camo jackets?"

"I suppose I could say both."

He adjusted the wiper speed, keeping his movements casual while he gave a low whistle. "So that wasn't a random mugging?"

"No."

"Why are they after you? What did you do?"

"Me? I did nothing. Absolutely nothing."

"Okay."

"It's true."

"Sure."

She shook her head. "It's complicated."

"Try me."

She remained silent.

"By the way, my name's Derek Stone." He held out his right hand. "And if you don't want to see a cop, that's fine by me."

32   Still no response.

"Okeydokey." He moved his hand to the heater and switched the blower on high, then turned on the CD player and pressed Play. Merle Haggard came on, singing about beer. Derek lowered the volume, just in case Lydia decided to divulge anything else, although at this stage, he was more concerned with winning her trust than with getting information.

It was a strategy that had always worked for him back in his FBI days. Once he gained a subject's trust, the rest would inevitably follow on its own. Judging by her speech and body language, Lydia was still high on adrenaline and not thinking straight, but she was bound to crash soon. His best bet was to make sure he was there when that happened.

Lydia gasped and twisted to look behind them again. "Oh, my God. I see lights."

He glanced in the rear view mirror. A halo of light swung through the rain, illuminating the brush at the edge of the trees and the gravel at the shoulder. Seconds later, a set of headlights streamed around the bend.

Derek swore under his breath and stepped on the gas. Those guys must have been tougher than he'd thought—he'd counted on them being out for longer than this. He'd deliberately stopped short of killing them, since that would have caused too many complications, both with the Brotherhood and the cops. They were merely foot soldiers; he was after the man at the top.

"It's the same van!" she cried. "I can tell by the lights. They cracked that orange light on the passenger side when they slammed into my car the second time. Oh, no! They're gaining on us!"

"Not if I can help it. Hang on!" He wrenched the wheel to the right. The Jeep tilted alarmingly as it bounced across the loose rocks at the foot of the slope. Spruce boughs scraped the roof and the window beside Lydia, making her jerk backward.

Derek maintained a death grip on the wheel to keep the Jeep from rolling. It had been years since he'd taken a group backpacking through this area. If he'd miscalculated his position…

Ah, there was the track, right where it should be.

His headlights picked out a dark gap in the trees. He steered directly for it, switched into four-wheel drive and gunned the engine.

"What are you doing?" Lydia shrieked.

"We're taking a shortcut."

She braced her feet against the floor and clutched the dashboard. "I'm sorry for yelling again. This isn't fair to you. I never meant to get you involved in my problems. No, that's not right, I hoped you would get involved, but—"

"Too late, ma'am. Whatever you're into, we're in it together now."

...NOT THE END...

Look for the continuation of this story in **Romancing the Renegade** *by Ingrid Weaver, available in October 2005 from Silhouette Intimate Moments.*

Here's a sneak peek...

FORBIDDEN CAPTOR

by
Julie Miller

Don't miss Julie Miller's contribution to Harlequin Intrigue's five-book continuity series BIG SKY BOUNTY HUNTERS *when Forbidden Captor comes out in November 2005. In this gripping series, rugged bounty hunters must track down a group of escaped convicts hell-bent on destroying America the only way they know how: through violence.*

FORBIDDEN CAPTOR

When she turned the corner to the last, most isolated of all the chambers, Tasiya Belov hesitated. The light-bulb here had burned out, leaving the only illumination to the bulb twenty feet behind her, and the moonlight that streamed in from what must be the cell itself.

Tasiya silently cursed her luck. She could either travel all the way back to the kitchen for a flashlight, or she could swallow her fear of the unknown enemy around the corner and follow the wall with her hand until it opened up onto the cell itself.

Weighing the options of retracing her steps through the dungeonlike chambers past sixteen prisoners versus checking on the welfare of one man made her decision a quick one. If she could face down the guns of Dimitri Mostek's men, she could certainly handle a shadowy passageway and an unarmed man who was locked safely behind bars.

The stones were smooth with age but sticky with moisture and dust as she trailed her fingers across them. Leaving her cart behind, Tasiya headed toward the shaft of moonlight. When she reached the end of the wall, she peeked around into the cell.

She caught a silent breath. And stared.

On the other side of those shiny steel bars stood the hardest looking man she'd ever seen. He wore only a pair of jeans that hung loosely enough on his hips to reveal a strip of the white briefs that hugged his waist. He stood with his back to her, his arms reaching above his head. He was fiddling with something at the base of the window, doing something with the rusty iron brace at his wrist. He wasn't any taller than her father's six feet of height, but he was massive across his shoulders, arms and back. Twice as broad as her father. Muscled and formed in a way that reminded her of tanks and mountains.

He was all male from the short clip of his dark brown hair to the flexing curve of his powerful thighs and buttocks.

And even in the moonlight that mottled his skin, she could see he was horribly disfigured.

Raised, keloid scars formed a meshwork pattern from his waistband up to his left shoulder, where the dimpled terrain of a faded burn mark took over and disappeared over into his chest, up the side of his neck and down to his elbow.

Tasiya pressed her fingers to her lips to stifle a gasp. Her stomach clenched and her heart turned over in compassion. My God, how this man had suffered.

To her horror, he froze at her nearly inaudible gasp. With a precise deliberation, he lowered his arms and slowly turned.

Shrinking back against the cold stone wall opposite his cell, Tasiya stared—rudely, curiously, compassionately. The front view was nearly as harsh as the back. She could see now that the shadows that dappled his skin weren't all tricks of the dim light, but from bruising as well. The old burn injury covered nearly a quarter of his chest and one side of his neck and jaw. His chin was square and pronounced. One carved cheekbone was bloody with the slash of an open wound. And the swelling around his left eye distorted the shape of a face that would have been harsh and forbidding under any circumstances.

Without a word, he took a step toward her. But when Tasiya, trapped in a circle of moonlight, flattened her back against the wall, he stopped. His mouth opened as if he wanted to say something, but he shrugged instead. Tasiya's gaze instantly darted to watch the fascinating ripple and subsequent control of all that muscle.

When she realized he'd stopped and was even retreating to the rear of his cell to alleviate her fear of him, Tasiya's breath seeped out on a deep, embarrassed sigh. This man knew he was frightening to look at, imposing to get close to. Others had cowered from him before.

What a lonely, terrible existence that must be.

Sensing some of his pain, Tasiya looked up into his face. The only thing not forbidding about the prisoner was his eyes. Enhanced by the glow of the moon, they were a cool, soothing shade of gray that reminded her of the quiet, wintry skies of her homeland.

And they meant her no harm.

Unlike the lechery she'd seen in Marcus and Dimitri's eyes, the cold condescension she'd seen in Boone Fowler's expression, or the blank, preoccupied stares she'd seen from the other prisoners, this man was making a point of putting her at ease.

Responding to that unexpected civility, Tasiya summoned her courage and retrieved her cart. She wrapped the last small, crusty loaf, which couldn't be more than a snack to a man his size, in a napkin and poured some water into the last metal cup. Then she knelt down in front of the steel bars and lay the bread and water just in front of them, the way she'd been instructed.

When she heard the rattle of his chains as he moved to pick up his meal, she shot to her feet and backed well out of arm's reach. Compassion or not, he still made two of her, he was still a prisoner, and he still frightened her.

But in her haste to put distance between them,

she'd kicked the cup over and spilled the water. Tasiya watched the puddle quickly seep into the cracks between the stones on the floor.

She couldn't leave the man without water.

She glanced up at him. He was staring at her, with ever-watchful eyes, but he wasn't condemning her. He glanced down at the cup and she knew what she had to do.

Shaking her head at her own skittishness, Tasiya picked up the pitcher of water from her cart. She had far greater things to fear from men far more handsome than this one. Good looks didn't make a hero. Scars didn't make an enemy.

This was her job. This was for her father.

"I am sorry," she whispered, picking up the cup and pouring him fresh water. "Here."

With a show of bravery, prompted by human compassion, she reached through the bars herself and held the cup out to him. He stared at it for a moment, as if he didn't understand the gesture. Long, silent moments passed. But she waited until his agile, nicked-up fingers closed around the cup. She quickly pulled away as he gently took it from her grasp.

"Thanks."

The deep-pitched voice startled her. The husky tone resonated in that big chest and washed over her like a warm caress.

Tasiya looked into those wintery gray eyes and felt the first human connection she'd known in the four

days since Dimitri Mostek had kidnapped her father.
She didn't know if making that connection with this
beast of a man should be a comfort or an omen. But
she sensed that when he looked at her, he saw *her*. Not
the *foreign trash* hired to cook and clean and be forgotten. Not a blackmailed mistress-to-be. Not the
look of betrayal.

Her.

"You are welcome."

He retreated to his cot and sank onto the bare mat-
tress to eat and drink.

Tasiya quickly replaced the pitcher and turned her
cart to leave.

"I'm Bryce Martin," he said between big bites.

She stopped midstride. He wanted to make personal conversation with her? No one else, not even
her employers, had. The idea was almost as discon-
certing as the darkened hallway and the threats she'd
received.

Turning back to his cell, she watched him take a
long drink. The ripple of muscles along his throat fascinated her. How could one man be so much…man?
The visible proof of all that physical and mental
strength was daunting. She didn't need any female in-
tuition to sense that Bryce Martin was a very dangerous man. And that she should be careful around
him.

She quickly returned her gaze to gauge the trust-

42

worthiness of those assessing eyes. "I am Anastasiya Belov. Tasiya to most."

"Your accent's foreign, isn't it?" His wasn't like any of the others she'd heard here in America yet, either. She detected a lazy articulation in his bass-deep drawl.

"I am from Lukinburg. In Europe." She wasn't revealing any secrets with that much information.

He stuffed the last bite of bread into his mouth and stood. She tilted her chin to keep those gray eyes in view, her heart rate doubling as his size and scars moved closer. His wrist chain grated across the bars as he thrust the empty cup between them.

The keys at her wrist jangled as Tasiya snatched the cup and hugged it to her chest, dodging back a step to avoid contact. Bryce Martin scowled, as if her aversion to touching him neither pleased nor surprised him.

"Next time, Tasiya Belov," he warned, "be more careful 'bout stickin' your hand inside the monster's cage."

...NOT THE END...

Look for the continuation of this story in Forbidden Captor *by Julie Miller, available in November 2005 from Harlequin Intrigue.*

SPOTLIGHT

**"Delightful and delicious...Cindi Myers
always satisfies!"**
—*USA TODAY bestselling author Julie Ortolon*

National bestselling author

Cindi Myers

She's got more than it takes for
the six o'clock news...

*Learning
Curves*

Tired of battling the image problems that her
size-twelve curves cause with her network news
job, Shelly Piper takes a position as co-anchor on
public television with Jack Halloran. But as they
work together on down-and-dirty hard-news
stories, all Shelly can think of is Jack!

Plus, exclusive bonus features inside!

On sale in October.

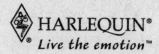

HARLEQUIN®
Live the emotion™

COLLECTION

Somewhere between good and evil…there's love.

Beyond the Dark

Three brand-new stories of otherworldly romance by…

Linda Winstead Jones

Evelyn Vaughn

Karen Whiddon

Evil looms but love conquers all in three gripping stories by award-winning authors.

Plus, exclusive bonus features inside!

On sale October

Silhouette®
Where love comes alive™